Longlive!

MENÁN DU PLESSIS

AFRICASOUTH PAPERBACKS
CAPE TOWN · JOHANNESBURG
DAVID PHILIP

First published 1989 in Southern Africa by
David Philip, Publisher (Pty) Ltd,
208 Werdmuller Centre, Claremont 7700, South Africa
ISBN 0–86486–125–7

Printed by Blackshaws (Pty) Ltd,
Kinghall Avenue, Epping, Cape

1

Allah uAkbar. The first cry came from somewhere close by in the night outside; and then there were two other voices calling more distantly. Hoping as much as declaring. God is great. The chants of praise mingled, unsynchronised yet always ending together on the same suppliant tone. A restless cadence, as though the song remained eternally unfinished. It must be an ancient thing. To think that the melody might be older even than the words – a hymn, perhaps, dating from a time even before the grasslands of the Sahara withered, dying away into wind and sand. With different words, the same imploring notes might have hung afterwards in the chilly air, like the invisible vector of a bird's flight – not seen, yet glimpsed by the imagination in the aftermath, distinctly remembered as a trace of light, as something that had only a moment before been present.

* * * * * * * * * * * *

Desiree lay with her head turned to one side on the pillow, listening, trying to think what had woken her. Coming from outside the window was a small, bristling noise of birds: stitching back together the chaos of the night.

Desi, Desi I can hear the birdies.

Shh. Sleep some more.

But we can go home now, Auntie Vivi said it will be all fine in the morning.

She was back in that unfamiliar bed, she dreamed: under the sheet still crisp with the clean sunlight of the yard. Her baby sister lay sleeping in the angle of her arm. Victor, though, was awake, staring at the window.

Desi, it's morning now, I heard *them, it's all right now, we can go home.*

* * * * * * * * * * * *

When André woke again, it seemed hours later; though there was still the echo of a drifting, spiralling phrase in his mind, pale as smoke from burning leaves. He stared across the room, watchful. Smears of light gleamed along the spines of the books on his shelves. It seemed to him that he'd been seeing these surfaces and objects for an eternity. Lifting himself on to one arm, he heaved the bedding away. Time to get up. Come on, come on.

His shoulder had dislodged a few cards from the wall above the narrow bed. Grumbling, he retrieved them and thumbed them back up amongst the others he kept there. *'Karl Marx as a man of action always spoke categorically, without warnings or reservations. As a scientist, however, his maxim was* de omnibus dubitandum.' – Stanislaw Ossowski. And this was one Desiree had written out for him: *'Once admit that human life can be guided by reason, and all possibility of life is annihilated.'* – Leo Tolstoy. (It was not quite clear what she'd meant by that offering.) The cards kept tumbling down these days: perhaps it was the spring warmth drying out the poster putty. Or else it was the autumn of his student days, he thought, giving an odd, soft groan of mirth.

The memory of his thesis invigorated him. He'd been

starting to get somewhere last night. Then that lot up in the house started to distract him. Marisa coming in; and all that chatter in the kitchen, with the music and the lights spilling out over the stoep, flowing across the yard.

He shook his head. Right: on your feet you lazy bastard. Shoving aside the blanket, he stood up.

Last night he'd tossed his shirt over the keyboard before slouching over to bed. Made a good dust-cover. He was recovering his humour. Another memory nudged him as he stood at the desk. He tried to ignore it. Dragging on the still-buttoned shirt over his head, he leaned forward to push a disc into the slot of the drive.

It was hard, though, to shake off the awareness of other, unfinished business. David had spoken to him earlier in the week, murmuring in his smooth way that the thing was fairly urgent. *Sorry to bother you, but we do need another question from you, just one, to cover your section of the course. Of course it's a nuisance for everyone, but since admin have gone and granted this option of deferred exams – well, we have to oblige.*

In fact, three students in their department had already applied for the concession, so there was no getting out of it. When David read out the names over the telephone, André realised that he knew all three quite well. (They'd taken the trouble to come and speak to him about the boycott.) He grunted, no longer really annoyed. It would have helped, though, if he could remember what he'd set for the November paper.

He began to clamber into his jeans, and pressed one of the scroll buttons on the keyboard. The words came up, flickering. He'd left himself a note before turning in last night.

NB: Possibly a fatal flaw here. Idealistic suppositions about 'humanness' could be Achilles heel of thesis. Need to pre-empt counter-argument that human beings are lazy, aggressive, inarticulate, irrational, selfish . . . so on: weak animals with thin, naked hides, preserved from extinction only by such features (unique to the species?) as their cunning, adaptability and an unlimited capacity for violence.

He stared at the monitor, poised to sit down and start developing this theme. But there was plenty of time. Better finish dressing first; get his act together.

As he was drawing his wristwatch on, a few hairs snagged under the strap, and he glanced down. It startled him to discover how early it was: not even five. Roused, he stalked over to open the door.

His room, separate from the main house, led out directly into a backyard filled with the quiet smell of grass. Along the eastern horizon there was a band of light, so tentative that it puzzled him where the general fullness of light was coming from.

Tucking in his shirt, he went back inside. Come to think of it, he might as well go up to his office now. At least then he'd be able to put in a long, uninterrupted stretch of work later.

At the hand-basin in the corner he splashed his face, and then had to grope, blinded, for a towel. Other memories were beginning to prickle at him. Damn damn. There was a flecked bit of mirror mounted above the tiles. Out of habit he kept his gaze on it, though in fact he disliked taking in his own features. He'd forgotten that Riaan was coming round this afternoon. He bared his gums, jiggling the dental floss between his teeth. Trust the kid to hit on today of all days. He spat out the toothpaste in a hurry. What the hell. It seemed his work was going to be disrupted one way or another. It would be good to talk to Riaan after all this time. He brushed a hand over his chin. The shave could wait.

It was true he hardly knew the boy. His own brother. He must be around nineteen by now, maybe even twenty. Pushing back the hair from his forehead, he turned, with a sudden obscure sense of bemusement.

Well, if there was something else, it couldn't be important.

He picked up his keys and crash helmet and left the room, crossing the damp, silvered grass to the back stoep. The wet floss of a dandelion head flung itself across one of his boots.

Christ, it was quiet inside the house. Unnerved by the idea of actually tip-toeing, he nonetheless tried to move noiselessly along the uncarpeted passage.

It was a relief to be outside again, standing in the front courtyard. Looking up at the mountain, he breathed in, filled with a deep sense of contentment. Now he understood where the light was coming from. A full moon was teetering there against the silhouette of the peak; immense, and hesitant, as if it were nervous of spilling its vast burden at this last moment, with the slow traversal of the night so nearly over.

As he watched, the glowing, pocked satellite began to slip down, rocking and blurring. Within seconds it was lost to sight, fallen down behind the mountain's shoulder.

He walked over to his bike under the tree, amused to notice the sports car next to the mini. Richard must have spent the night. Well, that was Marisa's problem.

It had been a mistake to park under the trailing leaves. Taking a chamois rag out of the side compartment, he wiped the dew from the cold metal. When he was ready he reached for his helmet, pausing while he threaded the chin strap to look up at the horizon again. With the western sky forming a pale screen behind it, the mountain remained a solid black shape, attracting the last stars towards it. As he watched them, they seemed to swarm slowly off, thick and lustrous, heading into a new night-time further on around the globe.

Suddenly he lifted the helmet back off his head. Turning, he went quickly back to the house to dump his things and then, pushing his keys into his pocket, he made a second start; setting out this time on foot.

* * * * * * * * * * * *

Something was bearing down on her, crowded with light and explosions. She tried to fight it off, tried to raise her hands, but they were impossibly heavy; and the mass of sound was choking her. *The bloody blighters. How can anyone sleep?* They were carrying someone down. Down from where? Up in the sky, that was where the workers had their quarters, where the tree brushed up against the fourth storey balconies. Up there it was pandemonium – yes, all hell's creations – with the mynah birds squalling and shrieking in the branches. Come down from that tree. *They ought to shoot the damn things.* And then they were dragging the body down.

Unable to scream, Marisa managed at last to thrust out a hand, breaking through the soft wall of muteness into the light. Still struggling to breathe, she blinked. What had made her hands powerless. There was something traced along the walls of the stairwell, all the way down.

Richard lay sleeping, face crushed into the pillow. She tried, not gently, to lift his arm away from her waist. Why wouldn't he wake and hold her. She stretched out her legs, extending her feet until she was pushing slightly against Richard's shins with her toes, treading there, stubbing against him.

She longed to huddle up to him, to feel his body comforting her; but he resisted her, even in his sleep, keeping his muscles rigidly bunched against her. She traced her fingertips over his body, stroking the sagging skin between his shoulder blades. (It was the region of a man's body that moved her most, for some reason.) He was beginning, just beginning to show signs of ageing, she thought. One day the skin there would slacken, just as it would begin to pucker over the vain tautness of his belly.

Stirring, he reached out, heavy and befuddled as a child, trying to draw her arm round him.

She moved closer against him, stroking his forehead. She knew how easy it was to re-assure him. Quietly her fingers strayed over the dry skin, following the lines that rayed out from the corners of his eyes.

Those eyes of his, she thought. Hazel, they seemed to brim over sometimes with grey light. When he was working hardest at being charming. She put her arm around his shoulder and held him tight, tossing her head so that her hair would spread in a blaze across his chest, over his throat. Keeping her eyes closed, she nuzzled against him, trying to imprint her breasts with the faint smell, wild as bush-smoke, of his sweat.

He could be such a bastard, too. *For a failed actress, Marisa, you do an awful lot of acting still.* Last night he'd come out with that.

She pulled away her arm, trying to get herself free. It was sordid, she thought; the way they bickered and attacked each other, saying such hard things. She tried to tug more of the blanket to her side, but it was pinned down under him.

Unable to turn away, she lay there stiffly for a moment, gazing upward, frightened by her own sudden graveness.

Overhead, suspended from its string, the tumbleweed turned on its own paper-light axis, stretching out its bleached spines.

It wasn't really a tumbleweed. Trust André to point

that out to her: strictly it was a dried-out lily head, the skeleton of the inflorescence. He was always so clumsily long-winded. The poor sod must have learnt to talk out of books. Thinking of his earnest insistence, she smiled. (*I'd guess a better word for it might be 'sporophore'. Because it carries the seeds off, you see, as it tumbles over the sand. After the flowers have died back.*)

Sporophore. Semaphore. Yawning, she stretched out her limbs again. Sorrow for. Metaphor. André was absurd, she thought happily. She rested her forehead on Richard's arm. Sporophore. Sparrowfor. What are sparrows for? Scatter seeds, of course. When they've eaten the fruit.

She'd been with Braam when she found it. Or was it Johan? The doubt drifted away to the verges of dreams; sand before the wind.

Look, oh can't we stop, please can't we stop the car. Look there. In a clearing, only metres from the roadside, there it was, fallen in the grey sand, in amongst the thin wattles. He'd stopped, ungrudgingly; slinging his arm across the back of the seat to reverse the bakkie till they reached the spot. And she'd gone racing over the chilly sand to fetch the giant spoked thing. Close-up, she saw for herself what she had never believed could be the truth, that the straw-coloured spines were the vestiges of flowers. Laughing, incredulous, she lifted it tenderly on to her hands, and came back slowly, walking with it balanced to her breasts, since her arms could hardly reach around its circumference. The sea must have been very near to her then: stepping carefully, feeling the cool sand spilling into her sandals, she could smell the saltiness of kelp lying tangled somewhere, rotting on a beach. Along the horizon, the sky still had the glaring blankness of the moments before the dawn. And all the time, trying to hurry, shouting out her triumph to Braam, she was gazing at the tips of the broken candelabrum in her arms, seeing the last shining tissue of its flowers gone out, crumpled, like old messages.

* * * * * * * * * * * *

As he walked past the site of the new hospital, André could have sworn he smelt damp sand, and a tang of iron. Gigantic cranes framed most of the construction area in a latticework of metal, and at the centre of the place, rising up from behind stacks of pre-cast concrete slabs, he made out a hill of builders' sand, shored up with boards.

He wondered about the fate of the old cemetery plots below the hospital. Through the broken-down hedge he caught glimpses of leaning tombstones, winged angels, obelisks and memorial urns, most of them cracked or tilting. Upheavals caused by earthworms, perhaps. (He was remembering Darwin's worm-stone, and the patient, admirable empiricism of the man.)

He was roused again from his thoughts only when he reached the gardens below the theatre, and the hidden sprinklers began to whir, blithely and without warning spattering out the earth's small secrets on to the footpath. Suddenly drenched, the blue agapanthus heads looked shaken and foolish. The path meandered on past the College of Music, with its complex lean-to of old and modern buildings. Once, on his way up to the campus, late for an afternoon tutorial, he'd taken a short route, cutting up here between the college buildings and the ballet school. He remembered passing a small group of dancers lolling there in a patch of sunlight on the grass, still in their practice things, while music drifted down from the studio. One of the girls was kneeling up, moving her arms though the air, curving and extending them. He'd tried hard to look away. They made him think of the moths (folded in sleep, white with dust) that he sometimes shook from his curtain in the morning.

Music, as a form of art, was mostly frustrating to him. While he was entranced by it, he was unable to fathom it, wordless in its presence. As a phenomenon, though, it fascinated him. Immaterial, surely, it was nonetheless a 'thing'; even though its mode of existence was so enigmatic. It embarrassed him to remember how he'd once tried to raise these ideas with Chris; wanting to talk about this elusiveness, about the nature of an 'object' that dwelled only in the human mind. It wasn't merely that it could not be perceived (like an emotion, or an abstraction). On the contrary, it was entirely a perception, something sensed. The question, in fact, was whether it was anything *other* than that. And if so, what? The discussion had not been successful. Instead he was left with an impression that he'd wounded Chris, offended him, in some way.

Perhaps he'd come across as pompous, with his long words, mad questions. Quite probably. People often took him up the wrong way, he knew. It used to bother him. He'd made an effort over the years to lighten up a bit, putting jokes into his lectures. Even so, he found that the students did not always smile straight away at his ironies. It usually took a term for it to dawn on them that his driest remarks were meant to be humorous; and then for the rest of the year they would reconstrue everything he said, occasionally bewildering him with unexpected laughter.

He shrugged. Up ahead of him, the mountain offered hints of rockface and a thin texture of vegetation.

He did regret it, though, that he never had anything coherent to say about music. The others in the house probably considered him a boor, of sorts, because of his silence. Chris at any rate. Marisa too, perhaps. Maybe even Desi (though he preferred to believe that at least she, out of the three, made an effort to understand him). But what could he say? That he enjoyed it when they played opera. (And he really did.) He'd never even found the words to say to Chris how much he'd liked hearing him, that time he sang in the City Hall.

Comfort ye.

He had a voice, all right. An extraordinary gift. Everyone said so. His teachers, the critics. But that wasn't really the point. He, André, should still make a personal effort to say something. Before the guy left for good. He could write a note, perhaps. Keep it short: less embarrassing that way.

The gradient of the footpath was beginning to stiffen. As his body responded, he seemed to feel himself coming alive. Perhaps if he walked fast, he would catch a glimpse of the daybreak from the campus. He glanced back towards the east, towards that rim of the distant mountain range.

Comfort ye, my people. Striding on, he waved his hands in the air, as if he could jog the tenor aria back into his memory.

Out of the corner of his eye he noticed the sprawl of vegetation down the clay embankments. Plenty of daisies, of course, though they were closed up at this hour. Already the summer weeds were starting to shoot up through everything, clambering over leaves, trying to get in on the act. Quaker grass, dandelions, lobelia, surings, wild oats. Well, he thought, amused, at least there were parts of the planned show still intact. The pincushions were managing to hold up their messy spines (with an air, a slight gleam, of finickiness), and the protea bushes kept up a fixed display of their large flowers, even though the burnt crowns were beginning to crack, spilling out darkened stamens and the last hints of their secret sugar.

He began to push himself harder, lengthening his pace.

Down there below the bridge was where the police had lined the road, waiting: twenty, perhaps thirty of them, restively fingering their tear-gas guns. Recollected, it seemed absurd: the serenity with which they'd set out that day, ambling down, you might say, along the winding drive from the campus. A band of academics at the head, black-gowned, with a few thousand students behind them, marching ten abreast, arm in arm, and singing. Hundreds more had come scrambling along in the wake, racing along this footpath, not wanting to come down and join the marchers, not wanting to miss out on any action either. Marching in the second row, André had regarded those spectators impassively, watching them as they slipped and slid down the embankments, trampling the bushes and watsonias in their struggle for footholds, faces bright as granite.

What had they hoped to witness, he wondered. What kind of bloody theatre?

As he neared the lower reaches of the campus the footpath changed direction, leading up to a track along the edge of the freeway. Now the vast, light-engraved mountain was to his right. He gazed up at its surfaces, feeling something within himself begin to clear.

I'm telling you, there are going to be a lot of tears. By the end of today there will be people dead. Dave Singer's angry prophecies had turned out to be correct.

Hard to believe; it was hard to believe that only a few weeks ago there was tear-gas blowing over this neat grass, drifting into the buildings of the sports centre up ahead.

He wiped the tang of sweat from his upper lip. God, it was good to get some exercise again. The lawns falling away below the track were still dark, faintly starred with oxalis. Was it the season for those, then? He felt a sudden nostalgia for the green taste of fruttangs. Did children today still look for the miniature fruit, tangled and secret under the tough stems?

He wondered how much time was left before the day would break. Strange. He would have expected it all to be over by now.

He looked out towards the east, out over the plain of the city's sleeping hinterland, sparkling in the dimness. There was something to be said for the university's situation up here on the lower slopes of the mountain. Not much, but something, he thought, warmed by a flash of amusement. If you wanted to be self-righteous you could say that it summed up the institution's lofty distance from the city; from reality. On the other hand, though, who would deny the fineness of the view?

Below him the Cape Flats stretched for miles, their shadowy entirety still smeared with artificial light: a million small points pricking out grids and freeways.

There was a patch of haziness drifting out there, across the sand-scoured region of lights and fires, blown bushes, glass buildings, lilies and iron. Was it mist, he wondered. Or smoke rising from the shacklands. Sign of war, or merely the teasing of wind and industry.

He moved on, heading for the road above the sports fields, keen to reach a good vantage point.

When he'd finally left, late in the afternoon of that day, dispirited, with a headache and smarting eyes, he'd walked along this route. Down there on the rugby field he'd seen a visiting team, waiting to begin their game, while the cans of tear-gas were still landing on the lawns below the centre, perhaps the length of a field away. Their kicker was practising; and each time the damn ball came down in that arc, André half expected to see a plume of vapour spurting out of it.

He'd reached the statue of Rhodes, now. After a glance round, he chose a stone step near it, stilling the creatures in the shrubs nearby as he settled. After a moment, though, they started hopping and flitting in the twigs again.

In the sky, towards the south, a faint scree of cloud turned red, and suddenly there were ribbons of colour above the eastern mountains. The leaves of the creeper were drenched all at once with stains of green light, and when he turned, André saw the streaks of corrosion in the statue taking on an acid tinge.

He stood up, rubbing his hands on his jeans to remove the gritty specks of dust and stone; wincing to find how stiff his joints were.

Now he was facing the mountain again. High up there, above the plateau, the sky remained dark, except for a last star, stubbornly stuck to the rim of the night.

He was beginning to grow restless, but it might be worth waiting a few more minutes. He walked back down a few of the steps, to stop at the base of the statue.

Inevitably there were students each year who derided this ponderous monument with its vacant gaze eternally cast over the dreams of empire. Some even wanted it removed. It was too heavy, though, to topple or cart away. Perhaps it was no more than a curio now, in any case. Now and then some original thinker would wedge an empty beer tin under the jaw; and every year the circling wasps would discover crevices for their discreet clay nests, behind the ears or in the metal folds at the elbow. One warm summer the insects had left even the hollow eyes encrusted with mud.

It occurred to him then that the sun might have risen already, without his noticing. Was that possible? He'd imagined that the event would be more spectacular than this.

Above the distant mountain range, surprisingly far to the south, there was a steady massing of luminosity, though it was hard to see any solid core to it. Small patches of cloud were turning dark against the gathering intensity – islands in that sea of rising light.

Still mildly hopeful of seeing something, he lingered.

* * * * * * * * * * * *

No, something *was* ringing. The telephone. Desiree leaped up, confused. It might be Kate. She darted to the door, catching up a shawl from the back of a chair as she ran, tossing it around her shoulders.

'Hullo?' She was a little out of breath.

'Hallo.'

She hesitated, recognising from the quality of the vowels that the greeting was in Afrikaans, not English. 'Hullo?' *'Uhh . . . goeie more, dame.'*

The speaker was a man: one who seemed accustomed to taking up space with the slow, self-admiringly modulated sounds of his voice.

'Hallo,' he said again. *'Kan ek met André Binneman praat assebelief?'*

'I'm sorry,' she said shortly. 'He's asleep.' She paused, waiting for a message. Desiree could hear the rasping, faintly whistling sound of breathing. The caller must be a heavy man. Or drunk, perhaps. One of the wings of her shawl had slipped down, and she drew it back, playing with its tassels.

'Please,' she began; but he put the phone down. She made a click with her tongue, close to anger; and for the first time she realised how fast her heart was beating.

She lifted a straggling end of the shawl. Oh well. With another tiny sound of annoyance, she tugged stiffly at the fringe. Oh well. Anyway. At least Chris hadn't been woken. That was lucky, considering the phone was right next to his room. He needed to rest before his performance this afternoon.

Silently she went back to her room, and climbed under her blankets again – keeping the shawl around her shoulders. It would be better to stay awake now: if she drowsed off again she might not hear the alarm. Trying not to sink too far down, she spread out part of the shawl over her pillow, and rested her cheek against the woollen pattern of shells and rosettes. (White as traceries of ash. What was it called? A gas mantle?)

He had come and lifted them out of bed far too early. *No, please, Uncle Theo. I want to go home now, our father is sick. I think Shireen wants my mommy.*

Don't be silly, you'll have a wonderful time. You kids can have the whole morning to swim; and we'll bring home fish for our lunch. He fastened the last button at the back of her dress, and gave her a hug. *There you are now, and where's your jersey? I'll make us a fire on the beach to keep you warm. And I'll roast you quinces.*

Quinces, Uncle Theo?

Yes, from our own back garden, we'll have them for breakfast. Frances and Dorothy will show you how we season them first in the waves. You'll see: they'll come tumbling back to you, rolling in the water. They get the tang of the sea that way. Brings out the taste, it's better than sugar. Food for the gods.

The sea came echoing back from the pitted, overhanging limestone. When they went running down across the cold sand, there were upended spikes and quills amongst the mussel shells and stranded kelp. Feathers, clotted with tarry lumps. They went on running, racing down to the edge of the waves with the knobbled quinces in their hands. The sea spread itself thinly over the firm, fine sand. There were flies crawling in the kelp.

Let's have the gas-lamp so we can see what we're doing till the fire gets going.

Quinces, sizzling, pink and glistening, steaming in the foil. *Don't get sand on them,* he teased. *Don't burn your mouth now.* The sky was whitening, with a harsh light that made her eyes ache. Overhead she saw the seagulls swooping, fleeting past, calling. They were far bigger than she had ever dreamed. *Please, please.* Their entreaties awed her. What if she tossed them some of the burning, stinging fruit? *We too: hear us, please.* Uncle Theo was busy adjusting a thick leather belt around his waist. It had a kind of pouch, where the rod rested. He took out a sinker from a cloth bag. She saw the puckered silveriness of the little lead weight.

Looking at the lantern made her feel a kind of terror. With its white heart, and that singing hush of the halo round it. What did Uncle Theo mean when he said that about her father? He was like the mantle of a gas lamp. After you've burned it in, all that's left is this little net of dead ash, so fragile; and yet it glows.

* * * * * * * * * * * *

On the point of giving up and heading for his office, André stopped himself, imagining he saw something at last.

Fire. Fire along the mountains: there it was, advancing all along the peaks and those darker, false crags of cloud. At the place where the light had been building, something was pushing up now, crackling with power. The shimmering increased, spilling over, blurring and shifting until it was molten, flowing finally into a single, blinding form.

Seconds later the clouds appeared ordinary again.

2

The sunlight was already spilling in through the tall sash window behind Mrs Scott's vacant desk. High up near the pelmet a tendril of the creeper had managed to find its way in from the outside. The wisp of vegetation even sported a few miniature leaves. André stared at the glistening thing suspended there in the light, and smiled. Undoubtedly, it was still spring.

With a file under one arm, taking gulps of his coffee as he walked, he wandered down the corridor to his office.

There was a neat pile of unopened mail on his desk, left as a reproach, perhaps, by one of the building attendants. Clear evidence he'd not been near his office in weeks. It occurred to him that he ought to feel a pricking of conscience. For a moment he watched the sunlight edge itself across the corner of a leaflet, intrigued by the way the white page flared up with light. Why not admit the truth, he thought. In reality he no longer had any desire to work in this place.

He swallowed some more coffee. Once acknowledged, the decision seemed simple enough. Yet it had taken weeks for him to get it clear in his mind. That he was disillusioned with the university – bored by its pretensions to be a liberal institution – he'd known for a long time. However, part of his current jadedness stemmed from a more recent, more personal crisis.

Crisis of faith.

He turned the phrase over in his mind, marvelling at it. Was that what it amounted to? Loss of trust in a mentor. Well, there was good reason for it. Which was not to say that the fault lay with David. No. He could not accuse the man of having deceived him. It had to be faced that he himself had been mistaken, blinded by hero-worship. Until a few months back, he'd never even heard him venture a political opinion. There had simply been no occasion. Yet he (André bloody naive Binneman) had taken it for granted that anyone with an intellect as fine and searching as David Harvest's was bound to be a progressive. Enlightened. There it was: he'd been misled by his own unfounded assumptions.

And if he'd made a fool of himself in his first, hectic admiration for David, no doubt there had been something equally irrational about his later mood of disenchantment. The thought was not a satisfying one.

He tilted his mug backwards and forwards. The instant creamer had formed lumps in the coffee, and for a moment he played, trying to make them dip and slide. While he had no desire to justify his lapse into emotionalism, it was fair to say he was not the only one who'd got fired up over the past year or so, as the regime acted countrywide to put down resistance.

Last spring the army had moved for the first time into civilian areas: into Sebokeng, Soweto, Kwanobuhle, Tembisa, Duduza, New Brighton, Galeshewe, Bongolethu, Joza, KwaThema, Guguletu, Langa. Strange to think it was only a year ago. These days it hardly drew much outrage any more when soldiers occupied a new suburb, surrounding the place with blade-wire, setting up searchlights overhead. In March this year, people in a crowd were shot dead for walking down a dust road, in remembrance of a massacre twenty-five years before, in the same town. In another town, more than thirty people were gunned down; and seventy-five thousand attended their funeral. There were new massacres, new murders. Mid-year, in Cradock, came still more murders, when the victims were dragged out into the veld, hacked to death and left there, charred and mutilated under the cold stars. (What shocked most, perhaps, was the openness of it: in the past, with few exceptions, people died in the secrecy of police cells, as though their killers still felt uneasy crawlings of shame and guilt.) Finally the suspension of ordinary law was made official; and after that the frightened weeks came tumbling over the country, harsh as stones, with daily reports of detentions, street riots, gunfire, stormings, mass arrests, murders and more murders.

Some kind of answering action was called for, there could be no doubt of that. In a special sense of the word, it was a question of responsibility. Yet what was a right response? What was right action? The old, evergreen problems obsessed André.

In the department, where people were accustomed to drinking their coffee in solitude, it soon became accepted that around mid-morning they would crowd together in Mrs Scott's small office. Someone would bring along the morning paper, and the rest would take turns to page through it; looking over the latest numbers of the dead, or at aerial photographs of razed, smoking suburbs. The government was certain to declare martial law if it went on much longer. What if they banned the UDF? And if Buthelezi joined up with Botha? God help us all.

The newspapers ran front page pictures of models in dresses for the summer evenings ahead. Silk roses, it appeared, were going to be the rage of the season. And this year in Namaqualand, the farmers promised, the daisies would take one's breath away. To prove it there were colour pictures (taken in previous years) of children playing in fields of them. Up in the north, a ranger had a more sombre prophecy: hundreds of animals were dead, or on the verge of dying, in the Kalahari Gemsbok Park, hit by the worst drought in the history of the region. The reason for the deaths, according to the report, was the absence of tsamma melons, gemsbok cucumbers and eland's root, the wild plants that provided moisture during rainless times. All this saving vegetation was withered, and the northern spring was not expected for another three months.

Economists, historians, politicians, journalists took it in turns to sketch possible scenarios, dismembering the present, trying to see what the future would hold.

At first David behaved as though he were offended by his staff's preoccupation with the news of the day and the rumours and auguries. He would break into their talk to show them a bundle of newly-arrived proofs from his publisher, or make an enquiry about the due-date for some assignment.

Eventually, though, he began to concede a little to the atmosphere of crisis. Preserving a slight distance from it all, he began to offer his opinions, beginning with a remark one morning that he would certainly not negotiate with any faceless mob.

A negotiator. Surely David did not think anyone required him to play such a role? André had wondered whether to remark that the perception of human beings as faceless was somewhat bizarre; suggestive, almost, of a deficiency in the faculties of the observer.

He said nothing, however.

Gradually it became clear that David's comments would all be in this vein. What was more, the others seemed to take comfort from them. Helen fell into a habit of fixing her wide (rather beautiful) dark eyes on him while he skimmed the morning editorial; and Julian (whom André had always cagily respected) started modifying his posture when he was around the man, lowering one shoulder to suggest an awkward deference. André did not find these scenes easy to stomach. It even began to irritate him the way Mrs Scott let her hand flutter up from the typewriter keys to tug at the neck of her dress when David was speaking (though that innocent revelation had always secretly amused him in the past).

For the most part he still said nothing, forcing himself to endure the swirl of words in his mouth.

In the meantime, in the world outside it was suddenly – prematurely – spring. Winter had hardly come at all that year. Despite months of bleakness and the early, sulky closing in of the nights, there was little rain and few if any storms. By the end of June, although there was still a thinness to the daylight, there were signs of surrender, and slowly the days began to admit small, if sullen, degrees of warmth. Walking up to campus one morning, André saw a spindly outcrop of new twigs clambering out impatiently from the top of a greyed, leafless tree. Soon the air softened, and as early as July there was blossom on the branches of the fruit trees.

With all these quickenings, it was hard to suppress a hope that something tremendous was about to happen. In the city there was a spate of public meetings, and André went to every one he could (even taking his mother once, after she'd phoned him one evening – desperately talkative, and scared).

Maddeningly, nothing seemed to emerge. And nothing changed, either, in the atmosphere of alarm. Only the numbers of the dead continued to rise, day by day.

* * * * * * * * * * * *

Desiree pushed open the small bathroom window; sending the starlings outside off on a spree of squeals and whistlings. The sunlight was already warming the grey flanks of the fig-tree.

Turning back to the mirror, she carried on tidying her hair, smoothing down the thick cloud with the edge of the brush, sliding in clips at the side of each temple. She looked at the effect uncertainly. Marisa was the one who knew how to do things. She would sit in the kitchen, talking away, meanwhile lifting up her hair into swirls, and then, laughing, ecstatic with self-derision, she'd fasten it all with a plastic teaspoon. On the shelf next to the mirror were the bottles of lotion Marisa used. Desiree studied some of the labels. What was skin freshener, she wondered. And why all these different cleansers? Marisa didn't need these things: her skin was perfect. *Bourgeois luxuries*. The damning phrase sounded itself in her head, in her younger brother's tone of voice. She smiled to herself. No, she thought. It was just that Marisa was a complicated creature; not always easy to understand.

It was true that she and Marisa had little in common. Well, how much had any of them? It didn't matter. You learned to accommodate.

Her thoughts were growing confused, stirred up by echoes of Victor's accusing voice again. It was only an arrangement. He knew as well as she did that they couldn't pick and choose where to live. Financially, it was convenient. And besides – she would not give Victor the satisfaction of denying this – she liked her housemates.

André could be morose. You accepted it, though. That was him: a private character. Still, it was a pity he could not lapse into a lighter mood occasionally. For one thing, ironies seemed to escape him. (Once she'd tried teasing him, copying out a quotation on to a card for him in imitation of his own meticulous method: but he'd accepted it in all solemnity.) There was another aspect of his heaviness that bothered her rather more. It was the way he listened so attentively to her whenever the topic veered to politics. As though she had some special, privileged access to truth. It made her uncomfortable to have so much weight attributed to her private opinions. Why did he burden her like that? Did he think there was something in the September genes that made them omniscient?

Chris was also a bit of an introvert. Quiet. Or maybe he just seemed quiet – because he wasn't really around all that much. If he wasn't up at the music school, practising, then he was out at Susan and Magnus Fine's place. Marisa often said it was a pity they didn't have a piano here in the house for him.

And Marisa. That one. Sometimes, when she was dressing up and laughing at herself, she seemed so confident. Dazzling. Yet there were also things that made you think she didn't believe in herself. She never liked to admit it when something was troubling her. If she mentioned anything at all, it was always lightly, as if she were scared that no one could possibly want to know. Or perhaps she simply felt it was safer to play the clown. If you made people laugh, they would like you? Maybe that was it. It was true she made them laugh.

Desiree took out one of the clips and slid it into her hair again at a different angle. She remembered Marisa arguing why Chris should have a woollen scarf for his farewell present.

He's going to New York in autumn, soon it'll be winter. I ask you. When they get blizzards there, and water-spouts, and they have ice-rinks, and their hair freezes. If Chris hasn't got something to protect him when he walks off that aeroplane, he is just going to die. (She was supposed to be watching the sauce, stirring it to keep out the lumps, but she kept turning round to demonstrate Chris's probable fate.) *Don't you know, in America they've got hail-stones bigger than sheep, and they kill people. Everyone knows what it's like over there: it's the other end of the world.* *It* is *the end of the world*. She lifted the spoon, as though she were alarmed by her own fantasy. *I promise you, if we don't give him a scarf, then he's going to lose his voice in America. It'll just freeze up in his throat. Aaaaaa. Like that. And then what'll he do when they ask him to sing at the Met? Snowflakes will come out.*

In the kitchen, the sunlight had begun to explore the old-fashioned linoleum, spilling pale rectangles over the fading marbled patterns, as if to sift through the dust and reveal the random, trivial evidence of their daily habits. Half a clothes-peg, a cent, a withered flower, a scrap of newspaper, a splinter of dried carrot.

On the table there was a heel of bread; and in the cracked blue and white dish that Marisa insisted on using, the brick of margarine was still out, forgotten, after last night's casual sandwiches. Observing one more ritual, Desiree spread the crust and then took it through with her, together with a cup of tea, into the front room.

They would hoot from the street, she thought. Or no, she recalled: Kate didn't like to do that. One of them would come to the door.

She settled into one of the dusty armchairs, cupping a hand under the crumbly slice of bread. For a while she concentrated on listening out for the car, hoping they were not going to be late.

Always they'd used to start those Saturday mornings at the Union in a rush. Arriving at the building, they'd have to leave Kate finding a place to park – while they ran up the stairs, trying to scramble up two at a time, handicapped by their load of boxes and files. Watched by the few workers already waiting, they would have to stand in the corridor, balancing things against their bodies, until Vanessa got the key to jiggle round in the lock.

If Maya heard them from across the way, she would probably come out from the Union offices, holding her cigarette in her hand. Trying to avoid saying anything. Desiree had an idea that she was shy, though she hid it behind a barrier of efficiency. Also, she seemed to know that her voice could gain an edge when people were slack around her. Maybe it distressed her to come across as sharp.

No. No, wait a bit. Maya wouldn't be around. She remembered now: they'd come for her at the same time as Teach Zwakala, three weeks ago.

Desiree stood up and went to the window for a while.

The shadow of the house still fell across most of the yard, but near the gate the dusty pebbles were warm with colour, and a clean, grass-white light was falling across the yard-wall. Immense in the foreground, the pepper tree glistened, already showing hints of the berries scattered in amongst its trailing leaves.

The street was empty.

At this moment perhaps Maya was also awake. Sitting on the edge of a metal-frame divan, sipping the black coffee they give you in prison. Or maybe she would be smoking, if she was allowed to have her cigarettes. Dressed in her track-suit, probably, with a bit of ribbon keeping her fine, wispy hair back from her forehead.

She would be sitting quietly, smoking.

Desiree looked at the tree again; at its burden of leaves. Brittle chevrons, sketchily imprinted. As though someone had distributed the bones of fishes amongst a class of children, letting them ink them, using their fingers; and then helped them, lifting them up to press the light-green shapes against the bark of the dusty branches.

'The greyness of the dogma, the greenness of the tree of life.' She'd found the quotation in one of her father's books, marked in the margin with a pencilled exclamation mark. Lenin had been fond of repeating those lines, or so the author claimed. They were from Goethe.

Sometimes she imagined she had a memory of her father sitting reading, with the lamp casting its light over his shoulder from behind the chair; and him wearing his dressing gown, resting that very book on his knee. Rose always said she'd invented it. Yet the scene was clear in her mind. He was wearing that old dressing gown, with the multi-coloured threads worn bare, and the small loops weaving in and out. She could see his hand lifting to turn the pages, and the metal of his watch-strap gleaming against his skin.

* * * * * * * * * * * *

Over the past weeks André had chosen more and more frequently to slip out to one of the student cafeterias for his morning break. At least it allowed him to think he was more in touch when he came across leaflets and student newspapers lying amongst the smeared plates. Sometimes a student would come barging through with a loudhailer, rallying people for a lunch-hour meeting, and he would go along there too.

As he stood listening to the speeches, nibbling his sandwiches at the back of the hall, he remembered the mass meetings he'd attended six, seven, eight years back as a keen (and troubled) undergraduate. The light in the place was still as he remembered it, filtering down through those austere, stained geometries in the high glass windows. Suspended from the ceiling was that same enormous lantern, like some architect's model upended, with its glass faces dirtied just as he recalled them always to have been, by the collected, mounting heap of broken moths and rose-beetles that tumbled down into its interior. And there were still the perennial red-wings that flew down, dipping and sweeping through the hall, calling to each other across the airy spaces under the intersecting vaults.

Yet there were differences, now. Back in his student days, the expressions of protest were often beyond his comprehension, syllables that slipped and echoed through the vast hall. Now he seemed to hear effortlessly.

On one occasion, shaking off unexpected rain from his clothes, he had squeezed a way in to find the hall packed with nearly three thousand students. There had been talk for days beforehand of a boycott, and he'd supposed the whole thing was more or less on the cards, merely to be ratified by the gathering. It took him by surprise, then, when a student stood up and began to speak, enraged.

The time is past for talking. We are sick of pleading for our freedom, for what is our natural right. We are no longer prepared to carry on begging, like dogs. We are no longer prepared to negotiate. Even though the speaker was standing at one of the microphones, the answering tumult in the hall forced him to raise his voice. He was objecting, it seemed, to the idea of a formal three-hour debate over the issue. *We are no longer prepared to discuss our freedom on terms dictated by a racist minority group. The people of Azania are no longer prepared to wait meekly, like dogs, until we are given freedom, like a bone.*

That use of the name Azania was a clue. The student must belong to one of the black consciousness groups that still survived on the campus, despite the renaissance of the congress movement over the past few years.

From now on, let it be understood, we will not be content until we have taken our freedom. We ourselves will seize our freedom, on our terms, in our time.

Near the speaker, students were beginning to surge together, picking up their things, drawing on anoraks. It seemed they were all members of the same organised group.

At the same time, the uproar of objections was worsening, and along with hundreds of others André craned foward to try and hear.

Another student, a girl, had fought her way to a microphone. As if to brace herself, she stuck her hands into the pockets of her pink jacket. She wanted to appeal to fellow students, she said. If they hurried this decision it might lead to less effective action in the end. It was important to discuss the whole thing thoroughly, before they launched into anything. Provided they planned properly, they might be able to draw in even more students than the three thousand of them already packed into this hall.

Finishing, she crouched down near the microphone, and as he listened to the dinning applause, André felt a slight prickle of awe down the back of his neck.

Another student was coming forward, touching people lightly on the shoulders as he made his way down the crowded aisle. Reaching the microphone, he stretched out both arms, in a gesture that seemed more to embrace the entire gathering than to ask for silence.

Comrades, he said; *comrades, please, let us not allow ourselves to be divided over such a trivial matter.* With a placating eye on the earlier, angry speaker he added, *I think we are losing sight of our broader aim, which is surely unity in action.* He smiled. *I think we are not naïve; we understand that the white students have their problems when it comes to organising. We know this reality. Even here today: there are thousands of students present at this assembly; but we see also that there are many many more thousands who are still attending lectures, who do not even seem to know or care what is happening in our country. So, what I am trying to say is, we see that there is still plenty of work to be done. Moreover, comrades, seeing as the issue of the boycott is due to be discussed in half an hour, according to the agenda for today, I think our struggle can afford to wait for thirty minutes, comrades.*

He gave another, softer smile: *If it was for longer, then perhaps I would think differently.*

Amidst the chanting and whistling approval that greeted his plea, there were shouts of '*Viva Sipho.*' So he was known. He must be another of the student leaders.

Sipho. A gift. Wasn't that what the name meant.

Yet even that speech failed to close the fissure that had opened in their midst. It seemed the disaffected group had no intention of being placated. Returning to the microphone, their spokesman announced that any decisions the assembly might come to now were irrelevant. Their committee had already taken its decision: they would be leaving the campus within minutes for Athlone, to join up with thousands of their fellow students who were already out on boycott and gathering there.

Questions began turning over in André's mind. How much of all this was coming out of genuine political differences? How much out of smaller, possibly even personal rivalries?

In the group around the speaker, some of the girls were neatening their scarves, swathing them over their hair and around their throats, as if they were readying themselves for the onslaught of the thin wind outside and the icy spring rain. André stared at their calm faces. Christ, they were so young. He was shaken by the turbulence of his own response.

Someone called urgently for a vote on procedure. Should they decide there and then whether to join the boycott, or should they let the discussion carry on for an hour, as originally planned?

The hands were already going up for the second option, when a student in front of André jumped to his feet and waved a lean arm for permission to speak. *Fellow students,* he called out, not waiting for a microphone: *Clearly things have changed. Earlier I would have agreed we should wait to discuss our whole strategy more thoroughly. No, no, please – please let me just say this before we vote. I want to say, I think now I agree with that speaker, that the time for talking is indeed over.* An uproar of impatience threatened to drown out his words. Leaping on to a chair, he continued, having to shout now across the echoing hall. *Surely any further plans we need we can make as we go along, while we're out on boycott. What we need now is action, and the time for that action is now. I say, let's decide this now.* When he gave his own vote, he thrust his arm high, as if his whole body were rebelling against any more formality. Already the breakaway students were filing from the hall, sticking to their word. Seeing their departure, André too leapt up to vote for an immediate decision.

The majority chose, however, to stick to the original agenda, which meant delaying the question of the boycott. Shortly after that André left the hall, finding all at once that he lacked the heart for any more debate.

Outside he'd found the air streaked with a cold, bright rain. It was only when he stumbled that he discovered how tense and hunched his body had become during the meeting inside; and he was suddenly grateful for the clarity of the elements. Straightening, he chose not to go directly back to his office, but carried on down several flights of the wide steps, noticing dazedly that even while the rain spattered down there was sunlight still glancing off the grey stone underfoot.

When he came to a halt, he found he was looking out across the flats, with his knuckles resting on a stone parapet. In the east, the distant mountains had raised up fists of whiteness. Snow, this late in the year.

The time for talking. So it was over.

His thoughts were becoming increasingly numb. As he stood there, with the rainwater beginning to trickle down into his eyes, he remembered the billowing, painted images on the students' banners. Colossal portraits of the president and the chiefs of the military and the police, caricatured with lighted sticks of dynamite stuffed into their ears – deliberately self-deafening.

In the normal course of things he did not care to invoke such categories as 'good' or 'evil'. They were terms that lacked elegance; too crude in the simple binarism they suggested, too murky in the moral framework they presupposed.

No, he thought, trying to reason with himself. It was impossible.

All he'd been able to tell, eventually, was that he'd grown tired of the rain and the stark light.

*   *   *   *   *   *   *   *   *   *   *   *

With a towel around her still-damp shoulders, Marisa stood at the open window, revelling in the spill of light over her body. She rested her finger-tips on the window ledge, practising a few exercises; rising up and down on the balls of her feet, feeling the tiny crackle of strength in her ankles, running under her arches. A few months ago she would have been bundling together her leotard and tights now, about to go off to meet her group of teenagers at the Art Centre. She wished she were busy again, working; even if it was only keeping others in training. Anything to be active again, fit, stretched to her limits.

They would come back. Lucas had said so, last night. One day when all this was over, the kids would start to come back, wanting classes again.

She turned away from the window.

Twisting on its string, the tumbleweed had caught some of the light in its dried-out arms. She watched its elongated keys casting streaks of shadow across the wall.

Her skin was starting to turn silvery-puce. She rubbed her arms, not without a small sense of delight. Time to get dressed.

Remembering something, she tugged open the bottom drawer of the chest. There, where she'd hidden it amongst her jerseys, was Chris's present. The silky wool glistened slightly. He was going to love it, she thought, with satisfaction, pushing the drawer back and opening another.

While she slipped on her scanty things, she looked at the child's jewellery box in front of her, and the fixed, outstretched arms of the tiny ballerina on its lid.

Marisa turned. On the bed, Richard still lay sprawled. In sleep, his face had taken on a heavy look. It bothered her that there were times when she almost disliked him.

You do an awful lot of acting. For a failed actress.

How could he have said something so harsh. He knew she had not failed. It was true there was that brief thing – ten days in the nursing home, suffering from exhaustion. It wasn't what you call a crack-up, though.

In any case, the whole episode was all over a year ago. What was more, she'd got herself out of it. All on her own. It wasn't something she would ever speak about, but her secret self took pride in that. It was mostly pretending, at first (oh yes, then I was a real little actress); but later the mask more or less fused with her real features. With time she'd more or less forgotten it was even a performance. She behaved like someone who was happy and well: therefore she *was* fine.

Just fine, thank you. Finish an' *klaar*. She smiled to herself. Failed actress *se voet*, Richard.

She went over to the wardrobe and pulled open both doors. If he wanted to end the affair, why couldn't he just come out with it. Directly. Instead of provoking arguments the whole night long.

Beneath the hint of mothballs there was some other, quieter fragrance. She remembered: the vague, mute sweetness of her mother's perfume – the same one she still brought back each year from Paris. Moving, she caught sight of her face in the mirror, and tried to look away, letting her hair tumble over her eyes, as though the heavy swirl of it would hide her from herself.

That hair. What did they say it was. The colour of amber. Every time she heard the word, it made her think of Aunt Renata's necklace. Stone-hard fragments of resin, murkily crusted, shot through with veins of greyness, memories of pines in the ancient sunlight.

She reached out and touched an old crêpe dress. As a child she'd used to totter round in it, rubbing her fingers over the tiny metal discs that encrusted the bodice, always surprised at their coldness. Pretending to her father, too: telling him they were diamonds.

An awful lot of acting, Marisa.

Slowly she smiled to herself. Awful. All at once she groaned out loud, exaggerating an English accent: Oh it was so awfully awful.

But still: even her aunt had said she was. *'n Klein aktrisetjie.* All those years ago.

She remembered the wide, cool voorkamer, where the grown-ups were. Where she'd gone threading her way, the quick, lithe child, perfectly aware of the way her dress floated round her (one of her mother's confections in broderie anglaise and satin ribbon). Running in, barefoot, gripping the cool tiles with her feet, she was wilfully deaf to her mother's timid reproaches. She heard the comments of the others, though – and lost her nerve. *She's like a little doll, isn't she.* Seeking a refuge she'd gone and pelted herself into Uncle Thys's arms, rubbing her hot cheek against the lapels of his jacket. But it was too late: she'd heard already. Almost crying with embarrassment, she snuffled against her saviour's chest. *Elsa, but the child is exquisite. Too enchanting.* What did it mean, she wanted to ask roughly. What? But she did not speak; and Uncle Thys, who was not her real uncle, helped her to make herself comfortable on his knee, assisting her over her stage-fright with parings from the sugar-coated fig on his plate. She took some of the crystallised fruit, but it was far too sweet and made her slip still further into a shaky state of imminent tearfulness. Beginning to hate him, to hate them all, wishing she could run away forever, she stayed there with her face pressed against the coarse fabric of his jacket, until the trembling went away.

Everyone was laughing. Even Renata paused on her way to the piano and looked down at her, amused. *What a little actress it is, Werner,* she said; speaking over Marisa's head to her father, who roared back, agreeing. *I can see poor Elsabe's going to have her hands full, later.*

Ever since, she'd lived with the unnerving impression that Ouma's sister had the power to see straight through her. With time, though, she learned that Renata's piercing thrusts could be avoided if one moved in first, quickly, and close. By the age of nine or so, she was competent enough to follow most music on the page, even when it was far too advanced for her to play herself. She was nervous, at first, to offer her skill, but one afternoon she found the courage and went up quietly to sit at Renata's side while she was playing one of the beloved three-part inventions. At the right instant precisely, she rose and flipped the page over, holding it for a second to be sure it was steady; and then as soon as Renata nodded, thankfully surprised, she'd sat unobtrusively down again. Afterwards she was favoured with a puckered look of appreciation. And from then on, Renata at least (out of all of them), stopped regarding her as a living toy, *'n regte klein poppie*.

She studied her face. Exquisite. No, she thought. They were mistaken there. Too bony; and the skin so bland. Only the dark eyebrows and lashes saved it from insipidity. Still, it was a good surface to paint on. Oh of course it was foolish, putting grease on one's face. Extract of dead whale and all that. But it was a kind of game. Make-believe. She loved it. Richard liked it too, she suspected. Even though he disparaged her for it.

She felt a tiredness behind her eyes. Perhaps he really did want to cast her off? Maybe he was afraid she was no longer fashionable enough.

She smiled at the mirror, determinedly vivacious.

The last time she'd been on stage was just before that – (there was nothing wrong with the word: say it, come on, say it) before that breakdown. Honestly: as though she were some kind of machine. She raised her shoulders, practising a quick gaiety. Of course, that was up in Johannesburg. Nobody here in Cape Town had seen her rehearsing Cordelia.

She had looked so really dead. That was what people said, admiringly. Suspended in Michael's arms, with her head thrown back, her arms trailing; while Michael raged, as the old, blind king. *0, you are men of stones. Had I your tongues and eyes, I'd use them so That heaven's vault should crack.* He would never let her fall, she knew that, she could feel the iron-hard muscles in his upper arms. Yet as she arched back, forcing herself to hang there, dangling limp as a rag-doll, the light seemed to come beading down, storming, with the driving grain of ice stones. The blood started singing in her head, and she was blinded. As Michael strode with her, her hands were brushing the splintered boards (she could smell dust, she was so near to the ground then). *I know when one is dead and when one lives – She's dead as earth.* Her throat dried out, and suddenly the craving sprang alive in her, seething through her veins: a compulsion to speak, to reach up and grab his hands, his hair, anything that would lift her up to safety, and hold her there.

She began to search through the clothes. That Indian cotton skirt would be right, if she could find it.

Richard had done it on purpose, last night, she was sure. He'd wanted them to fight. She flushed a little, conscious that she had not, perhaps, been completely blameless herself. But the evening *was* such a bore, she thought (knowing that this was a childish tremor of self-justification).

The performance had turned out to be brief, and people lingered on in the foyer afterwards, as if to compensate for an unexpressed sense of let-down. She would have liked to leave, but Richard soon gathered a small group around himself, and then she'd had to be introduced.

Marisa Siervogel, he announced, sounding off-handed, yet taking care, she observed, not to slur his pronunciation. She did not miss the glances, that were instantly followed up by a pretended lack of interest. She'd been recognised. Unhappily, she put on a vivid smile for them, and the conversation turned back to the play.

Well I did think we were, ah, beginning to get beyond this level of naked agitprop.

Indeed. I know I found myself wondering –

Richard was building up to one of his aphorisms, she guessed.

– wondering whether there really is a difference, after all, between art that draws on politics for its material –

She leaned against his arm, still smiling, aware of the other women secretly appraising her, searching for a blemish, some consoling flaw. She hated being exposed to this kind of adjudication. She'd never pretended to be some kind of beauty queen. She was an actress. Sometimes people's vindictiveness bewildered her. The minute they think you're setting up as a high-flier, they try to shoot you down.

– whether there is a difference between that – and politics that makes raids on art, as though it were a kind of arsenal.

No doubt the line would be polished up a bit and used in the next issue of his little magazine.

Richard, you don't think that in another context, perhaps, the thing might work? I don't know, but let's say, ah, somewhere out in the community. I mean, let's face it. The man kept looking at Marisa as he spoke. *We're a pretty uptight bunch.* He smiled comfortably, pleased with his easygoing candour. *Look, I'm a bourgeois type. I can't kid myself. I'm afraid I really can't bring myself to sing along when they go into these protest songs. Freedom songs.*

He gave Marisa another – surely salacious – smile. *What do you say, my dear? What's the struggle to us or we to the struggle?*

'That we should weep for her.' The line whispered itself in her mind.

The man continued, conscious that the others were listening to him.

A few nights ago I had some friends round and we were sitting outside on the verandah: we had a glass of whisky each, it was that time of day and we were looking out, admiring the twilight over the Cape Flats. The view from my place is tremendous. God, you can see from Table Bay to False Bay. Anyway, this night there was a whole series of barricades up, there must have been nine of them down Prince George's Drive. It was spectacular: as far as you could see, there were these racks of fire, receding one behind the other, like images in a set of winged mirrors. Oh Christ yes, and it was one of those glimmering, slightly sparkling evenings. There was something quite beautiful about it. Unearthly. And there we were – sipping our drinks, watching it all. I tell you, it gives you an eerie feeling. Something tells you it's decadent. And you start to feel as guilty as hell. But – and this is what I'm getting at: if you are really honest with yourself, you realise there's nothing you can do. You can't very well drive out there to go and give the comrades a hand. All you can do is watch. And while you're about it, you might as well acknowledge the pleasure involved.

He turned slightly to Marisa again. *Perhaps I'm shocking you? But to feel guilty is a kind of deception one pulls on oneself.*

Marisa put her fingertips lightly on the shoulder of Richard's jacket. *Sien jou later,* she whispered, knowing how much he disliked it when she played up her Afrikaans side. Not allowing him time to respond, she slipped away, offering his friends a charming smile of apology, a little wave with her fingertips.

That was when she'd come across Lucas trying to squeeze his way through the crowd around the bar. With a shout he reached for her and hugged her, hugely, lifting her off her feet. She clung to him, while he laughed and staggered, having to hold up his wine glass so as not to spill anything over her.

You look so lovely, Marisa.

She hugged him again, tightly, loving him for the way he delighted in her. Didn't he think her dress was too decadent, she demanded; too bourgeois? She knew her hair must be thick with light, glistening around her bare shoulders.

He held his wine glass for her to take a sip, then knocked back the rest himself. *O ja,* he said; *Ja, Marisa I'm sure it's terribly bourgeois. God ja, I don't know. I don't even know what the word means.* He laughed again. *I haven't got time to worry about these* hooggeleerde *names for things.* He stroked her arm. *No I think it's beautiful.*

She saw the tiredness in his face then. Perhaps he felt as insecure as she did in this crowd of glamorous people. Out of contrition she hugged him again, and left her arm around his neck this time.

Are you still so busy at the Art Centre these days, she asked.

He kissed her shoulder, and laughed, ignoring the question. *No, what about you. What are you doing?*

He seemed taken aback when she told him. Even slightly cynical for a moment. Then he nodded, not unkindly. *Ja, it seems everybody is running around looking for some organisation to join these days. We call them the* amajoini.

Despite his earnest expression, she knew that he was teasing her. To show him that she had caught the pun, she began singing the easier part of the marching song. It was a simple ground – you sang the word on the tonic, dropped down to the sub-dominant, *amajoni,* moved up a tone, *amajoni,* then went back to the tonic – and then you started the little four-stage tune again. *Amajoni, amajoni.*

My jinne, jy ken mos even die songs *ook.*

Amajoni, amajoni. She was beginning to run out of breath. *They told us that word comes from the days of the British. They used to call the soldiers 'johnnies'.*

So you're going to be a soldier now.

She shook her head, still singing. *Amajoni. That just goes round and round. I wish I knew the main tune they sing over it. I mean, I do, but I don't know the words.*

Mildly, he laughed at her; beginning to look pleased.

Maar goed, that's great Marisa. I think everybody needs to be involved somewhere, it's good if you've found a place for yourself. Hoe sê hulle: a niche. Me, I'm busy enough as it is. I'm on my way back now to the Centre. We're still busy trying to get these tee-shirts out for tomorrow.

For the funeral. Are you going to be there?

But he shook his head. *I'm not one for big crowd scenes. In any case, I'm probably going to be too tired, we're going to be working all night still.*

When Richard came up to take her away, she noticed that he gave Lucas a curt look.

Thinking about it now, she supposed she might well have been partly to blame for the squabble on the way home. Takes two to tango.

You were just using that guy, Marisa. Making a complete exhibition of yourself, hanging all over him like that, to make some kind of sick point about how liberated you are.

He turned his head to look at her. They were waiting for the lights to change at an intersection, and for a moment she had a fantasy of leaping out of the car.

You don't know when to stop, Marisa: your whole life is just one big act after another. You're the worst kind of actress; and I'm not referring to your brief career in the theatre.

The memory of his words – she could hear the tone of his voice still – made her feel shaky again. She'd found the skirt she wanted. Now she began to drape it around her hips, tugging the waist tie through its loops. The flimsy cotton felt so light against her skin. It *was* spring, it was nearly, nearly summertime, she thought, swishing the soft folds around herself. She looked into the mirror, enchanted by the small flecks of gilt printed aross the border frieze of crimson birds.

At least when I'm pretending, she thought, it's for a good reason. I know what I'm doing.

You have to pull yourself up by your own bootstraps.

For those few days she'd felt as if she were composed of nothing but flickers, moments of shifting light: lying there, she would see a petal suddenly fall from the bowl of roses on her locker; or there would be the shadows of bamboos streaked across the curtains. *Asseblief, Papa, kom terug, kom haal vir my.* And it was hard, appallingly hard, then, not to cry. Of course she'd fought back, pushing the corner of the pillow into her mouth, biting it. It was a role she did not want, she knew. Such vapid fragility. God, no. Yet there was no one to fetch her.

When they finally came, straight from the airport, her mother was pale, worn out from the long flight home, as well as from fright, no doubt. Staring back at them from the bed, Marisa guessed that they had been fighting throughout the journey, in that silent, taut way of theirs. She felt the tension begin to burn again, achingly, between her own shoulder blades. *Risa, toe nou, Papa is mos nou hier.* Oh, he was playing his role so finely, with such bravura. *What happened? What the hell happened?* His voice seemed to break with the noble, stirring anger of love. And all the time she could feel him trying not to recoil as he felt the stiff thinness, the hot, childish despair of her body.

Her mother watched, frantic to know what she had done wrong. *But my darling, we thought you were so happy in Johannesburg.* She searched her daughter's eyes for forgiveness. *Why didn't you tell us?*

The next morning, when they came again, she had her things packed (the toothbrush still damp and smelling of mint in the sponge-bag). There was a tedious hour of argument; but finally the psychologist shrugged, and her parents could no longer protest. Of course, she was an adult. She had a right to make her own decisions.

Yes: and she had decided that she was an invalid, a casualty, only so long as she remained in that nursing home. It was driving her mad, to lie in that private room, sedated, biting down against a languid sense of horror – at the sweet cleanliness of the linen, the grace of the slowly spilling flowers. She had to pull herself together. (Either that, or she was dead.) Pull yourself up by your own strings, like a marionette: as if you're a puppet and there's no one left to hold you anymore, and animate you, except yourself. Against the sunfilter curtains, the shadows of bamboos and papyrus grass had seemed to criss-cross and fall and rise again, lightly, in the wind.

She spun round, trying to make the skirt flare out. *I only do it to survive, Richard. At least I'm not after status.* As the skirt floated down, a deeper voice spoke inside her, rebukingly. *Toe nou, genoeg nou, Marisa, enough.*

All right, that last thought was unkind, she admitted. Maybe insincere as well. It was a criticism she'd learnt from André. What did he call Richard? A poser. She was not even sure she understood what he meant by it.

She did not want to feel contempt for Richard. Contempt was only the bitter stop-gap of people who had no imagination, and no generosity. How could she have taken up with him in the first place if he weren't, in some way, admirable. André could be so quickly dismissive of people. There were plenty of other people who spoke about Richard with respect. His editorials might sometimes be a bit off the mark, but his magazine was courageous; and at least he was literate and witty, if somewhat brittle.

Even when it came to the occasional other women in his life, he would never, if he could help it, go out of his way to lie to her. Usually he'd taken the neutral course of saying nothing; and the few times she'd been unwise enough to push him, he'd told her only as much as prevented him from being actually evasive. It wasn't deceit in the strict sense. If he'd hidden part of the truth from her, it had been entirely for her sake – to spare her feelings. The fact that he took the precaution endeared him to her (perversely, perhaps). It must have been a sacrifice, of sorts, since Richard was not the type to live comfortably with tiny untruths scouring away at the fine, haughty sense he had of himself and his own integrity. Yes, she thought. She was beginning to feel calmer now. Underneath all the facade, Richard was an intelligent, feeling person.

Yes, it was enough now.

She pulled on a top, and bent hurriedly to fasten the thin straps of her sandals. She looked again at Richard. Why wouldn't he wake up, and go. Yes, go. She really did want him to leave her now.

All at once she longed to be doing something. Perhaps she should go and make some coffee. Maybe he would open his eyes if she brought some in and left it near him, where he could smell it. The picture of it made her smile.

* * * * * * * * * * * *

The empty coffee cup was lolling in his hand. André stood up, deriding himself. What on earth had he been thinking of, coming up here at the bloody break of the day.

This place had seemed bleak to him ever since he discovered the real nature of David's beliefs. No doubt a major conflict between them was still looming. Was it even possible to carry on writing his thesis under the man's supervision? The thought was painful. The keenness of David's intellect had never been in question. And one of the things André had admired him for was his crusty, glittering determination to live by the tenets of liberalism. Diligently, almost fastidiously, he had seemed to keep his mind constantly open. His academic work indeed affirmed the many fine aspects of that tradition; and as an individual, he had seemed living proof to André that rational debate between human beings was always possible, no matter how much they might differ. When David first began voicing political opinions in the office, André had kept silent, uncomfortably.

He personally had no time for apartheid, David assured them. Anyone who'd read his books would know that. Actually, he thought a lot of it had already gone; he'd never come across any of the really nasty racial stuff – not since his return from Oxford, anyway, twelve years ago. A liberal himself, he believed in the right to protest. Absolutely. But any reasonable person would concede that protest had to be sensibly directed. And it escaped him how missing a few lectures was going to accomplish anything.

André refused to be drawn.

Another time, though, when David made a remark about a 'bunch of radicals dictating to the rest', he found it impossible not to respond.

Careful not to raise his voice, he mentioned that the students had taken the decision democratically. *The debate beforehand was quite extensive. Heated, even.*

David gave him a small stare. He had no time for democracy, he said, recovering easily. It was a noble idea, but in practice, what did it mean. The rule of mediocrity. Ignoring André he carried on. *Maybe it's arrogant of me, but I've never liked meetings and that sort of thing, sitting on committees. I'm not your born bureaucrat, I'm afraid. Call it a personal quirk, but it's my way of preserving what I – what I like to think of as my integrity.* Always, David had that disarming capacity for self-deprecation. *It seems to me that if I'm forced to abide by some kind of collective decision, it entails a sacrificing of – of myself. It has something to do with surrendering one's individuality.*

André kept his own tone of voice equally mild. If David refused to participate, was he not indeed guaranteeing that others would make decisions on his behalf?

For once David seemed to consider before replying. *Oh, I suppose you have a point,* he said eventually, baring his teeth in a smile of glittering politeness. *Of sorts.*

Later that morning Mrs Scott had sent a typed message round the department. Concerning the cancellation of classes, Professor Harvest had no desire to impose his own views on anyone, and suggested that individual staff members should act according to personal conscience. At the same time he wanted to point out that if any group of students wished to have a class, this was no doubt their democratic entitlement, and, as such, a right he would like to see respected.

André went to the small departmental classroom at the usual time; with no intention, though, of giving his scheduled lecture. (It was only correct, he supposed, to explain his position to any of the students who might turn up.)

Sithembile, he noticed, was absent, but the remaining seven were all there, looking perhaps slightly uneasy.

They met his self-conscious speech with a short silence. Then Steve made an effort to reply. *Okay,* he said. *Okay.* Ducking his chin nervously up and down. But would they have a class next week then?

Not thinking, André nodded, determined to remain friendly; while Catherine chipped in, *Well, of course, the boycott is only for three days, isn't it?*

André nodded again, with less certainty. Who could say what might happen over the next few days and weeks. Unfairly, perhaps, and a bit grittily, he reminded the small band in front of him that the boycott was not some extrinsic thing, imposed upon them.

The student body – you – decided this, he told them

(wishing he did not sound so irritated).

We *didn't*, Gina and Michael said, both with the same bright stare of indignation.

Well, why not? he came back, driving them, he knew.

We don't all go to mass meetings, André. Offended, Steve glared at him. The others stayed silent, warily conscious, perhaps, of the point André was trying to make.

Speaking in a rush, Gina came out with it: *Oh, it's that thing about the* idiotes *and the* polites, *I bet*. (He could not help noting how poised she sounded, even in her disdain.) *He's saying we ought to have been there. I suppose it was our duty as responsible* human *beings*.

The satirical intent of the stress was unmistakeable. Well, perhaps he did tend to harp on the word. Suddenly it was difficult not to smile. *Okay*, he said, *okay I'm sorry. Maybe I was being heavy. But I'm still not prepared to teach today. Ethical reasons, all right? For me it's a question of right conduct*

This time they all smiled – even Steve, despite his flushed, grudging expression.

* * * * * * * * * * * *

Marisa appeared in the doorway.

'Hullo, hey Desi, hullo.' I'm glad somebody else is awake. It's so quiet in this house, it's like a grave. Why don't you come and sit in the kitchen and talk to me. I'll make you some coffee. Come; I'm just organising something for Richard.'

Desiree was surprised to feel herself warmed by the sound of Marisa's voice. She hesitated, though.

'I'm being fetched, I don't want to miss –'

'But you'll hear them, won't you? They'll come to the door. Come on, the kitchen is so sunny and warm at this time of the day.' As Desiree followed her through, Marisa kept talking. It made conversation simple at least.

'Okay, now. You sit over there, Desi. Coffee for you. Or would you prefer tea? Yes. Wouldn't you like one of these?' She had a packet open and was lifting out the chunky rusks on to a plate.

Desiree took one to appease Marisa. She did not want more tea either, but accepted the cup, smiling confusedly, with one hand to her lips, momentarily unable to speak because of the dry crumbs in her throat.

'I love that dress of yours, Desi, it's so happy with that bright braid on it, it's like a paintbox. Oh.' Looking embarrassed, she stopped. 'Oh no, that sounds corny. But I do mean it, all the same. That red seems to sing. It makes me think of when I was a child, and outside it was raining and dark, but we would have a fire in the front room, and my mother would be busy with her sewing, and I'd lie on the rug with my paints; and everything seemed safe.'

As she spoke, Marisa was moving around, drying plates, fetching things from the cupboard. Now she paused and stared at the tray she'd been setting, drawing her lips tight, into the dry kiss of dissatisfaction. 'Wait,' she said; and went out through the kitchen door.

Desiree looked down at the frieze of faded indigo elephants along the border of her skirt. She was fond of this dress, even if it was old now, worn soft with washing.

When Marisa came back inside she was beating the air with long, dangling sprays of leaves and trumpets.

'Cape honeysuckle, did you know that's what they call it.' She lifted her encumbered hands, trying to gesture. 'Everything else is closed. All the daisies, everything's curled up.' She sounded half indignant. 'Why do they do that, do you think?'

Desiree was beginning to feel slightly overwhelmed.

Marisa in one of her flighty states was not always easy to follow. Yet she did not seem to expect any serious answers – and soon enough she answered her own question.

'Afraid of the night, maybe. Never mind, anyway, I got these. Look, aren't they exquisite, Desi, smell them. Now this is going to wake him.' She dropped the flowers on to the tray, letting them lie there haphazardly over the cutlery. 'Okay, I'll be right back.'

While Marisa was out, Desiree dipped her finger into her tea and ran it slowly round the rim of the cup, trying to remember how you got it to sing.

Like a paint-box.

The paintbrush she'd had as a child had a metal clasp to hold the bristles in place; but even so, single hairs kept escaping and sticking to the paper. And there was a clay-like smell to the solid little blocks of colour in the tin.

She knelt on the carpet, crouching forward in her concentration, as she painted in the letters on the large sheet of paper.

Really, you children need poster paints if you're going to do that. Water colours. Oh dear, Martin. Their mother was trying to pay attention to something their father was reading out, but the baby kept crying.

That thin little wail of Shireen's. It was 'the formula' again, Desiree thought, vaguely. 'CAKE SALE', she had painted. The remaining words were written out lightly in pencil, to be filled in still with colours. *'In aid of the TLSA'.*

Imitating their father, perhaps, Anthony, who was eight years old then, began to quiz her. *Desi, tell me now, what does TLSA stand for?*

The question flustered her (though secretly she was positive she knew the answer). She dipped the brush into the jar of water beside her; and watched the murky swirl. Suddenly she whispered, *Teachers' League of South Africa.*

My word she knows, Anthony said. *Well, that's pretty good. All right, here's a harder question. What does league mean, Desi? What's a league?*

Confident then, she'd shouted happily back. *Seven league boots.*

There was a burst of laughter from their father. *Dorothy, listen to the child. We give our time, our sweat, not to say our blood and tears to keep the League alive, and this one can only associate it all with fairy tales, fantasies.* His eyes, though, were brimming with delight.

Boots? Boots? Anthony took his cue from their father and pretended, irritatingly, to be convulsed with laughter.

There, sweetheart. Her father was consoling her. *Just ignore him. I tell you what, why don't you find out the real meaning. You can use my dictionary to look it up, how's that?*

Anthony calmed down and got to his feet, as if he were bored with his own febrile behaviour. Going over to their father, he raised the lean wrist to inspect the gold watch. (He was showing off, Desiree thought, despairing. When would she learn how to tell the time?)

Daddy, it's nearly time for the concert, shall I put the radio on? With a funny, lanky dignity, Anthony went to the mantelpiece and stretched up his thin arms to reach the dials of the wireless.

Their mother lifted the sobbing baby to her shoulder and began massaging the tiny back. *That's a good idea, Anthony. They're playing the Pastoral symphony today. Don't you want to go and fetch Rosie? Tell her I'll help her with the rest of her homework tonight. And Desi, be an angel for Mommy and see if Victor is awake yet.*

'Can't we put on some music, or do you think the others will murder us if we wake them?'

Why was Marisa so agitated this morning.

'Let's, let's . . . What about all these records Chris came home with last night?' She pointed to the cardboard box on the floor.

Desiree hesitated, not wanting to be a kill-joy.

'Okay, you're worried about disturbing Chris. Look, I'll tell you what we do. Why don't we bring that one speaker through, the one with miles and miles of cord, and then we can close the door, and no one will hear.'

'But the records are probably stereo,' Desiree said, beginning to feel light-hearted.

'Never mind.' Marisa's eyes were shining as she too tried not to laugh. 'We'll get an idea of it.'

Desiree followed her into the living-room, going over to wait at the window while Marisa lifted out the tangle of flex from behind the armchairs.

'When are they supposed to be fetching you?' Marisa was busy looping the wire in untidy skeins around her forearm. 'I bet they'll be late.'

Back in the kitchen, Marisa set the speaker up on the table. 'Oh, we forgot to put a record on.' She crouched down next to the bursting, slightly mildewed box. 'All this stuff.' She looked up at Desiree, an expression of openness and expectation suddenly in her face. As though for a moment she were a child, hoping to be told a story.

'They belonged to his mother. His father gave him a whole lot of things last night,' Desiree explained. 'You know he went there for supper, to say goodbye to them.'

Marisa broke in again, as she was lifting out an album from the front of the box.

'Let's play this one. Leontyne Price. It says, "one of the most beautiful voices in the world today". I don't think I've ever heard her.' She tugged out the disc in its paper envelope and went off to put it on the turntable, leaving Desiree with the outer sleeve.

It was the record Chris had insisted on playing last night. His mother's name was written in the top corner, with a carefully scrolling flourish underneath it. Grace Braaf.

I was a bit confused when I was a boy. I fell in love with all of this; her face as well as her voice.

Desiree gazed at the sketch of the American soprano. As if to avoid bold shapes, the artist had used a fine stippling to suggest the sweep of the cheekbones. Yet the very delicacy of the technique created something extra. A muted impression of some dreaming, unearthly power in the singer's face.

Even the songs were a part of who she was. I believed she really was the most beautiful woman in the world. And – of course you can guess – I thought she was simply the image of my mother.

The speaker on the table had been issuing a faint, rumbling hiss. Now, almost before she was aware of the music beginning, something silvery seemed to be rushing below her skin. It was hard to believe it was a human voice carrying the thin shaft of that phrase. As she listened, she had a sense of the hairs stirring along her arms: the notes seemed to be floating, high above the blur of orchestral sound.

She turned over the record sleeve, to follow the words. *'Sul l'estremo con fin del mare . . .'* On the horizon, at the far edge of the sea . . .

The sea. What was it she'd been dreaming? Early this morning – something about gulls, and the tide coming in, and the yellow quinces tumbling in the transparent water.

What had made her remember those things, she wondered. Uncle Theo wading out to cast with his rod; leaving them huddled on the rug, with the steaming, knobbly fruit in their hands, and the gas lantern burning beside them, propped in the sand.

Desi, do you know what it is that makes the glow? That little thing you see in there is the mantle, and the way it works, you have to singe it first, to change it into ash. Isn't that a thought? Pure ash. That's why it's so fragile.

And I'll tell you something else. I always used to think your father was like that mantle. He had a radiance. I won't say he didn't anger me at times – because he did. You must know that grown-ups don't always agree over everything. I used to think, here was a man who'd been through the fire. And the miracle was that it didn't destroy him. No. It changed him into something purer and finer than the rest of us. I wonder if you're old enough to get my meaning? Towards the end of his life, there was something about him. He had a quality, he burned. Only it wasn't fire, but something much quieter: a kind of light.

As the aria came to its unquiet end, the voice soared up in a raging of hope.

She'd seldom seen Chris as talkative as he'd been last night when he came home. Perhaps it was his way of taking leave. Getting all the unsaid things off his chest, before he was gone for good. That might explain why he'd gone on so much about his family's removal. As though to say: we also suffered, Desiree. You Septembers weren't the only ones.

The notion made her flinch slightly. Perhaps it was simpler. Perhaps he'd just needed to talk – after that unexpected performance of his father's.

I can't say I know what I wanted from him. I don't think I expected a hero's send-off. No; I think I was always my mother's hero. Seriously, I can see that now. She thought I would be the one to save us all. I was going to be rich and famous, and get back our old house, her beloved garden. Also, I think it was a question of pride for her. I was going to be the

Braaf who made it; the one who lifted up the rest of the family.

(Chris had looked her in the eye, almost as if to ward off any silent judgement she might be making.)

But my dad, well: I don't think he needed any of that. I mean, he got on in his own way, in the end. No, don't get me wrong. I don't begrudge him. I think he deserved his success. He was good as an overseer, when they first promoted him. I suppose because he understood the work. The craft side. Because that was how he started out, when he was still his own man, he had a carpentry business. I remember, in the evenings, him coming home, and he would always take off his hat first thing and hang it up. It had this little feather in the band. Then he'd swing us up, each of us would get a turn, first me, and then my little sisters, and of course he'd hold them up high, because they were little. I remember, his hands always had that warm smell, I suppose from the wood, and the oil. But then he sold up. It was a pity in a way, because it was in the family for a long time, it was my grandfather's business. But then he went over to the factory, and eventually he took on more of the other side, the managing. I think it was only natural. He had that kind of mind. He knew how to look ahead. He could see how a thing would turn out. Not just one piece of furniture, but the whole prospect of a thing. Whole ranges. He knew what people wanted, too.

And my sisters. Oh, Cynthia's engaged now. I'm happy for her, too. But she's also changed. She and Julia. It's all going to discos, or if they're at home, the television is on all the time. They never used to be like that. I don't know. They used to care about music. They even did ballet when they were little; and they always used to come, faithfully, with my mother, to hear me when I was singing.

He *didn't, you know. My dad. It's a funny thing. He's never heard me, ever. Last night I suddenly felt, I don't understand him. At all. It's a hard thing, that: when you stop one day and all at once, you realise – you have nothing in common with that person. Even though he's your father.*

'Desi, what can I do, he just refuses to wake up. That man has got about as much self-propulsion as the plankton in the sea. Seriously, I must tell you, Des, I'm thinking of breaking up with him.'

Desiree looked at Marisa, unsure whether she was joking or not.

'Oh never mind. Change the subject. Desi, what do you think is going to happen?'

'What, to Chris?' (Marisa's eyes were unexpectedly quiet now, Desiree noticed.) 'I think he'll be fine. I'm sure it's just nerves. I mean, wouldn't you think so? Maybe it's a gigantic version of stage-fright, for him.'

'Oh. Oh yes, yes I'm sure it is.' Marisa looked faintly guilty for some reason.

'Apart from everything else, I don't think he's ever flown before, not even to Johannesburg. So of course he's probably feeling a bit afraid and lonely, on top of all the excitement and this rush at the last moment.'

'Yes. Desi: actually, I meant politically.'

'Politically? But he's not – Chris has never been involved in anything.'

'No.' Marisa looked still more flustered. 'We're at cross purposes. I meant – I wasn't really thinking about Chris at all – I just meant: What do you think's going to happen in the country?' She hesitated. 'Some people in our Area were saying there's a rumour they might extend the emergency to Cape Town.'

What made Marisa imagine that she, Desiree, had any special ability to predict the future? Suddenly she felt shy.

'I don't know,' she said. 'I don't know any more than you do. I'm sure your people have got as good an idea as anyone.'

Now Marisa seemed confused. 'Which people?'

There was a rustling in the background, while the empty groove between tracks was spinning under the needle.

Marisa held out the plate of rusks, offering Desiree another (as if she were at a loss for any other kind of overture).

The opening arpeggios were instantly familiar.

'No, no thanks, Marisa, really.'

Desiree wanted to listen to this song. Chris had been talking about it last night. Aloud, she said: 'What do you do, anyway?'

'What do I do?'

'No, I mean what do *you* do – your Area Committee?'

'Oh. Well, heavens, lots of things. We give out pamphlets, or we go out and help to collect signatures for petitions. There always seems to be a lot of fund-raising on the go, so we're forever selling tickets for things – movies, braais.'

I don't know how to put it, you know I'm not good with words. It's a melody that your mind hears, that it thinks it hears, it invents it, when it isn't really there. When you listen to that prelude – the original thing of Bach's, I mean – it's so quiet, you think it's so simple. It's this gentle progression of harmonies, like a single gigantic chord being unfolded in time, spread out across thirty-five bars. But somehow as your mind is taking it in it starts finding this silent extra part: you imagine you're hearing a melody, like another voice, breathing through the piece. As though it had a soul. Or, what do you say – a quick?

But then as soon as you try to grasp it, or you write it out in notes, you know, literally: then you kill it.

What is the name for that. There's a word for it, people use it about rhythm sometimes.

(Inferred, Desiree guessed privately.)

Anyway, with this piece, what Gounod did was he went

and put words to that silent part that was never meant to be exposed. And it beats the living day-light out of the thing.

'Oh I nearly forgot. Marisa. Talking of Chris, will you be able to go to his recital this afternoon? I wish I could, but I don't think I'll be free in time: sometimes the bureau is busy till the middle of the afternoon.'

The distress in Marisa's face was quick, and honest.

'Do you really think we have to? I thought it was just for all those lady patrons of his with their blue hair and purple jewels. It's not really a concert, you know: more like a tea party with a song or two thrown in. I don't think Chris is nervous about it.'

They were both still.

Desiree wondered. From the sound of it, Mr Braaf had said some harsh things last night. Things about Chris's mother.

Mrs Braaf used to reminisce, apparently, about their old family home, about the creeper that grew over it, tumbling thick and white as cascading water, filling the front rooms with scent in the spring.

And there was a palm tree in the middle of the street that used to be draped with jasmine in springtime. The whole height of it, right up to the huge crown of heavy spined fronds, would come alive, rustling with the flimsy, shimmering tangle.

But last night my father was saying she just dreamed it all up: that jasmine never existed. She couldn't face up to the reality that we were forced to leave. So, to cope, she came to live more and more in a world she invented for herself. She believed she was remembering, but really she just imagined it all.

I don't know, Desi: I was only four when we left. Actually, it wasn't even that the Group came for us. We knew it was going to come sooner or later, so my dad decided we would move first, before they came and told us. But the thing is, I could swear I also remember the jasmine. I know I can see that tree still.

While Chris was struggling to remember, Desiree had begun to think she too could see a bright, untidy mass of beaded strings spilling down from the crown of a date palm.

'Marisa, please won't you try to be there? I think it would mean a lot to him. I get the impression he's feeling terribly alone right now; almost abandoned.'

* * * * * * * * * * * *

Back outside in the daylight, André studied the mountain again (though from here it was half obscured by the library buildings). Overhead, the sky had a kind of innocence to it now.

Taking the steps down, he could hear the birds still at it in the shrubs and creepers.

He took the route over the footbridge this time, and then carried on past the old Dutch mill. Half way down, set back behind the quiet eucalyptus trees that lined the road, he passed what he'd heard was a government building. He'd often come by in the late afternoons and seen people leaving for home. Girls with lots of make-up and smiles, waving goodbye to each other. Once or twice he'd seen camouflage-painted vehicles drive out past the security checkpoint.

Well, did these details signal anything? What did they mean? That the country was heading for civil war? That was what so many of the pamphlets said. He'd even seen it written on a wall: *'Braaivleis, rugby, sunny skies and civil war.'* Actually, go on, admit it, that was clever. He remembered the old advertising jingle. *DA da, DA da, sunny skies and Chevrolet.*

DA da. He reached out and snapped off a spear of grass that was sticking out through the neatness of a hedge. Rhetoric was all very well amongst activists. Like marching songs, and war-cries, the slogans of 'the struggle' no doubt had a real function. But he was not interested in listening to people psyche themselves: he wanted facts, rational assessments. Was it true? That was what he wanted to know.

The flicker of irritation was dying down. Truth? You could call a proposition true; and you could say that a situation obtained: but if he'd learnt anything at all over the past few months, it was to forget about things like truth, and correctness. Especially when it came to action. Political action. It might be appropriate or inappropriate. But right? What was that?

When the idea of a march on Pollsmoor Prison was first rumoured around, his own response had been one of elation. Action at last.

Yet, talking to Desiree, he'd found that there were some who thought the idea crazy.

But it's irresponsible, André. Sheer adventurism. We've seen stunts like this before. It's putting people's lives at risk. For what? For a spectacle. For a day's pageantry. It reduces our struggle to the level of – of . . . amateur theatricals.

The remarks pricked, since he'd always treated Desiree's point of view with respect. And then, a few days later, wandering into a meeting of concerned academics, he found others expressing the same anger, even in similar phrases.

He wanted to march. For weeks he'd been yearning, seething to get out there and do something. It appeared, though, that he was being irrational – seeking immediate gratification in an action that was 'political' only in the most specious sense.

He turned the accusation over and over for several days before that Wednesday. Finally he came to a private, almost belligerent decision that he would follow the majority. The ultra-Leftists might be right, in principle – the plan might well be misguided. But if tens of thousands of ordinary people were going to get out there and do something, then he wanted to join them.

He was up at sunrise on the day; and it was hard to suppress a thrill at the thought that thousands of others must be readying themselves in the same way at that moment, throughout the city.

Already there were hundreds of students waiting inside the hall when he arrived on campus.

Did you hear, it's probably not up.

Because they've taken Dr Boesak in?

Ja. There's going to be a vote, but apparently the co-ordinators and the SRC are going to propose we call it off.

Listening to the informed young people around him, André felt a pang of frustration. He'd come prepared for action, finally determined to do something. Damn it, he was not going to be thwarted now. Yes, he'd heard the news. Dr Boesak had been arrested. Well, surely that was all the more reason to take a stand.

As he stood there chafing in the gathering crowd, a girl brushed past him, with something carefully huddled in her cupped hands. He could not help following her with his gaze, taking in the fine hair that streamed down around her face. Then he recognised what she was carrying. A tiny posy. For Christ's sake. She'd sealed the stems of the daisies in damp cotton wool, wrapped with tin-foil, as if to make sure they would last out a long journey. She must have been reading about the Hippies in the Sixties. (Twenty years back: she wouldn't even have been born.) Perhaps she dreamed of walking calmly up to a line of policemen, to put flowers in the barrels of their rifles? Or perhaps the little offering was just a talisman, for protection.

Two thousand, three thousand students had turned up for the march, and there seemed to be at least a hundred members of staff dotted amongst them. André was wondering whether to make his way over to a small group of lecturers, when the organisers swept on to the platform – one of them heading straight for the waiting microphone.

The plan was now far too dangerous, they were told. In the absence of Dr Boesak, no one could guarantee that the march would not end in catastrophe.

A few other speakers took their turn. Then John Bannister sprang up on to the stage and asked the staff to meet outside in the courtyard.

The day was already brilliant, and the sun had sent soft, smoothing hands over the bulges of the bronze statue that stood there looming – a strange god-beast cast in enigmas, implacably hailing the mountain.

Go on Alan, chair for us.

Yes yes go on.

Alan Findlay climbed a couple of steps. In the light his hair glittered with a surprising amount of silver. He would chair, but – elegantly he apologised – he would not pretend to be neutral. In his own view the organisers were correct to call a halt to the plan.

Hear hear.

It was a bloody senseless idea in the first place.

Stocky Dave Singer spoke from the lower step. *I can guarantee you now, if we allow the students to go ahead with his insane idea, what we'll have at the end of the day is a lot of spilled tears and a lot of spilled blood.*

One of the women had had her hand raised for about a minute. The chairman nodded to her.

She for one was tired of all this caution, she said,

projecting her voice boldly. All these endless intellectual excuses for inertia. *I think the day has finally arrived for us to take a stand, to put our beliefs into action. For once.*

André took in the bulging tote bag she was lugging over one shoulder, and wondered whether she, out of all of them, had had the sense to bring along supplies of food and extra clothing, perhaps even plasters for blistered feet, and disprins. He guessed she might be from the English department: hair in a fringe, arty blouse over her trousers.

Well, none of them, surely, disputed the need to put beliefs into practice. (There was an edge to Prof. Findlay's polite reply.) However, the issue was how to do so in the most effective way.

Dave Singer broke in again. What would the march achieve? *It seems we've got a few people suffering from a personal, emotional craving to recapture the heyday of their youth.* But this was 1985, not 1955. It was naive to think that conditions today were even remotely similar. *Let's not kid ourselves. As far as the government is concerned they're sitting with a potential revolution on their hands and make no mistake, they will act on that assumption. They've got the entire army out there today. Their aim is going to be to stop us, and if they have to kill, they will do so. If we go ahead with this march, I'm telling you now, by the end of today there will be people dead.*

Voting, after that, did not take long.

As soon as they had filed back into the hall, Alan Findlay announced the academics' decision to the gathering. André had expected the students to respond with jeers or groans. Instead, they listened quietly, with an almost desperate politeness.

The students for their part had come to the opposite decision. Many of them were already coming forward to collect posters of Mandela, and there were surgings of preparation around the hall.

Unhappily, the academics regrouped themselves; and when Ian Bannister shrugged and headed for the door, the others followed him out into the courtyard again.

Warding off the harassing glare of the sun with his forearm, Alan Findlay spoke immediately.

Well, I think it's clear that the situation has changed. I think that our earlier decision was correct. Indeed, I believe it remains so, in principle. However, it is my own view that under the new circumstances, that decision is no longer appropriate. I believe, in fact, that we now have no choice but to march with the students.

There it was: the only responsible course of action.

To save time, if there are no objections, I would like to move immediately that we do so. Can we take a show of hands?

Moments later the small group of staff went back in. This time they headed straight for the academic gowns that lay bundled in readiness on the stage. Findlay and Bannister went to confer with the students on the platform: as they spoke to the young leaders, they were fastening the red armbands of marshals around their jacket sleeves, pulling them on with a rough, bitter haste.

Almost casually, the two or three thousand students began spilling out through the doors into the sunlight, ambling down the stone steps to where the procession was forming up.

Ten abreast. And if we could have academics to the front, please. Academics at the head.

André watched Dave Singer walk up to take his place in the front row. He was angry: sweating with it. A girl went and joined him, almost tripping over the long black robe that fell back from her shoulders. She was wearing a flimsy pair of sandals. To walk to Pollsmoor in. Did no one realise how far away the prison was from the campus? It must be fifteen kilometres, at least. He watched her as she turned to link arms with the man on her other side. It was that chap from African Languages. Thembile Khalane. André had never spoken to him, but he'd seen a paper by him in the quarterly staff journal. The girl looked rather young. She probably wasn't really staff; more likely just a tutor.

From somewhere behind them came a tentative scatter of song. *Mandela prescribes for freedom, Mandela says freedom now.*

André watched the windows going up in the buildings along the university avenue, as students leaned out to stare at the gathering mass. It was extraordinary how many photographers were present that day: twenty or thirty of them, and a couple of television camera crews. One of the men came up close and crouched down in front of them, squinting up at Thembile and the girl through his lens. She was pale. (Scared, probably.) The photographer looked as though he wished she would lay her breasts proudly bare and go striding directly into some glorious, technicoloured revolution.

If we go ahead with this march, I'm telling you now, by the end of today there will be people dead.

Two students took up their positions at the head of the column, with a banner portrait of Mandela slung between them on wooden posts.

The buzz was beginning to obtrude into André's thoughts.

Okay, people please, if we can have everybody linking arms.

Mandela prescribes for freedom, in our land of Africa.

At last, preceded by the giant banner, the procession set off. (For an instant the calico sail dipped between the two bearers, dragging back to reveal a cameraman lying there, filming the marchers as they streamed forward, almost trampling him.)

To André it seemed as though they were walking through a wall of shimmering, unreal light. This was an instant in history? It felt like nothing. There was nothing between his fingers; only the sunlight everywhere, and even that had no weight to it.

The banner obscured the view ahead, but it hardly mattered. In a way, André thought, it simplified things: there was nothing for it but to walk blindly forward. It was better, too, not to think ahead, about what the coming hours might hold.

One of the two young bearers had tied his sweater round his waist, and the tee-shirt he wore was little more than a vest. The wooden posts were ragged with splinters, André noticed. The timber was going to chafe that student's shoulders terribly.

Show us the way to freedom, in our land of Africa.

A marshal came up and started trotting along beside the standard-bearers, pointing back. They nodded, then veered away to the edge of the road, leaving the academics in front.

A helicopter had come puttering out of the sky and was hovering over the enormous column. Police?

Probably a press charter, someone said.

Finally they were heading off university property, out on to the public road. All along the bend there were police vans and cars pulled up. There was no sign, though, of a riot squad.

What happens, happens, André told himself. There was a curve ahead; and beyond that they would pass under the fly-over bridge. Out of the corner of his eye he noticed students swarming down, racing across the lawns, heading for vantage points along the embankments. Voyeurs. Where had they come from, he wondered, calmly walking on.

Then, rounding the corner, they saw: this was the

point the police had chosen. There they were waiting, lined up across the road.

Christ, let people keep calm.

They've got guns, someone whispered.

No, no those are just for the tear-gas. There's one over there that is for rubber bullets, but that's all.

Someone called a halt. From behind the small vanguard of staff there were angry shouts, and the heaving, jostling momentum of the marching students seemed to keep on coming. *No, forward, forward.*

Dave Singer folded his burly arms, as though bracing himself to hold back any renegades who tried to break past him. Stiffening his pace now, André remembered. The moment he'd felt that pressing at his back, he'd squared his shoulders too, instinctively readying himself.

For what? he wondered. Readying himself for what? In the end, what a damned anti-climax the whole show had come to.

The girl in front of him had stood very still; her face suddenly gone the glittering white of quartz.

Then a student marshal came up from somewhere further down the column and began to address them through a loud-hailer. That was Nick Burger. (He was regional head of the National Students' Union: André had heard his name before.)

Fellow students, comrades. The police have issued us a warning. We have five minutes in which to turn around and go back up to campus. Under the light anorak he wore, his tee-shirt was clinging to his body, darkened with sweat. *Please, I appeal to you to remember the decision of our assembly, that we would avoid confrontation.*

Out of the corner of his eye, André saw Alan Findlay rush up, robe flying.

However, before we turn around, I am going to read out our message for Mandela, as we agreed.

What was this now, the police were notorious for their impatience. Further down the line, marshals were relaying the announcement.

The papers shook in the student's hands as he read aloud, taking his time. It all seemed a bit high-flown. Something about hailing the eagle. Never mind. Just get on with it. The students behind them were trying to thrust forward again. Angered, André stretched his arms out firmly.

Ahead of them, the police had struck ironic attitudes of boredom. One or two were practising slashes through the air with their sjamboks.

At last Nick gave the word for them to turn.

As the procession reversed, the gowned academics this time brought up the rear. With a few thousand students ahead of them, reluctantly retracing their steps, the last few ranks could only move at a serene pace. Close behind them walked the police, trying to hurry them on with showy (yet restrained) sweeps of their whips through the bright air.

And that was that. Days afterwards, surveying the general events throughout the city that Wednesday, a columnist wrote that the little escapade at UCT had been a mere Sunday School outing.

André was nearing Observatory now: the mountain had turned more of its shoulder to him. The lower slopes, he noticed, already had that withered, dun colour of summer grass.

Squinting, he looked up at the ruin of the old blockhouse, square against the skyline, still stonily commanding its views of the south and north, as well as the west. As a teenager he'd used to wander up there and clamber around. Looking for relics. He'd never found much, though. An occasional cartridge gone astray from the shooting range in the quarry. Otherwise there were only weeds and lizards in the place. A bit barren.

The words of the tenor's aria came back to him. *Comfort ye my people.* The damn thing was going to stick in his head now.

The march had been a let-down. Everyone felt it. Later that same day the thwarted students had gone down to hold pickets along the edges of the freeway, where it bordered on the campus.

Wearily, a few of the staff decided once again to go as escorts. And they must have looked like a handful of fools, running around in academic bat-suits, slipping on the grassy slopes, trying to reason with a few hundred unmoving students.

Of course the bloody police came back.

They're going to attack, come on, you must get out of here.

He'd caught up with Bannister, briefly. *These kids are going to get hurt, they don't want to listen, they won't budge.*

Bitterly, Bannister sneered back at him. *They're not kids, they make their own decisions.*

And then of course the cans of tear-gas started flying over, bouncing like stones in their midst.

The corrosive smoke was leaking from a can at his feet as he shouted, running with his arms wide, flailing, trying to shepherd people. Instantly his eyes were blistering with the fiery, streaming light.

Later, resting against a wall, sick and shaken, he'd thought over that comment of John's. All right, so they weren't kids. But, Christ, they still needed protection, didn't they? André could remember screwing up his burning eyes, fighting the desire to rub them.

Indeed, a mere picnic.

And yet, looking back, there was no doubt that the attempt to march on Pollsmoor had triggered off something – a new phase. (People threw around the word 'watershed'. Maybe it even fitted.)

In other parts of the city that day the police had acted with less restraint: by midnight there were eight dead, and hundreds more wounded; and a day later the toll of the dead had risen to seventeen. Within a week, thousands of teenagers had abandoned school and taken to the streets of their neighbourhoods. There might be a lull of two or three days, but then the barriers of oil-drums, old bicycle frames, crates, branches and burning tyres would rise up again. The Casspirs would come cruising back down the streets; and the stones and bottles of petrol would once again start flying.

About time, some said. Finally the Western Cape has got its act together. All these years this part of the country has been 'the home of the intellectuals', so-called. Long on theory, short on action. At last it's getting through that we can't sit forever, waiting for the 'right moment'. Finally Cape Town has woken up and joined the struggle.

Even the walls began to proclaim things. *Umkhonto weSizwe calls. Time to take up the spear.* In the wind there were rumours, restless as sparks of glinting dust, that if you wanted to answer that call, you no longer even needed to leave the country.

Oh yes. He'd played with that idea. (For a time he'd been obsessed with it.) On one level it seemed the obvious thing. History had landed them with a particular problem; and perhaps the simplest, most elegant solution would be to join the army of resistance. His personal beliefs compelled him to make some response.

Yet, he kept telling himself, those beliefs also imposed limits on the kind of action he could undertake. (This was his old theme tune, as his students knew.) Anything that was not stamped with the quality of humanness was beyond the pale. The difficulty, though, was to define that 'humanness'. These days it seemed to him nothing more than a set of latent powers. It was always only a potential. To realise that humanness required the active achieving of all the strengths unique to the species – the gifts of speech and reason, the faculty of memory, the power of imagination. Surely a resort to violence instead of these things would imply that he had failed to be fully human in his actions?

As he struggled with himself, he'd begun to hate his own pedantry. If only he could just go out, take a running jump and land firmly on the far side of all those bristling, self-constructed barricades of words. The café was already open, he saw, as he crossed the main road below the hospital. Perhaps he should pick up a newspaper. Get some milk for the house.

From a wall across the street there was a shout of red paint: *Longlive UDF!*

Two delivery men came out as he reached the entrance. Holding back to let them pass, he happened to glance at the plate-glass that ran down the length of the small building. What were those leaflets doing pasted all along the shop windows?

He peered more closely at one of them. The sketch, in cartoon style, showed a man writhing, wide-eyed, while a tyre blazed around his neck. God. To caricature such horror. In the background there were youths depicted in crazed jubilation; wearing UDF tee-shirts.

The hairs were stirring on André's forearms as he went inside.

The shopkeeper met his gaze with an expression of mingled sombreness and frustration. 'You saw those things? Right-wingers. I just want to know what kind of glue they used. We're going to have to scrape them off, man.'

While André was standing at the counter, the two delivery men re-entered with a pallet between them, carrying in the morning's bread. The loaves must still be warm, he thought, noticing the sheen of moisture under the filmy stuff that wrapped them. All at once he felt the hunger scouring at his insides. Christ, it was as though he'd forgotten the existence of food until this minute. He picked up one of the loaves and added it to his purchases.

Ravenously thinking of breakfast, he hurried on home.

Where is the border now, Boetie? The question confronted him silently from another wall half way down the street, where someone had sprayed it up in gigantic letters.

Good question.

3

Vanessa turned round in the passenger seat. 'Desi, it's good to see you again.'

Kate nodded, 'Yes we've missed you.'

'I must just warn you people,' Vanessa said, 'I'm on a diet and I'm starving, so I'm afraid I can't be held responsible for anything I do or say today.'

'When can you ever,' Kate teased.

Desiree felt a small springing of shyness. This world of constantly playful talk was still quite alien to her. She stared at the two in front of her, wondering what it was like to be them. Wondering whether the drift of their ordinary thinking and dreaming was the same as her own. Of course it must be. Yet she still allowed herself to look at Kate's dusty-blue dress, as though there might be some clue in its fine flower print. No, she was being foolish. She leaned forward, to try and match Vanessa's friendliness. 'It's only because I'm not tutoring at the moment. We've stopped teaching at the college.'

Did they know about these things, she wondered.

'Yes I heard,' Kate said, elaborating (perhaps for Vanessa's benefit): 'Because of the boycotts.'

'Oh, oh I see,' Vanessa said, trying to curl up more comfortably in the front seat. 'I suppose in solidarity. Oh. So you're not back with us permanently? That's a pity.' Desiree smiled back, not wanting to speak. She hardly knew herself what her plans were now.

'Oh Desi, I forgot – have you heard the news, you know Kate's bitten the dust? She and Nick have finally decided.'

Kate slipped in, rather dry: 'Vanessa was so pleased when we told her, she burst into tears. You can imagine how that made us feel.'

'No, no you idiot, it was just . . . I was just so relieved. Desi, I was beginning to think they never would.' Kate, who was plainly happy, pretended to dampen Vanessa's pleasure. Of course the wedding wouldn't be for a while still. She still had her bar exams to write.

Looking over her shoulder at Desiree, Vanessa whispered: 'I'm making Katie's dress – that's why they have to wait.'

'Well, you better finish it before Nick's call-up papers come. Otherwise you'll have to post it to us in Ireland -'

'In a parcel,' Vanessa exclaimed, laughing.

'And we'll get married there, and you won't get to be bridesmaid.'

For a few moments there was an amiable silence in the car. They were travelling along the freeway now, passing the outskirts of the golf links. Desiree stared at the dense bushes, thick with gold blossom, that grew along the boundaries. What were those trees called. Wattles? Mimosa?

Vanessa sneezed and had to fumble for a tissue. 'Damn, it's the pollen, it's this time of year again.'

Kate wound her side-window up, for Vanessa's sake, and for a while there was silence again. The glass of the windscreen seemed to intensify the warmth of the sunlight (which on its own was pale, cautious as new grass).

'Put on some music, Kate?'

'Oh . . . yes, if you like. There's a tape in already, if

you can stand Brahms at this time of day.'

Still holding a tissue to her nose, Vanessa fiddled with the small metal tabs of the cassette player.

Desiree leaned forward a little, to rest her folded arms on the back of the passenger seat. She was beginning to get used to these two again. She wanted to say something now. My father had the same thing. The words were there waiting. He also used to get hay-fever, maybe because he was asthmatic. She looked at the bland sheen of the little pearls that swung from Vanessa's earlobes. That was why. It was the asthma, why he died. The words remained stuck in her thoughts, refusing to be spoken.

The music broke through: a few quiet bars of pulsing notes, and then the beginning of a tender, elegiac melody. Vanessa leaned back again, sprawling against the sun-warmed vinyl. When the singers came in, she breathed out the first words of the chorus with them. 'Blessed . . . blessed, blessed are they that mourn.'

'I hope nobody minds listening to a requiem at this time of the morning. So, Desi, how's everyone in your family? How's Rose?'

'For they shall be com . . . forted'

The silent sentences still crowded inside Desiree's mind. They didn't help him. We always thought, maybe he tried to call out, but he couldn't, of course, he couldn't breathe. Or maybe they didn't want to hear.

'She's still working for Barney and Ghaironesa at Legal Resources, isn't she?'

They claimed it was pneumonia, brought on because he'd weakened himself, with his fasting.

'Yes,' she said quickly. Wishing she did not have to be reminded, just then, of her older sister. 'She's finishing her degree this year, by correspondence, and next year she wants to carry on with the Ll.B.'

Kate inclined her head slightly, listening. 'I'm glad, she said. I'm sure it must drive her crazy, working as a secretary.'

Desiree wanted to object. Rose was not the sort to dwell on her own frustrations. She did not know how to say it, though, in a way that would be light and unaccusing. She rested her head on her arms again.

'And your brother, the older one, is it Victor? I'm sorry, it's Anthony, isn't it? He must be qualified now?'

'Well, he has been for a year now,' Desiree explained mildly. 'He's working at Groote Schuur now. In Casualty.' She remembered something, and added, suddenly feeling less shy: 'He was on stand-by last night. Rose phoned to tell me, she said they were warned the army was going into Guguletu.'

'What, why?' Vanessa swung round to look at Desiree.

Desiree shook her head, and shrugged, unable to answer. 'Oh yes, we heard something too, at the firm late yesterday,' Kate offered. 'Apparently they were planning to go round on one of their door-to-door operations. Sometimes they give out pamphlets as they go, but I think the main idea is to search.'

'But for what, Katie?'

'Who knows. It actually goes on all the time. People just don't always get to hear about it – I mean, people outside the townships. Maybe it was because of the funeral today. Bit of intimidation.'

'I'd forgotten the funeral.' Vanessa settled back in her seat again. 'I suppose,' she said, 'it figures. In a way. I bet they're feeling jumpy – the police, or the army, whoever it is.'

'Damn sure they are. At that last funeral, the one in Athlone, when they had six thousand, seven thousand people out on the field. I don't know if you were there, Desi. Not? We heard afterwards there were more than a thousand guns there that day. You know how the men wear those long white robes? Well they had them under those. Apparently people discussed it very carefully beforehand, and it was strictly agreed they weren't going to use them except in self-defence. But a thousand guns.'

'Do you think there's likely to be trouble today? Desi, are you going to go?'

'Oh no,' Kate said sharply, amused. 'Desi wouldn't go to that. It's all been organised by the UDF. Ness, don't you know: the Septembers are old-time members of the Unity Movement.'

Vanessa looked at Kate, her face open, attentive.

But that's nonsense, Desiree longed to protest. How can you make such simple statements? Quickly, softly, she said over Vanessa's shoulder: 'No, that really isn't the full story. We've always been opposed to sectarianism.'

Kate frowned, but it seemed to be because of the sun in her eyes as she rounded the bend of the clover-leaf. 'I know the magistrate has ordered restrictions on today's funeral. The usual.' (She could not have heard Desiree.) 'No loudspeakers outside the church, no banners to be displayed, only two hundred mourners allowed in at the cemetery. Of course I don't think people will pay much attention. They never do. Let's just hope the police keep away for once.'

'Let's hope,' Vanessa said. 'Me, I don't mind admitting that I'm scared to go to those things. I know one ought to, you know, to show solidarity and everything. But after that Salt River one, when the crowd just turned on that guy and lynched him. Can you say 'lynched'? Or is that only for when somebody gets hanged?' She shook her head. 'Well, anyway. Ever since then I've felt . . . . I don't know. I'm really not sure about all these mass movements and huge big rallies and so on. I'm sorry. But I don't think they are always under control. I know that man in Salt River was a policeman, and maybe he was provocative in some way. But you can't justify murdering him like that. It was so obviously retribution, for the first man's death. No, I just . . . .' She let her words peter out.

Desiree looked again at the little stones, snared in silver-wire, that dangled from Vanessa's ears. She was thinking of the woman who'd run into the street that day, trying to plead with those youths. *It is wrong of you. In Allah's name, stop, stop.*

'I never did make out what happened there,' Kate said. 'The newspaper reports were terribly confusing. Was he stabbed or what? The story said he was also bludgeoned. With kerbstones – but somehow that seems hard to believe. And then there was something about a shot being fired; and how that Muslim priest tried to save his life, and they nearly killed him as well – there was a picture of him with his robes all covered in blood.'

No, Desiree thought. They did haul up kerbstones from the side of the road. There was a man staggering around with one in his arms, holding it to his belly.

The mourners had gathered on the soccer field behind the mosque, four thousand people at least. *Women please wait till the end.* After the service, the bearers left first, keeping the coffin high on their shoulders as they made their way through the crowd. *Allah uAkbar.* Studded with a few bright flowers, the white cloth over the coffin shimmered in the wintry, crystalline light. Softly, over and over, the low chant was repeated. *Allah uAkbar. Allah uAkbar.*

People fell in behind the coffin, walking slowly, in a column that took up the width of the street. *Women, please keep to the end.*

While she waited for the men to pass, Desiree had gazed up at the buildings opposite. The factory girls had come outside and were leaning over the iron railings of the fire escapes, five or six of them crowded on to every landing. The sunlight kept catching glints of sequins in their headscarves.

Allah uAkbar. Allah uAkbar. As the last straggling ranks crossed the main road, cars were beginning to move again slowly, hooting. By-standers lined the pavements, holding up clenched fists.

For a moment the murmurs of praise were interrupted by shouts from the street corner: *Amandla!*

Ngawethu!

Alongside Desiree, a few women joined in.

But they were instantly rebuked. *No, comrades, please: discipline, remember.*

Now they were heading up a steep road lined with the huge, blind buildings of warehouses. Desiree caught a glimpse of tall pine trees to one side; but beyond those she could see nothing, blocked by the crowd ahead of her.

Suddenly the ranks were scattering, pell-mell, and a child came racing past, screaming with fright. All around Desiree, people turned to flee without knowing why.

No be calm, don't run. Shrill voices halted them, and the strange eddy of panic subsided.

What has happened, what's going on?

There's been an accident, someone's dead.

Near Desiree, no one could see anything. People began pushing forward, trying to get nearer to the gates of the cemetery. Then the rumours came scurrying down the hill, seething through the dense crowd.

Someone's been killed.

No.

What?

They stabbed him, he's dead, man, he's covered in blood.

No, no.

It can't be.

It's a policeman. He moved like he was going to shoot and then they got him.

Jammed into a standstill, the crowd was packing itself tighter, with people still jostling to see for themselves. Now an ambulance appeared, coming up the steep road, trying to make its way through. It stopped; and then, in another rush, people were falling back, clearing the street. Pressed back, Desiree found herself pinned against the high concrete wall of a warehouse.

A group of young men had encircled the white-painted, official-looking vehicle. Behind the windscreen, the driver lifted both hands and shook his head. Then, slowly, he began to reverse down the hill.

While some of the youths followed it, one of them came staggering into the street with a concrete kerbstone clutched in his hands, balanced against his belly.

Shrieking, a young woman broke away from the crowd and darted towards him, thin arms raised, and hair streaming down her back. *It is wrong of you, it is wrong of you.* Caught up in a shrill hysteria, she went on and on, until friends dragged her back into the crowd.

Desiree felt the chill of fright beginning to sting her cheeks. Forcing herself not to run, she began to pick her way through the crowd, heading back to the main road.

Once she was free, she kept on walking, afraid that if she stopped for a moment, her limbs would seize up. Around her the light was blinding, though it was so quiet, resting in the weeds along fences and walls. A man had just been killed. It was unthinkable. Keep on moving. Alongside her in the street there were butterflies tumbling uncertainly through the air. The sun was out. She was trembling with cold.

Kate leaned forward to get a clear view of the intersection ahead. As her eyes narrowed involuntarily against the sunlight, Desiree noticed the fine dry lines in her skin.

Suddenly, quietly, Vanessa pretended to groan. 'I must tell you I'm so hungry I could die. Do you think we're going to be here till three again, like last time? Kate? Do you think we'll have many clients today? Didn't you say something about the townships being sealed off?'

'Solomon phoned me this morning, to say there might be problems. But he's going to try and come in the back way, along Lansdowne Road. He says the interpreters will try to make their own way through to the terminus. Someone will have to go and fetch them from there.'

Vanessa straightened up in her seat. 'Remember on Pollsmoor Day, they had this place lined with troop carriers.'

'A "ring of steel around Athlone", to quote.'

'And they had soldiers standing every ten metres along here.'

Later that day of the Salt River funeral, Desiree had gone home to her family. Shireen and Victor had just come in when the police began delivering their answer to the statement made in the cemetery that morning.

It started with a heavy droning racket in the sky to bring out the residents from their houses. There was a helicopter circling the suburb. While everyone stood in the streets, staring up, children began running along, shouting out warnings.

Salt River was being invaded: patrol cars and police vans were cruising in, driving around the blocks.

Within moments, the first yellow patrol car entered Dove Street. As it passed their gate, Desiree could see the men crammed inside: six or seven of them, huge-bodied. They seemed to leer as they stared back at her through the windows.

Overhead, the helicopter kept circling.

Ghostbusters, ghostbusters, two small boys came yelling.

Ghostbusters.

Casspirs? Surely not, Desiree thought. And then an insect-shaped vehicle appeared at the bottom of their narrow street. It was hard to believe. Armoured cars in Dove Street.

Slowly the long, tank-like thing came lumbering past. Clinging on at the back was a policeman. His head had been turned into a glinting mask by his helmet; but he wore the visor lifted, and behind it Desiree could see his eyes. He looked young; perhaps no more than nineteen.

At the corner, unexpectedly, the Casspir stopped: unable to make the turn in the narrow street. There was a scatter of laughter down the street.

Warily, the young policeman climbed down and walked out into the middle of the street, keeping a hand on his tear-gas gun, casually. With a scowl of warning set on his face, he began beckoning the driver on.

As though to mock the policeman's worst fear, someone called out jeeringly from the pavement: *Vat hom*.

Plainly, though, no one had any interest in grabbing the man.

Still guiding the driver, the policeman allowed himself a quick glance over his shoulder. There was a small, tight-mouthed sneer on his face. Once the Casspir had rounded the corner, he stalked back to it, slowly, with the stiffness of offended pride.

The clattering, chopping blades in the sky seemed to be killing what little warmth and light there was left of the day.

Eventually the police seemed to get bored with driving up and down and around the blocks, meeting no response; and as the last light died, they left.

'What a country.' Vanessa was shaking her head.

'Sometimes it's hard to believe all this is real. You know, there was this young woman we saw at the Law Clinic on Monday night. I couldn't make sense of her story at first, because she seemed so young, I couldn't believe she was a mother. But anyway, it turned out she has this thirteen-year-old child who's been detained. The police came into the schoolgrounds last week, made all the kids assemble, and then picked out the ones they decided were 'ringleaders'. One of the teachers told her afterwards he tried to speak to the kids in the back of the van, but most of them were so terrified they were crying. Screaming. Anyway, she swears her child has never been involved in anything. The only reason they might have taken him is because she sent him to school that morning in his ordinary clothes – because she didn't have a clean uniform for him. And then when she went to the police station that evening to take him some supper, apparently these people who were on duty just swore at her. But really: calling her such names, using the most disgusting language she'd ever heard in her life. She says she was so shocked she felt ill. She left the food there, but when she came away she was shaking, as if they'd hit her. Now, she says, she's never been to any of these UDF meetings, she's not interested in making any trouble; and she's completely against violence, as a Christian. But now she's all for the consumer boycott, she's even got her neighbours to join her.'

Desiree looked out at the roadside. There were faint streaks of wild flowers, miniature flares of light, floating as if they had no stems, above the blonde grass.

* * * * * * * * * * * *

André put down the phone feeling tired. The poor woman was lonely and frightened. If only that voice of hers didn't irritate him so much. (No doubt she believed its rasping, cigarette-induced huskiness was attractive.) He was not a good son, he thought, trying to remember when he'd last been round to her flat for tea. She probably wanted to see him, but couldn't bring herself to ask him outright. Perhaps he intimidated her. His own mother? (He hoped not.)

Hang on, what was that? Something was grinding repeatedly, round and round, making a small, periodic thudding sound.

But he had, he reminded himself, made several efforts to help her. A few months back, when there was a public meeting at one of the suburban civic centres, he'd taken her along, thinking it might help to dispel some of her fears.

Afterwards as they were leaving he'd been amused by the intentness with which she hurried him along in the direction of the car-park, past the crowd of people who were starting to dance and chant outside the hall. It was only when they were safely on the road that she would admit she'd been afraid of a riot breaking out.

Yes, no, she was glad he'd dragged her along. She hadn't realised how much was going on in the country, she had no idea. That the police could go around behaving like that. There was only one word for it, when they shot that child, point-blank in the jail. She'd been impressed by the speakers, especially the man, what was his name? Trevor Manuel. He seemed quite young, but he wasn't a rabble-rouser, she could respect someone like that. And it was a good thing to have those others, from the Black Sash and so on, because they were older, obviously more experienced, they would keep a moderating influence. And when that woman was talking about her son in detention, she could really identify with her, as another mother. It just showed you. Under the skin we're all the same. Of course it was a cliché, but it really was so true, wasn't it. It was quite funny when she was going on like that, and the interpreter had to keep breaking in. But even if people laughed, they were really laughing with her, they were all sympathetic.

Also, one thing that really did surprise her was seeing so many other people, oldies (she giggled) like herself in the audience. She would tell André honestly, she'd expected the place to be full of young radicals.

There you are, he'd said; and seized the chance to suggest that she join the Black Sash. *I'm sure you'd find it comforting, mother. It would give you a sense of belonging. You'll find you're not alone. And once you start to get involved – doing things, practically – I'm sure it'll take away your feeling of helplessness.*

He must have timed his proposal badly, though.

Oh no, André, it wouldn't be me.

For no reason that he could see, she lapsed back into a doubtful, protesting state. *No really, I couldn't.*

At least he'd had the sense not to push the issue.

What on earth was that sound?

He decided to follow it; and tracked it down finally to the living-room, giving a click of annoyance when he realised what the source was. The thing must have been left on all night. He switched the machine off and lifted the record from the slightly warm turntable. Where was its cover, damn it. He frowned at the label. Leontyne Price. Perhaps it was one of those from the box he'd seen in the kitchen.

He strolled through, balancing the disc between the thumb and fingertips of one hand. Of course. He was beginning to remember. Last night, when he came in for coffee and found Chris and Desi sitting up, they'd mentioned something about a whole bunch of old stuff – records and papers – that Chris's father had landed him with.

The sleeve was there. As he slipped the record back inside it, he glanced at the drawing of the singer; and paused for a moment, before returning it to the box. What else was in the collection, he wondered. Chris wouldn't mind, surely, if he had a look. He flipped through the records, and as they fell forward, one after another, he noticed how heavy they were.

There were also a few old albums wedged into the box, and loose pages of music.

He'd never learnt to read music, and it tantalised him when he detected what seemed to be patterns in the curving graphs formed by the black dots. Their significance remained an enigma to him. Curious, he touched one of the sheets. Stained with age, and almost powdery, the page seemed to disintegrate further under his clumsy fingers, flying up in miniature fragments of paper and music, fine as dust.

Rummaging further, he discovered something wedged right at the back of the box, pushed down flat as if to hold everything else in place. It was a book – a score, André supposed. The paper cover was half torn away, revealing more sprinkles of that dry, mysterious code of printed music.

André lifted it out; and his hand stopped dead.

Lying there in the exposed space was an object; compact, and glinting with the subtle sheen of metal.

Out on the stoep, Richard had taken occupation of the weatherbeaten deck-chair. 'Don't mind my company?' He waved, as if to chase the sun from his eyes. 'Oh, here, I borrowed your newspaper. Not much in it.'

André took it silently back, and spread the pages open on the ground at his feet; at the same time taking a large bite of the sandwich he'd abandoned when the telephone rang.

What the hell did Chris want to bring that bloody thing into the house for? (He almost choked on his own tight-throated anger.) It brought them all down to the level of those paranoics who slept with guns under their pillows, scared of being murdered in their beds by 'the blacks'.

'Marisa's gone out on a vital mission. Looking for honey. Can you believe it. She knows some hawker in Mowbray who gets a few jars from the farm where he fetches his produce. She says it comes along with a chunk of the waxcomb in it.'

André grunted, and shook his head, trying to immerse himself in the meagre news reports. His mind was still on the revolver. Perhaps it belonged to Mr Braaf. Chris might have brought it back by accident, along with all that other junk. It was possible. Give the guy the benefit of the doubt, anyway.

'There's something extravagantly futile, don't you think, about Marisa's pursuits. I ask you: honeycomb. It's just wax. Far as I know, the human digestive system doesn't have the slightest clue what to do with the stuff.'

Taking another bite of bread, André turned his thoughts deliberately back to his mother, and her phone call. She hadn't said it, but it was possible she was hurt by Riaan's decision to spend the weekend with his father. And now the old man was pestering her. Ringing her up in a fury, demanding to know how she could let Riaan visit their other son. Calling André names.

It wasn't good for him to carry on like that, with his heart. He'd had another two angina attacks recently, did André know?

In his mind, he heard her ruined voice again. *He's convinced you're a Communist, André. You aren't, are you?* She smoked incessantly these days, supposedly to keep her figure. He remembered his teenage anger, even shame, at the way her fine, white-gold hair used to be dirtied by the staleness of smoke. It was a smell he secretly understood to belong to the lavatories at school, something associated with furtiveness. What a little puritan he must have been, he thought.

She must be approaching fifty now. Not exactly an oldie.

André smiled faintly. He thought of the slanting cheekbones; the eyes constantly glancing up, appeasing, still shining with flirtatious light. She'd put on weight over the years, but the bold angles and planes of her face had hardly changed. It was easy to see why his father had fallen in love with her. In fact, if there hadn't been such obvious grounds for physical attraction (both ways, no doubt), it would have been difficult to explain the marriage, given the differences in their backgrounds.

He'd pieced together some of his mother's history. Once her schooldays were over, she'd left home at the earliest chance, coming to work as a junior typist in Cape Town. At sixteen she knew how to look after herself, she'd told him once. On Saturday nights she used to make sure she tagged along with the older girls from the office, wearing one of the party dresses she'd sewed for herself. She was the one – in the snapshot of the five practising a can-can kick, arms around each other's shoulders – she was the one with the wide satin belt that emphasized her tiny waist.

It was one of the other typists who'd introduced her to the tall clerk from Promotions. Marthinus Adriaan Binneman.

Dark-haired, the way some Afrikaners are, with skin deeply tanned over the protruding bones of his cheeks. With his broad shoulders, he looked awkward in those early photographs (there was no mistaking the air of the country boy come to town), yet there was something appealing about the eagerness in his clear, intelligent eyes. Dressed in a suit, with his hair smoothed back, he managed to look almost debonaire. It was rumoured that the top brass had started to notice him.

The company had set up shortly after the war, and prospered. By the early fifties it was already expanding its markets. It was possible, André supposed, that the directors (all Americans) were starting to need local go-betweens: people who'd acquired some urbanity, without losing the ability to speak easily to farmers and business-men from the country districts. Perhaps his father struck them as an ideal candidate. He'd impressed the rest of his department by mastering an ornately fluent English within months of joining them. (The faint tinge of an American accent had never disappeared from his speech.) No doubt his other assets were also noticed: his gregariousness, and a robust self-esteem that would easily (and usefully) spill over into admiration for the company and its products.

His father had always had a gift for enjoying life, André thought, a little stiffly. When Rosemary Ashton caught his eye, he'd embarked on a lavish campaign of courtship. Tucked into his mother's album there were still the stubs of old theatre tickets, along with brownish fragments of pressed flowers, and carefully straightened chocolate papers.

André could recall his mother confiding to him once that the real passion of her youth had been dancing.

Your father was very good at it, he could have been a professional. But then his idea of a night on the town was a trip to the cinema. (I used to think it was thrilling, the way he said 'cinema' like that: everybody else just said 'bioscope'.) Or else we'd go and eat at a restaurant in Sea Point. Your father did always like to eat. And to talk: he had a real love affair with words, it didn't matter what language. In those days I never used to get bored, I could listen to him for hours, especially if there was candle-light.

After their marriage, though, those conversations gradually lost their soft halo of romance. So his mother said.

Eventually, she and André's father would settle almost automatically for a film when they wanted an evening's entertainment.

Once André arrived, it wasn't so easy any more, of course.

But you get past that stage, somehow. And as soon as he was toddling, they used to put him in the back of the little Morris Minor on Saturday nights, and go off to the drive-in cinema.

A modest enough form of hedonism, André thought. He could even dimly remember some of those nights, from around the age of four or five. Dressed in his pyjamas, with his pillow and his bear next to him, he usually drowsed off on the backseat, lulled by the heat of the summer night and the enigmatic tumult of music and gunfire, and American voices. Sometimes, though, the sounds and the gigantic images used to excite him and he would stay awake watching everything, earnest, and feverish. During the interval his mother would take him to the cafeteria at the heart of the vast parking ground (he would swear he could remember walking with her over those artificial, tarred undulations.) They'd take back cokes and chips and, always, for his father, a kingsize hamburger. While the advertisements flashed across the screen, the interior of their small car would fill up with a reek of fried onions, meat, tomato, toasted bread, warm fat and spices. Then, when the feature film finally started, his father would turn up the crackling sound and lean back in his seat, settling himself for serious enjoyment.

When André was slightly older, his parents allowed

him to wander off before the start of the show, down to the swings at the foot of the screen. At the height of summer the sky would still be light, even at eight o'clock, and the flickering beam from the projection room managed to cast only faint, spectral figures over the ash-silver sail of the screen. Underneath those wordless phantoms, André would swing himself up higher and higher, until the chains jarred vigorously at the limit of each arc. As the stars came out, and the smell of grass and creosote grew richer, the gigantic myths continued to play silently over his head, washing across the screen in colours that steadily deepened until they had the reddish tinge of reality – and the continued absence of sound and dialogue suddenly struck him as frightening.

Even then, there were still times – to his mother's delight – when his parents went out dancing.

He remembered one of those evenings. While he dawdled outside, waiting for the friend who was coming to spend the night, a strange, gaping moment had opened up in front of him.

He seemed to see the light receding from the marigolds; and when the neighour came out to water his lawn, André discovered quite suddenly the unbearable, stupefying ordinariness of things.

Filled with a vague, suffocating listlessness, he'd wandered slowly back inside, to stand in the doorway of his parents' bedroom. His father was standing at the long mirror, leaning away as he adjusted his tie. He seemed to be in a good mood.

André tried calling to his mother, who was seated at her dressing-table, but she did not hear him.

He watched her slip on her stockings, tugging at the dark top part, and snapping down the little buttons that dangled from shiny white things. She smoothed down the rustling skirt of her evening dress and sat forward on the little stool, with its ruffle of net. Tilting the mirror so as to catch the light, she peered into it. André watched her draw over her eyebrows with a pencil.

Mommy, he tried again, and stepped into the room; longing to touch her, but reluctant to go up and clasp her around the neck, in case she pushed him away as she sometimes did, to protect her make-up. Still, he edged himself close enough to smell the scent of her. A vagueness of flowers, and something like wax, that seemed to sing, mingling in with the fragrance from under her arms and between her warm bosoms. He could remember how he'd reached out to stroke the soft waves of her hair, so soft and fine, floating out away from her cheeks, and down towards her neck.

All the time his thoughts kept returning guiltily to the memory of the acrid marigolds, and the light outside that had seemed to turn tepid before trickling away.

His father must have been watching in the mirror. From across the room he called out in that rich voice of his. *Hallo, seun. Tell Mommy she looks like a film star.*

Yes, he'd thought. She was beautiful.

He remembered how he'd stepped nearer and touched her skirt, filled with breathless hope. *Mommy, are you a film star?*

What had happened to it all?

There were many things he could ask, if he cared to. What had made his parents decide to have a second child so late, almost ten years after André was born?

Where was it his father used to disappear to, for those long stretches when he abandoned them, failing to come home for weeks, sometimes even for months?

His mother's face would become curiously unreadable during those times. Even when she met her older son's gaze, her eyes were opaque, if proud. Lighting up another cigarette, she would walk past him and wander out to the swimming pool in the dusk. Flopped into one of the garden chairs, with her plump, blonde legs stretched out in front of her, she would stare though the cigarette smoke at Riaan as he thrashed around in the sparkling water, boastful and wiry even at five years.

It was not that she'd refused to answer André's questions: she'd made it impossible for him to ask any.

Richard lay there in the deck-chair, frowning as he concentrated on sunning himself. (A skimming glance from behind his newspaper was enough to confirm for André that he was more powerfully built than Marisa's lover. Broader in the shoulders, thicker in the torso.)

There was a flicker of the dark eyelashes. 'You should have seen Marisa making a spectacle of herself last night. Wreathed around the neck of this poor sod she probably wouldn't deign to say two words to – if he happened to be, ah, as they say, white. It really gets to me, the way these little *verligte* Afrikaans types think the cure for apartheid is to love every black they meet: literally, that is. It betrays such a damned obsession with race.'

He paused. 'There's another layer to it as well, I sometimes think.'

With pained attentiveness, André gazed at Richard.

'It's this notion that if you want to end oppression you start by changing racist attitudes, as though the one flows from the other: when in fact it's the other way around. You think about it. What is it that makes one group contemptible to another? It's something about abjectness, wouldn't you agree? The condition of being downtrodden. It's the oppression, in other words, that provokes the hatred.'

André gave a slight nod. 'Oh agreed,' he said; and paused. 'I'm sure that's a fine aphorism. But what does one do with it? What are you are actually saying?' He was being rude, but then he was under no obligation to be polite to this man.

Richard shrugged. 'Not much I suppose. When I thought of it the first time I was full of whisky – and perhaps I had a somewhat fortified sense of my own grandeur. I imagined I was contributing something to the argument that the struggle is not about ending apartheid.' He made his mouth twitch.

André refused to let himself be disarmed by the handsome, facile glitter of the man.

Oblivious, Richard continued. 'It's this guilt trip that really angers me. And maybe here I'm not even talking about Marisa in particular. It's people like her in general, really. Always the anguish, always this belief that they have to make amends.'

'Guilt, you reckon?' André shrugged. 'Sounds a trifle too easy for me. I mean, to be a convincing explanation. Personally – and at the risk of sounding equally fatuous, no doubt – I'd say a more likely motivation for Marisa is her need to be loved. Seems to me it haunts her, it's a craving: this insatiable desire to be admired always, adored by everybody.'

'Oh indeed yes, that's bound to be a part of it, in her particular case. She has to be the most insecure woman I've ever known. But I was generalising. Wouldn't you say, on the whole, it's guilt that makes people, ah, cross the tracks – so to speak?'

Would he now. Would he say anything so damn simplistic. Carefully, André marshalled his own ideas. There was nothing intrinsically wrong with an occasional prod of guilt. He found himself staring across the low wall of the stoep.

The sunlight was flaring up, shimmering in the thin, bristling petals of the opened vygies. But then: if one did not act, yet at the same time persisted in nursing the moral hurt – well, that he would be inclined to call a form of bad faith. Restlessly he looked across at Richard, trying to determine whether it was worth having this discussion with him.

'Oh I can see you're not going to give. Well anyway. We were talking about Marisa's motives. All I'm saying is that they are selfish. Come on, André, you can't deny that she's simply trying to shake off the burden of her origins. It's an entirely personal need she's fulfilling.'

'Well. And is that so reprehensible?' André kept his tone bland. 'Actually, I suspect it's not altogether unnatural. How else could it be? She *is* an individual – inescapably, just as you are, and I am. And after all, human beings aren't historical forces. They are merely actors. In fact they're seldom even that: "agents" might be a better word.'

Richard placed his hands behind his neck so that he could raise his head to stare, deliberately, at André.

* * * * * * * * * * * *

As they came along the corridor they could hear a woman's voice ringing out from one of the offices.

'Cora's here,' Kate murmured. 'She must have let people in, thank goodness.'

About ten workers were already waiting in the first of the two interleading rooms. Seated on wooden benches, they gazed up at Cora Ndzube, listening to her deep, bell-like voice as she explained something.

Kate went to speak to her, while the rest of the group made their way to the desk and cabinets near the window.

'Desi? Maybe we should try and get the admin underway. Would you like to take the names?' Vanessa allowed the heavy box of files to slide from her arms on to the desk. One of the workers offered her a look of commiseration. 'There should be paper in one of the drawers. Oh and here are the tickets with the numbers, I think they're in order. Now let's see what else. Someone will have to go through the correspondence. Maybe Katie, or Indran when he arrives. You know Indran's coming in this morning? He agreed to swop over from Group B this week, because poor old Dave's starting to panic about exams.'

She was a generous creature, Desiree thought, remembering that Vanessa was also a law student, also due to write her finals in a few week's time.

'Oh and the cheques file. Desi, do you think you could take a quick squiz through that when you've got a list of all the names, just in case there's money waiting for someone. Or maybe I can do that later. I'll leave the file on top here so we don't forget.'

If Maya had been around the correspondence would already have been sorted. It wasn't part of her job (she was full-time with the Union now), but because she'd started out working for the Bureau, she was familiar with the things that had to be done. Also, she knew how disorganised the volunteer groups could be. If she had a free moment during the week she used to slip across the corridor and clear their in-tray, in preparation for Saturday morning. Desiree imagined her standing at the desk, holding a lighted cigarette in one hand, running through a sheaf of opened letters with the other. Her face would be rather pale; the small, fragile features steadily tightening with exasperation.

What did the police want to take her away for. Bastards.

More workers were coming into the room, and suddenly Indran emerged from their midst, out of breath, as though he'd run up the stairs. 'Hullo, everybody, sorry

I'm late. So what's happening? What do you want me to do?'

'Such zeal.' Vanessa was teasing, but Indran blinked acknowledgement, obviously pleased.

He noticed Desiree then, and from the small rushing of warmth in her face, she knew that her skin must be deepening in colour. She ducked her head until she felt able to look straight at him: 'I thought you would have computerised us all out of existence by now.'

He smiled back. 'Hey give me a chance, I'm still working on it.'

As Cora and Kate approached, Vanessa turned to Desi, prompting her. 'Let's make a start with taking the names. At least we can give people their numbers, and start digging out the files.'

Cora had been looking their group over. 'Mmm,' she said. 'Vanessa, Indran. And Desiree. You are back with us, that's very nice. How are you?' Nodding her head, she turned to share her approval with the others. 'But it seems to me you are very few today? Where is Dave, isn't he also with your group?'

Kate explained the swop, and Cora nodded again, keeping her eyelids slightly lowered, as though to withhold a fraction of her approval.

'Just tell me, who is going to fetch the interpreters, because you know they will be waiting for you this morning at the Nyanga bus terminus, did Solomon get you on the phone?'

'Yes he . . .'

'So well, maybe you should send somebody soon, I don't know. Because I am afraid if you make them to wait too long, they may think there is some difficulty. You know with the funeral today, and all this thing.' She pursed her lips, and looked at them consideringly.

'Look if you want to get on with the admin in the

meantime?' Indran was volunteering. 'I could go, I've got my car here.'

'Indran, would you?' Kate made an effort to sound brisk.

'It's Mr Nkosi from the controlling committee. Cora, isn't that right? And Siphiwo. You know them, don't you?'

'Oh I know Siphiwo.'

'They'll be looking out for you, anyway.'

Cora looked them over one more time, with a trace of indulgence this time in her clear eyes.

'Okay,' she said. 'So you can carry on now on your own. I have to go to my office. We are very busy this morning with the Union, seeing as Teach and Maya are . . .' She hesitated, as if she did not want to put it into words. Still silent, she raised her hands and mimed someone using their finger-tips to seize two objects and whip them away.

'Is there any news?' Vanessa asked. 'Has anyone been able to visit them?'

'Yes,' Cora said. 'Maya is getting maybe a visit next week, from her mother. But for Teach, there is still nothing, nothing.'

'Where is he?' Kate asked. 'I know Maya's in Pollsmoor, is he there too? Or have they taken him to Victor Verster?'

'No, our information is, he is still in Pollsmoor. His sister, maybe you know Mrs Dlikidla, she took food and clothes for him on Tuesday. But now we don't know, with these people, we have no guarantee that they will let him have those things. And of course we are worried, because you know he is not a young man, and he has problems with his chest.'

She finished with a look of practical cheerfulness on her face. 'Anyway, so we all have to work harder.'

After Cora had left them, Kate began rallying the group. 'Okay, where are we?' She leaned over to read the first name on Desiree's list, then turned to the row of tickler boxes on the nearby shelf.

'I'm so hungry,' Vanessa whispered, reaching past Desiree for her cigarettes.

'I heard that,' Kate said crisply. 'If you want to be thin, you have to suffer.'

'Would you like one?' Vanessa answered, handing her the packet along with a lighter.

The smoke from their cigarettes drifted up in small, blueish plumes. By the end of the afternoon, Desiree thought, her head would be throbbing. This was one aspect of the work she had forgotten. She turned her head, hoping the others had not noticed her distress. It was no use objecting: they needed the nicotine, or whatever it was that soothed them, helping them through these Saturday sessions. Behind her the window was open as far as it would go. It allowed some fresh air into the place, but meant also that the noise from the streets below came drifting up.

Once again she thought of Maya, and Teach Zwakala. *Because you know he is not a young man . . .*

In the middle of the night, when their mother's soft groaning had died down at last (leaving them with the shame of relief); and the ambulance came (and the lights were flashing outside), and Rose was there in her dressing-gown. Someone was whispering in anger. There were people speaking on the telephone, and then the doorbell was ringing again, and Shireen kept crying in a tiny, blinded rage in her cot. When the men were coming in with Mr Abrahams from next door, and Anthony looked suddenly like a grown-up, like their father resurrected perhaps. Victor came running to find her, his small body rigid, hot; hitting her with his fists and screaming, tears blistering from his eyes. *They coming to detain mommy.* That was what he must have thought.

Still more workers were coming in, some evidently here for the first time, to guess from the way they paused in the doorway, studying the place, trying to read the faces of those already waiting. One of them began a conversation with a young man about his own age, speaking casually, as if he knew him, though he avoided fixing his eyes too inquisitively on the other's face.

'I can see us having to rope Cora in,' Kate said, exhaling smoke. 'I just hope Solomon manages to get here soon.'

'It's not as many as it looks.' Desiree held up the list. 'These five are all from the same company. They were all dismissed on the same day, so I only opened one file for them. I hope that's right?'

'Good. Yes. We'll take it as a group case.'

'Desi, won't you give me a file number?'

'2556. Have you got that?'

'Oh, hang on, here's Solomon now.'

At the sight of the elderly man entering the room, Desiree felt a sudden lightening of mood. Things might start to get better now. As she watched, he stopped to speak to a client, greeting the man with infinite carefulness.

'Found it,' Vanessa announced. 'Oh, would you believe it's one of Andrew's, I'll kill him. Desi I'm sorry, could you perhaps give him a ring. We should have his number. Where's the list?'

The phone was kept on the window ledge, balanced on top of a batch of envelopes. Once she'd finished dialling, Desiree gazed out through the glass pane, trying to make out which of the dingy buildings opposite might house the club, or whatever place it was that broadcast the monotonous disco music. She recalled Alan saying once that it came from the furniture shop on the corner. Maybe there was a theory that it would attract customers inside. She smiled.

'Okay next one, 3014, Langa.'

'Mr Langa? Oh no, is he in this morning?'

At the other end of the line, the phone rang over and over.

'But Kate, what am I going to say to him, it's hopeless. He was with those people for twenty-three years, do you know that, and the bastards aren't prepared to give him a gold watch. Okay, so he was just the cleaner and tea-maker, and they've got their policy, gold watches are for their senior staff only. But you'd think: after twenty-three years. I've written this Mr McKenzie a letter now, trying to appeal to his heart – I thought maybe as a last resort we could reach him on a purely human level. But there's been no joy out of it so far. We haven't had a reply.'

Desiree put the phone down. Someone would have to explain to Mr Gagwana that the consultant was out, and ask him to return in a few weeks' time. The procedures were slowly coming back to her.

* * * * * * * * * * * *

Marisa parked the car in Main Road, and sat for a while, trying to shake off a racing sense of panic. She leaned her head against the side window. Across the street, near the Mowbray library, the leaves of a giant fig were clasping at the light.

She could not carry on pretending there was no problem. The difficulty lay in working out what it was, exactly.

Perhaps Richard was heading for some minor crisis of his own. Although he did not talk about it, he was heading for his thirty-fifth birthday, for one thing. Maybe he was frightened. Conscious of a need to make choices. Well, it was about time, wasn't it? People settled so easily into patterns of existence. If he didn't make some fundamental change soon, he might reach forty and still be the eternally restless, dissatisfied rake. On aesthetic grounds alone, she thought, the image could hardly seem appealing to him.

She must speak to him. Alternatively, perhaps she should say nothing at all, and simply leave him.

Flit away, one more time. Same old butterfly behaviour. The thought hurt her. She had been trying so hard this time to avoid the easy course. Self-mocking, she used the clichés deliberately, lightly. Trying to turn over a new leaf. It was a decision she'd taken even before that episode in the nursing home.

She could remember walking in downtown Johannesburg, and glimpsing a familiar face in the crowd. Yes: one of her father's friends. And the man had turned his face away, with a cruel shortness. The snub was terrible to her, searing as the poisonous scratch of a wild thorn. Did people gossip so much? And judge so harshly? That man had written her off – just like that – at twenty-four. The notion shocked her into a state of inner stillness.

Braam had tried to warn her, of course; long before. Funny how you can fail to understand what people are telling you. But then Braam was always wanting to point out her failings. It was maddening. Even after everything was over, long after they'd stopped being lovers, he carried on doing it, behaving as though he bore some kind of moral responsibility for her.

There was that time when he phoned her up, inviting her out for a walk, quite formally, as if to warn her that he had something serious on his mind.

It had been windy at Sunrise Beach that day, and the

sand had a dry edge to it, so that the powdery grains made a squeaking noise underfoot.

Marisa, I want you to listen. We've got to talk about this craving of yours, this mad desire to be admired all the time. His straight hair had kept whipping across his eyes, and he'd had to scrape it back with his fingers. *No, no listen.*

Ja ja I'm vain, Braam, I know.

No. I don't really think you are. He'd managed to silence her there. *It's something else I wanted to say.*

The sheets of water were racing in fast, swirling wide across one another, before drawing back to leave a sheen across the sand. You could gather up nautiluses here, someone had told her once. (Etienne. Wasn't it him?) If you came down in the stormy season, at dawn, and if the wind was right it would be driving the paper nautiluses in off the waves, sending them scudding and flying on to the sand, or leaving them to tumble in the stiff eddies, cracked and shattered by the foam. You could gather them up, armfuls of them, though mostly they would be broken, unless you managed to catch them flying out of the wind. She started telling Braam; but he went back to his own theme, patiently.

It was about her behaviour of course. He took pains to explain to her: he was not overly bothered by other people's opinions – although it hurt him to hear what they were saying about her.

She knew; she didn't need him to grind it out. *Ek weet mos.* Running on ahead, she turned to shout, happily. *Hulle sê, hulle sê . . . I've got the morals of an alley cat.*

He refused to smile back. He was, she realised, angry with her.

For a while she walked alongside him in silence, reluctant to admit that she had taken fright. That heavy honesty of his.

He persisted. Promiscuity was – *sometimes in a person it*

seems like the other side of frigidity. The substance of it is the same thing.

She raised her face to the wind, wondering why the light seemed so harsh, when there was nothing to see in the sky except glistening cloud and a vast, diffused sweep of greyness.

What is the common element. Come on Marisa, stop trying to avoid me. It's an inability: Marisa? An inability to make a lasting commitment. Of stem jy nie saam nie? Kom, hoe sê jy?

Hating him, she'd raced ahead again, bending to pick up a length of kelp. Watching him from a distance, making her eyes sparkle, she put the tube to her mouth and blew, hard, till she managed to produce a low sound.

What bothers me, Marisa, he called doggedly across the sand, *is this craving of yours all the time for more admirers.*

I can't hear you, she cried back, breathless. *The wind, it's just blowing all your words away.*

What is it, why can you never be content in yourself, why do you need all this constant affirmation from outside?

She lifted the kelp-horn and tried to make that noise again; secretly thinking how the thing stank of salt-water and flies.

Braam, asseblief, she said, when he caught up with her again. *It's no use. We always talk so much and the words are so long, and in the end they've only pushed us miles apart from each other.* She ridiculed him. *They just keep coming, buzzing, buzzing, booming out of you, but it doesn't . . . there's no connection, in the end there is nothing to hold on to, they don't even hold us together.*

He tried to put an arm around her, but she'd stepped lightly aside. *Marisa, I don't mean to attack you. It's just that you bewilder me. It seems to me as if you want more than anything to be loved; but as soon as someone does, does love you – you run away, you feel you have to fly. You need more, someone else. It's never enough. Marisa, why?*

She lifted the instrument again, and this time managed to sustain a lowing, bellowing note; looking at him all the time, with her eyebrows raised, as she kept her cheeks puffed out.

Braam steadily ignored the game. It was true he knew her far too well. Eventually he took the crazy instrument from her, and stood facing her, using his free hand to shade his face, so that he could look into her eyes. *Can you not see, no? If you are always seeking confirmation from others, it can only mean you have no faith inside yourself, no solid core where you know who you are, where you can accept that you are loved.*

Frowning, he put his hand on her shoulder, trying in his clumsy way to be gentle with her. *You think you can make people love you, worship you. But what you don't understand is that your need for little puppet admirers turns you into a . . . a robot, an automaton. 'n Pop. Ja dis jy wat die klein poppie is, Marisa. You are the little toy dancing creature: not the latest man you've captivated.*

She could tell the depth of his anger from the mordant articulacy of his speech. Beginning to feel helpless, she shouted, pushing him away. He had no right. He *was* attacking her. Just because he denied it, it didn't mean he wasn't.

You think you are in control, Marisa; but you are making a mistake. You are easier to twist than a bendy-man. Anyone, anything seems to influence you. One day you will wake up to discover reality flooding right through you, and it will carry you away.

She'd refused to hear any more.

It was becoming unbearably warm inside the car. Perhaps she should get a move on.

Marisa got out and walked down one of the side-streets, heading towards the bus terminus, where the street-sellers usually stationed themselves.

'Here's your potatoes onions for the braai mummy-girl.'

'Rand a bag,'

There weren't many people out on the streets. Too early still, perhaps. Or perhaps it was because of the funeral today?

'Here's your pototoes onions for the braai.'

No; she'd bought vegetables for the house only yesterday.

Another roving seller caught her eye, raising a cluster of bananas for her inspection. 'Rand a bunch, lady, rand a bunch.'

Smiling, she shook her head.

'Soeter as heuning soeter as stroop.'

Most of the sellers were still setting up their trestles, balancing them on top of crates, old drums or up-ended pallets. One stall looked as though it were the weathered body of an old hawker's cart, without wheels, but with the wooden shafts still protruding from the front.

'Kom kyk hierdie soet bananas hier.'

As he sang, the merchant kept at work, building up bright pyramids of naartjies and apricots.

'Peach time peach time, alweer peach time. Lovely peaches lady, three for a rand.'

She hesitated, and the hawker, thinking he'd caught her attention, tried again:

'Come try some,
It's good for your gums.'

Shaking her head, she walked on.

'Spring time, peach time.'

The man she was looking for usually set up his stall over there at the far end of the traffic island. Always dressed in a white overall, always with a hat on his head. He seemed to be the most organised seller in the area, with his own bakkie, and a beach-umbrella to shade his stall. He'd told her his name once, slipping an orange into her slingbag, refusing to take her money.

'Rand a bag rand a bag, lady, rand a bag.'

Richard thought she was frivolous. Well then, she might as well confirm it for him. She'd told him she was coming out to see if Adam had any honey this morning. And it was perfectly true, too. Sometimes he kept a few jars of it behind his pineapples and shied-up naartjies. Pale and thick, with a rough chunk of the comb included. Perfect for a feast, for a farewell supper.

'Kyk hoe lekker koop die mense die bananas
Lekker spotted bananas
Kyk hoe lekker koop die mense die kant.'

In the distance, on the other side of the road, she noticed two young men selling what seemed to be strands of pure, blazing light. Attracted, she went across.

The two merchants seemed rather shy of her. Silently, they watched as she picked through the jewellery. The sunlight shot through the glass, making the beads slip with fire and brilliant hints of metal.

The stall was little more than a wooden tray, balanced across two old oil-drums. On each drum was a poster for a soccer match: 'All proceeds to families of victims of police violence'.

She touched one of the glittering necklaces. 'It's pretty,' she said, hoping they would not think her patronising. They stared back. Perhaps they were unable to speak English, just as she was unable to speak Xhosa. 'How much?'

The taller one responded this time. 'Four rand.'

She smiled again, regretfully, and turned to walk away. She would have liked to buy something, but a vestige of sense told her it would be a waste of money.

Suddenly she changed her mind. Damn caution, she thought, reaching into her bag. She took out four rand in coins and held the money out to the men, lifting up a string. The glass beads flashed and trembled with a watery, faintly crimson light. Like pomegranate seeds, she thought.

'Is there tax?'

They shook their heads.

'It's beautiful,' the taller one said, watching her fasten the thing around her neck.

The clasp would not last very long. Never mind. She could almost feel the rose-coloured light flickering through her fingers.

In a dreaming state, she wandered back up the road.

'Lekker avocado pere,
Drie vir 'n rand three for a rand.'

She was starting to hear how the cries were orchestrated. One hawker would begin, ending his chant on a rising tone; and then another man would come in on a low note, making his own cry overlap the dying sound of the last singer's phrase.

A woman with a small boy at her side stood at the stop for the city-bound buses.

'Hier's lekker avocado pere.'

Two hawkers were competing for the woman's attention, each holding up an avocado pear.

'Three for a rand, only three for a rand.'

The child stared over his shoulder at the men, keeping a section of his mother's skirt tightly balled in his fist.

'Hier's een vir die kind,
Een vir die man,
En een vir die vrou –
Dis 'n ene vir jou.'

The woman took no notice.

'En die mummy weet waar . . .'

Perhaps it was meant to be an obscure insult. Without a pause, the hawker pretended to direct his cries elsewhere. Marisa saw the quick spark of a grin he exchanged with the other seller, before a new bus-load of customers arrived, and the cries became fast and professional again.

'Lekker soet bananas
Soeter as heuning sweet as honey
What will it be?'

Seeing the child made her remember a scene she'd witnessed here one afternoon, when Adam was feeding the pigeons.

It was a daily ritual: fetching the bag of grain from the back of his bakkie, he would give a whistle; and there would be a shimmer across the sky as the waiting birds took off from the roofs and ledges, coming in on angled wings to snatch at the rolling, hard yellow seeds in the dust.

Once, though, one of the birds had come plunging down, misjudged its flight – and landed on the shoulder of a tiny girl; causing a clamour of terror while its claws stuck for an instant in the miniature collar of her dress, and small hands shot up to tear the thing away. Within seconds, though, the battering creature had broken free and fluttered to the ground. As it waddled greedily off after the scattering grains, the child recovered her balance too, and started to laugh with the rest of the crowd.

Who fed them, Marisa wondered, on days when Adam did not come?

Who would feed them today?

'Lovely bananas pick any bunch
Only a rand, just pick any bunch
Hier's spotted bananas
Die's lekker spotted bananas hier.'

A bus came racing around the traffic island, and braked sharply in the middle of the road. They weren't supposed to do that, were they?

The driver already had his door half open. He was shouting something.

Two or three inspectors ran up.

What was the excitement? As the passengers clambered down they were all talking, loudly. Some of them had dazed, almost bashful expressions of amusement on their faces.

'Skollies. Alweer skollies.'

'Waar't dit dan gebeur?'

'It was just there by Hanover Park. *Ek het so geskrik.'*

'All over again, it's starting. *'n Mens raak so moeg.'*

From shelters across the road, more inspectors began to converge on the bus, calling to one another, walkie-talkies crackling in their hands. Marisa saw them follow the driver round to the back of the bus to look at something.

One of the inspectors looked at her. 'It's nothing, lady. Just a . . . a cracked window, that's all.'

Voices were still calling out, as people dispelled the fright of that moment.

'It's a TV, *nou's die bus 'n TV.'*

'Ja and we had to be the pictures inside.'

Marisa felt shaky. If there were stones being thrown now in Hanover Park, what might happen at the funeral?

'Here's your potatoes onions mummy-girl
Some is for the slaai
The rest you can put it in the braai:
Buy
your potatoes onions here mummy-girl.'

The antiphonal cries were breaking out again, as the hawkers rushed to catch some trade before the crowd dispersed.

'Lovely bananas nice and soft
Just pick any bunch
Lovely and soft -'

The first singer seemed to miss his beat, but then came in deliberately fast, trying to keep his expression steady:

'For haarders kyk in die fish-shop.'

The notion of hard bananas lying on a marble slab made Marisa smile, and suddenly it was a relief to laugh.

'Spring time, peach time
Peaches for a teacher.'

Oh, she thought, smiling at the seller. She might as well buy here. A pity about the honey, but never mind.

The seller unfurled a plastic bag and nodded to her to choose the fruit she wanted. A pineapple. Naartjies and apricots for tartness. Or peaches? Four of those oranges. Definitely some of those spotted bananas.

As he packed the fruit for her, the man kept his shrewd eyes fastened on the passing crowd, still inserting his own cries into the medley.

'Lovely bananas die kant
Kyk hoe lekker koop die mense die kant.'

* * * * * * * * * * * *

The phone rang almost under Desiree's hand. 'Hullo, Transport and Allied Workers Union Advice Bureau.'

'Hullo?' The person at the other end was phoning from a call-box.

'Mm, hullo,' Desiree repeated. 'This is the Advice Bureau, can we help you.'

'Aaa, hullo, please, who am I speaking to?'

'This is the Union's Advice Bureau, this is Desiree September, from Group C. Maybe . . . can I take your phone number?'

'Hullo?'

'mNumzana?' Hesitantly she tried: *'Ufunani ukuthetha nonobhala wethu, uSolomon Mzamane?'*

She turned slightly, and tried to catch Solomon's eye.

The caller was speaking rapidly in Xhosa now, mistakenly believing that she could follow him.

Trying to shut out the noise in the place, she pressed her hand against her ear.

She waved across the room to Solomon, holding up the receiver. He was still concerned with the plight of the man at his side. Slowly, he turned, seeming to address Kate and Desi indifferently. The worker talking to Solomon had the feverish, glistening eyes of someone who'd been ill for a long time. Perhaps he was another one with tuberculosis, she thought, remembering the dozens of sufferers they'd seen in this office.

'He's coming now, I'm sorry,' she said into the receiver; and returned her gaze to Solomon. 'Please, won't you tell me your phone number, in case.'

Solomon moved across to speak to Kate. 'Well now, you see, he says, he is nearly at retiring age, so now you see, he can't get his contract renewed if he is unfit for work.'

When the bleeps started, there was a moment's clattering and slamming; then the man was pleading with her again. He must have had extra coins ready.

'So now, we have referred him to the Black Sash, because we feel if we try to get permission for him to stay in the city, it may be better for him because of his illness.'

'Hullo, hullo?'

'I'm sorry, I promise, he's coming.'

Her gaze strayed round the room, taking in the posters on the dingy walls. There was a chart someone had thought to stick up, on the dangers of asbestosis. The text was in German. More usefully, there was an illustrated wall calendar hanging near the telephone. It carried the logo of the Front, Desiree noticed, vaguely amused. Perhaps it had been placed there as an act of defiance. (The Union had chosen not to affiliate to the Front, and there were some who translated the different concerns and tactics of the two movements into supposed conflict between them. In reality, the Union encouraged its members to join community organisations as well.) She studied the collage of photographs above the neat blocks of numbers. A child with both tiny hands made into fists, pushed against its eyes, and the mouth wide open, wailing. A crowd of people on the march, with a makeshift banner held high. The Reverend Allan Boesak, standing behind a rostrum and smiling, radiantly, with one hand raised. Students etched on to film by a split second of sunlight as they ran, one of them ducking to catch up the canister bouncing at his feet.

Solomon was finally making his way over to Desiree, stepping carefully past the crowded benches.

'Desi?'

While Solomon was busy on the phone, Kate explained to Desiree what had to be done. 'Could you? The client's name is Kula. Got that? Mr Kula. With a kay. He just needs a covering letter to take to the Sash. The letterheads are somewhere up here, yes – that box, and I think there's carbon next door.' In a quieter voice, she added, 'I don't know if Solomon's going to be able to help with the interpreting, he's got too many cases of his own to handle as it is.'

The elderly secretary-general put down the phone and turned to them, with a mild expression on his face. 'That was Mr Nkosi,' he said. 'He is still trying to get through, he is at the terminus: he thinks he will come on his own now and not wait for you to fetch him.'

Kate frowned. 'No. No, Indran's already gone, Solomon. They've probably missed each other.'

'Oh,' he said, with a patient, faintly sceptical look. 'But now Mr Nkosi is thinking there is some problem.'

'Yes, I'm sorry, we were a bit on the late side this

morning.'

'Mmm,' Solomon said.

'I'm sure Indran will be there any minute, seriously.'

'Well then, so it's all right, maybe, if you say.' He shrugged, as if to heave the problem off his shoulders, and walked away to speak to another client.

The pounding noise of the disco music intruded again. Pretending to be searching for something, Desiree turned away and let her gaze rest on the dust-silvered pane of the window. A trick of the shifting sun, or the angle of her own glance revealed something she had failed to see earlier: an image written there of a spread wing, of feathers blurred against the clarity, the shimmer of the glass. The imprint of some split-second's explosive error.

She wished now that she'd gone with Indran. It would have been a brief escape, of sorts.

In the past she'd always enjoyed going out to fetch the interpreters or take them home afterwards. During the consultations, while they were working, there was seldom a chance for conversation. It was on one of those journeys, in Debra's car, that she'd first heard Mr Nkosi speaking – really speaking.

Exhausted after the morning's work, he could hardly have been comfortable in the back of the car, crushed in along with Siphiwo, Desiree and Mr Gxishe. He made no complaint, though, and merely dried his glittering cheeks with a handkerchief. After struggling out of his jacket, he'd offered everyone cigarettes, and finally lit one contentedly for himself. Within a few moments he seemed to have recovered, and was asking Debra about her studies.

Desiree had paid little attention at first. Her skull was in the grip of a blazing headache, and Debra's thesis, as far as she knew, involved some obscure survey of church attendance in the townships. Drowsing, she allowed herself to be rocked slightly from side to side, wedged between two warm bodies.

So now, when you talk to these people, do you find they are interested in, for example, the trade unions?

Debra gave one of her laughs, unexpectedly husky, and seemed to meet Mr Nkosi's eyes in the rear-view mirror. Desiree sensed that he was laughing too, quietly.

He mimicked someone replying to Debra. *"Everything will come right in heaven, so why should we bother to get involved in this politics."*

You've got it, Debra said.

Solomon, who was with them, travelling in front in the seat of honour, joined sleepily in the conversation.

Yes, this is always a big problem that we have, when we come to organising.

The other interpreters were listening too, and after a while Siphiwo interrupted, to ask if Debra wouldn't carry straight on to Nyanga East. She had to come past his place again on the way back anyway, so she could drop him off last.

Eventually they stopped in a sandy square, near some buildings that looked like barracks. Men's hostels. There was nothing but blowing sand in the neighbourhood. Neither Mr Nkosi nor Mr Gxishe seemed in a hurry to get out, and Debra switched off the engine so that they could carry on talking, sitting there in the car. Siphiwo wound down his window and leaned an elbow out, accepting another of Mr Nkosi's cigarettes.

But now Debra. In a way, I think we can still say there is a heaven. Because, as we know, even though we may transform our present society, that will only be the beginning. In fact, there will never be an end to it, to the work, because human beings are not perfect. We know ourselves.

Delicately he'd teased, turning slightly to catch Desiree's eye. *Even in our advice bureau we find this. We will always be making mistakes, there will always be new things we can tackle, where we can improve.*

He pretended to push back the sleeves of his shirt, as if he were about to grapple with something.

So, if people believe there is a heaven, perhaps they are not too wrong. (Almost shyly, he smiled.) *Perhaps we can say that heaven is an idea that people have. Yes. Because it is our idea of the perfect society, that we will never find on this earth. But it is this thing we will always be striving for.*

A new client was standing at the desk, patiently waiting for Desiree to notice him. She glanced up, about to ask his name – and then recognized him. It was Liso, wearing a yellow tee-shirt with the UDF's logo printed across it.

He gave a casual smile. 'I thought maybe you people might need some help this morning, you know.'

Vanessa came out of the second room. Seeing Liso, she raced over to throw her arms around him. 'Do we need you.' Touching his tee-shirt, she laughed, incredulous and admiring at the same time. 'How did you get through, wearing that?'

He did not bother to answer; more concerned to look around. 'So are you busy? Did any of the interpreters get through? Is Siphiwo here?'

'So far, no. Indran was supposed to pick him up with Mr Nkosi at the bus terminus, but there seems to have been some mix-up.'

'Ja,' Liso drawled. 'There are roadblocks.'

He strolled over to peer into the adjacent room.

When Mr Nkosi arrived a few minutes later, he looked hot and troubled. His journey, it seemed, had involved a crowded mini-bus and several thumbed lifts. He smiled, plainly struggling not to seem accusing.

'Did Siphiwo come?' he asked. Otherwise I think he won't make it today.'

Finally Indran returned.

'Hey I'm sorry, I couldn't find them. In the end I just didn't know whether to carry on waiting or come back here and help, I'm sorry.'

Mr Nkosi raised a hand and waved, to show that he was there. 'No, it's okay,' he called, easily.

Indran relaxed a little. 'Anyway,' he said. 'Anyway, I bought milk. So we can have coffee just now.'

Sounding hurt, he added: 'Hey you know I was stopped by the *boere*.'

'What did they want?' Vanessa asked, startled.

'No, they just had a good look inside the car. They asked me where I was going: so I told them I was going to fetch my father's labourers.' His mouth quirked. 'They believed me.'

* * * * * * * * * * * *

With the fruit on her lap, Marisa sat quietly in the car for a while. Be honest, she thought. She was afraid to go to that funeral this afternoon. But it had to be done.

Quickly she unloaded the plastic bags onto the passenger seat. Well, so it's lucky I'm an actress. Isn't it? Ja, Richard. Sometimes a person fakes things because it's necessary.

Survival purposes. So you can do the things you believe in.

Leaning across, she turned down the passenger's sun-visor and inspected her face in the mirror. She'd forgotten about the necklace. Catching a glimpse of it now, she felt gratified.

Pretentious people would say it was kitsch, but she didn't care, it was beautiful. Maybe she was being childish. But what the hell, what the hell. Who was she harming?

She met her own reflected eyes. Something flickered there, sea-grey and unquiet. She was looking pale. Not enough sleep.

You look like a ghost. Annoyed with herself, she reached for her handbag.

The little lipstick holder felt clammy under her fingers. *'She's dead as earth. Lend me a looking-glass; If that her breath will mist or stain the stone, Why, then she lives.'* She breathed at the mirror, through her mouth. Haaaaa. It didn't leave much of a mist; but then, it was a warm day. Making her mouth gape, she slicked a bit of colour over her lips.

'Is this the promis'd end? Or image of that horror?'

Heavens, no, be still. Drawing her lips together, she tried to bring out a sound, but the vague, unformed memories seemed to interfere. Should have been a boyscout, she thought, growing impatient with these fluttery hintings of panic. Isn't this what they do? Go around whistling to keep up their spirits.

Uncomfortably, she remembered Lucas. Every time he walked away, he would start whistling a long, elaborate tune. Not jaunty, or even very loud. What fears did he have to ward off? Maybe it was something about saying goodbye, parting from people. She felt quietened. Ten years, Lucas had done. Ten years on Robben Island.

Other people's suffering. It was impossible to know it directly. Perhaps that was where you reached the boundaries of the imagination.

She hoped she had not hurt Lucas's feelings last night. Richard was too crude, surely, to say she'd just been using him. He'd said he was glad she was involved now; and his approval mattered. She did, she really did want to make a commitment now.

Of course the word was awful. Banal, Richard would say. But it still meant something. How else could she put it? She wanted to change herself: to become more of a serious person, bound by certain things. She wanted to do the right thing.

Of course Richard would belittle such simple aspirations. They didn't have the required tinge of clever world-weariness. Did it matter? What did he know? He dismissed the UDF; but he'd never been near any one of the affiliates; he had no idea what it was really like.

Funny that it was Desiree who'd sounded cynical this morning. *So what do you do in that Area Committee of yours?*

Basta nou. A sudden fit of impatience made Marisa sit up. It was crippling to let herself be haunted by this constant fear of criticism. She reached out to check the gear lever, and turned the key in the ignition.

Where to, she wondered vaguely. Rondebosch? She had almost no money left now. Anywhere, go on, just move, do something.

She headed off into the traffic.

Anyway, the Area did plenty, she thought. There was a list that went round every few weeks, for people to give out some community newspaper to workers coming off the early trains. (She hadn't personally volunteered yet. Just recently two of their members had been detained for it). Still, she'd been to hand out pamphlets outside the Baxter theatre.

And she'd gone along once to the Art Centre, to help with the screening of posters. Dressed in a borrowed art-smock, she'd caught the sticky sheets as they came out from under the squeegee. She remembered Danny, enveloped in a billowing smock, wearing a beret that he'd discovered behind some paint tins. He'd spent the morning arguing about history with Rex and Steve. And then later he'd begun singing modestly to himself, in a rich, quite unexpectedly beautiful voice. Marisa stood quietly under the lines of strung-up damp posters, listening, while she raised her arms to peg up another just-inked sheet. *Tshona, tshona malanga*. Soon she was able to sing along. *Tshona malanga, tsho*. It meant 'at sunset', Danny explained. *Tshona malanga*. The rest of the song told how they were going to meet Tambo in the forest – *ehlatini,* armed with bazookas – *nebazuka*.

Under her breath, she sang it again now, turning to smile at the motorist alongside her. Nodding her head. *Nebazuka*. Oh yes, she thought.

Another time she'd helped to put up posters. It had meant getting up at five-thirty, pulling on a tracksuit, and stumbling outside to wait at the yard gate. She remembered standing there, rising up and down on the balls of her feet, while her breath turned to white mist in the crisp half-light.

When Rona finally pulled up, she had Karin with her already. They drove off fast, wanting to reach their zone before the streets started to fill with traffic.

It was work that gained a rhythm, as the three of them ran from streetpole to streetpole, then back to the car to fetch more posters. The rough sisal soon was burning her palms; while the chill of the metal poles drew out another, ringing kind of fire.

The sun came up, and they'd driven on further.

Increasingly, each sprint towards a pole became a race against the light. A truck drove past, with men standing up in the back, their heads muffled against the chilly air. Looking back at her, they'd raised their fists in sudden salute, shouting something that was lost in the wind. Breathless, she stumbled on, with the huge posters cutting into her arms, battering against her thighs. And as she ran there were light-filled instants of floating time in between, when she glimpsed the small sheen of new grass, and the Chinese lanterns rustling, still fat and green-gold in the field beside the road. Even while she grappled with the rough knots there was time: to stare through a rusted fence, to frown at scraps of yellowed paper, and the empty bottles wedged amongst stones and broken chunks of builder's rubble.

She pulled up at the lights near the old Rondebosch fountain. Perhaps she should find a place to stop here, and blow the last of her money on flowers. Masses of them. All the bulbs were out at this time of year – there should be freesias, ranunculi, poppies.

Imagining their scent and the paint-bright colours, she felt a kind of radiance streaming through her. Wasn't there a saying: if you only have money for a loaf of bread, rather buy half a loaf – and spend the rest on lilies.

Yes, she thought, peering through the windscreen for a parking place. Bread and lilies.

* * * * * * * * * * * *

'Desi? Desi? You speak a bit of Afrikaans, *ne?'*

Clinging close to Cora was a young woman, wearing a factory worker's coat over her skirt and blouse. Plump in a warm, vital way, she might even have been in her teens still. Despite her anxiety, she had a trusting look of hope in her face; and there was something carefree about the bright scarf she wore rolled up and knotted into a band around her forehead.

She was facing eviction, Cora explained. 'She shouldn't really have come to us, seeing as it's not a labour difficulty, but it seems to be an emergency. But maybe you can try one of the community advice bureaus. There is a list somewhere. If it's not in the desk, you can ask Solomon.'

The girl reached out to touch Desiree's hand, and

started explaining her trouble again.

As she leaned close to catch the soft words, Desiree wished that her Afrikaans were better. She could still follow it with ease, but when she tried to speak it, it became confused with the German she'd studied at school.

'Sorry, what's your name?'

'Heather,' came the answer. There was alarm in the girl's dark eyes, and yet there was a light in them too.

She'd been renting a back-room from a family. But now last night, it was so unexpected, they told her she must go. She *had* sometimes been late with her rent, but she always paid back as soon as she could; and she was a neat person, her room was always very neat. She thinks there is someone else they want the room for. And now they are going to put her things out on the pavement – this afternoon.

Desiree tried to think. Reluctant to pull away, she patted the girl's hand. In practical terms, there was probably nothing they could do to help.

Cora came back, moving in her calm way past the other workers. 'So now, I've found that list for you. I think you can try the Grassy Park bureau.'

Drawing the girl along with her, Desiree moved to the phone. There was no reply from the office; but the list gave home numbers as well. Keeping the receiver close to her ear, she turned a little, to smile at Heather while she waited for some answer.

Eventually someone at the other end picked up the phone – asked something, and went to call Mr Jansen. (His wife, perhaps, or a daughter.)

At last she was speaking to him.

As soon as he'd got the gist of the case, Mr Jansen took control, demanding details that Desiree had not even thought to ask.

'What is her address? Now, just ask her, do these people own the property, the people she's staying with?'

Desiree relayed each question to the girl at her side, struggling slightly to put them into the other language.

'And when does she say they want to put her out?'

It was only as she mediated Mr Jansen's questions that Desiree began to grasp the urgency of the situation. Please let him be able to help, she thought. Please let him have a plan.

When he asked to have a word with the client, the girl seemed unwilling to take the receiver. For the first time a hint of helplessness appeared in her eyes.

'Praat hy Afrikaans?' she whispered.

Desiree spoke to Mr Jansen again, cautiously. 'By the way, she is Afrikaans-speaking, is that all right?'

'Yes yes of course yes, put her on, we've got a bit of a time problem here you know.'

The girl's face smoothed as she stood there listening to the voice on the other end. After a few moments she handed the phone back to Desiree.

Mr Jansen explained what he'd suggested to the client. Their office in Grassy Park was not officially open this morning, but he'd given her directions and he would go down there, personally, now, to meet her. He would see to it that something was sorted out.

'It's difficult, you see, if she's a sub-tenant. The law doesn't really protect her.'

Desiree tried to thank him.

'No, no, this is what we're here for. Can't leave the poor girl on the pavement. It's inhuman. Please tell her I'm on my way.'

* * * * * * * * * * * *

Marisa left the car in a loading zone, and went quickly, humming, to the street corner where the flowersellers sat under their canvas umbrellas.

There were poppies, she saw, with bees fumbling and dithering in them; and daffodils, asters, Canterbury bells, marigolds, rosebuds, tulips, anemones.

And freesias – there *were,* she'd known they would have them.

And ranunculi. A smell of cold, iron-tainted water came from the dense-packed tubs and buckets. Oh, and *sewejaartjies.* Everlastings. Those were her favourites.

'Lovely anemones and poppies, lady.'

The flowerseller must have followed her gaze, shrewdly.

'Beautiful roses, only four rand a bunch, lady.'

Freesias. Were they a kind of lily? Well, you didn't have to be literal about it. Any kind of flower, anything at all that was beautiful would do. There was a smell of spice. Cloves. Puzzled, she looked down, and saw the streaked carnations, with their petals still tightly held in the green bindings of the calyces. Maybe anemones? But we have to have freesias also, when will he ever see those again. Were there freesias in America, she wondered. And rosebuds.

She was being extravagant of course. Reckless. Suddenly she felt shaky again. She was quite seriously broke. At home she kept joking about it, but so flippantly that neither Richard nor André quite believed her, she suspected. In fact, she had sixteen rand to her name, plus the copper coins and five-cent pieces in her top drawer. Never mind, what the hell. Things would work out. Live for the day, especially this day.

She wanted a bunch of those tiny white flowers. (She would have to go to the restaurant and beg for her old job back, that was all.) She pointed out the fragile sprays to the flowerseller.

'And some of the *weeskindertjies*, please.' She did not know their English name. Baby's breath? In Afrikaans they were called orphans.

The woman lifted the bunches from their pails and swathed them in newspaper. The whole lot she could have for ten rand: it came to twelve, but she could have them for ten. She must have noticed the anxiousness with which Marisa counted out the second five in coins. Turning away, she bent and picked up a tiny bunch of creased, almost transparent freesias.

'Put them with,' she said, wrapping them in a twist of damp newsprint. 'For a bonsella.' She held them out to Marisa, with a smile that deepened the lines of weary generosity in her face.

Something in the air – all that fragrance, or the pollen, perhaps – made Marisa's eyes smart, and she wanted, suddenly, to hug the woman. But her arms were confusingly full, laden with newspaper and damp flowers. 'Thank you,' she said. 'Thank you.'

* * * * * * * * * * * *

Vanessa already had a pale, slightly glistening look of tiredness on her face. She was putting off that phone call, Desiree knew. Something about a gold watch that the client had set his heart on.

If the admin had eased up enough, could Desiree possibly take the next case?

'Of course.'

'I have to phone this man, he hasn't replied to our letter. But I can tell you now what he's going to say. Des, you're a honey, thank you. It's Mrs Ntuli. There's a cheque waiting for her from the Department of Manpower, it's a Workman's Compensation, all you have to do is give it to her. I had a look at Alan's figures, and the amount seems to be right. I don't know which of the interpreters is available. Oh, wait, here's Mr Nkosi.'

Desiree glanced at the cheque. With petty exactness, it was made out for one hundred and seventy-six rand and twenty-three cents.

Explaining to Mr Nkosi what it was for, she asked him to present it to the client.

Under Maria Nontobeko Ntuli's eyes, the pouched skin was streaked with a deep colour, as though she were profoundly tired, or grieving. According to the file, she was thirty-four; yet she looked closer to fifty. When the interpreter had finished speaking to her, she turned her face away, mutely.

Murmuring something, Mr Nkosi tried to place the cheque between the woman's fingers, patting her hand encouragingly.

She remained passive, refusing to grip the piece of paper.

Mr Nkosi turned back to Desiree, helpless. 'She thought it would be more, you see.'

Mrs Ntuli kept her face averted, so that they could see only her dull cheek, and the line of her miserably clamped jaw.

Desiree looked down at the folder again. Alan kept all his files faultlessly organised, with typed, up-to-date summaries in the front, and the correspondence neatly pinned in sequence.

Perhaps Mr Nkosi would be able to explain things better than she could. She put the file into his hands. 'See, what she had was not a permanent disability. She had an injury to her foot, a cracked bone, so she was off work for five weeks, until it got better. But it was only a temporary injury. That's what they call it, at the Department of Manpower. A temporary partial disablement.'

Mr Nkosi seemed to be memorising the terms as she spoke. (At least, Desiree thought thankfully, she wasn't telling him what he already knew.)

'All right, I think I am with you. So now, how do they work out the money that she is actually getting, in this case?'

'Yes,' she said, 'they use a formula. You can see, this is where Alan worked it out.'

Leaning forward, she used her pen to show him the neat calculations. Three-quarters of the normal wage, for the duration of the sick-leave. Pinned inside the cover of the file were half a dozen old pay-slips: the client had earned a weekly wage of forty-eight rand.

'So that comes to, here.' Alan had estimated compensation of around one hundred and eighty rand. 'I know it's very little, but the cheque is probably right, by their formula.'

Mr Nkosi turned back to Mrs Ntuli. This time he spoke to her at length, even taking her stiff hands in his as he tried to persuade her. Showing her the file, he went over the calculations again.

He was calling her 'sister', Desiree noticed. *Sisi*.

Still Mrs Ntuli sat there, expressionless, with her thin shoulders drawn up high.

Then, unexpectedly, she pulled away one of her hands and reached into her bosom, to fetch out a neat, hand-hemmed square of cloth. Staring ahead of her, into nothingness, she began dabbing at her face, using small, unobtrusive strokes.

Desiree sensed the futility of their words. All this careful talk of three-quarter wages being multiplied by weeks must seem like tormenting nonsense to the woman. (She'd signed one of the forms in the file with a cross. And if she could not read or write, how much less would she know the elements of arithmetic?)

Kate had been looking their way. Now, seeing the client start to weep, she came over.

'Mrs Ntuli, look, I'm sorry, but that is all you are entitled to get. I agree with you that it's very little. But I'm afraid there's nothing more we can do.'

The small, bitter tears continued to spill from the woman's blank eyes. Nearby, some of the other workers were leaning forward, watching.

Kate pleaded with Mr Nkosi. 'Can you try to explain to her that we're not against her. It's not us trying to refuse her, it's the law.'

Weaving his way slowly past the clients at the other desks, Solomon came over.

Mr Nkosi looked relieved to be able to report to him.

'Mmmm.' Solomon stooped and began to speak to the woman.

Almost inaudibly, she answered his careful questions.

Eventually he straightened up. 'Well you see, she has a problem. She says, the injury is still painful, it is still preventing her to work. She says, where she works they are making the ice-cream. The floor is always cold, they are working with water in the machine all the time, and it makes her feet ache. Now, the doctor says her injury is better, but it is not, the bone is still hurting her where it was broken.'

Kate frowned.

Fumbling, Solomon reached down to pat the woman's shoulder.

'I don't know,' Kate said, with a flicker of weariness in her face.

'Perhaps. Mmmm. It is just an idea now. Maybe she can get a second opinion? She says this foot is still hurting her, so now it seems to me she should be seeing a doctor.'

No but it wouldn't help, Desiree thought, remembering something. No, Solomon. Inside the file there was already a doctor's memo, saying that the last X-rays had shown a complete healing of the fracture.

'Solomon?'

He did not seem to hear her. Sometimes she wished she knew how to interrupt more forcefully.

Solomon continued. 'Now why don't you ask Mike if he will see her?'

Mike Davis, that must be. So he was still with the bureau. When Desiree first joined, he'd already been working as a volunteer for four years.

'You mean see her at the hospital?' Kate was doubtful. 'I'm not sure if Mike's still working in Out-Patients, Solomon. Or were you thinking he should see her here? I suppose it's not a bad idea.'

'Kate,' Desiree tried.

'Okay, Mike's in Group B. When are they out again?'

'Kate, I could ask my brother.'

Desiree gave up. Perhaps Kate's arrangement was better, in any case. Anthony wouldn't know the ins and outs of Workman's Compensation.

Solomon spoke to Mrs Ntuli again.

Submissively, she listened; and when he held out the cheque to her, she let herself be coaxed this time into taking it. She folded it, and tucked it away into her bodice. Then, standing up, she drew her thin brown cardigan close around her shoulders. Somehow, despite the stifling warmth in the room, she looked cold.

Solomon and Mr Nkosi walked with her to the door.

When they came back, Solomon was looking tired. 'These people. They hear in the townships that Workman's Compensation is going to give them big money. We find, the young workers now, they don't really know, and they spread these stories, misleading the people, like this poor mother.'

Desiree touched his arm. 'Solomon. I'm going to make the coffee. Can I bring you yours?'

His face warmed.

'Yes,' Mr Nkosi said, following up Solomon's thought. 'But nonetheless I think it is useful, now, because in this way the people will start to learn. With the bureau, we can help them, but only in terms of the laws. When the people realise, it is the laws that are the problem, then they will see that there is only going to be an end to this thing when the laws are changed. And so we see, the workers will learn that they must play a part in changing the laws. In fact, they must be the ones who make the laws.'

He paused. 'In the meantime we must just help as far as we are able to.'

As if to breathe more freely, he drew back his shoulders; and then gave Desiree a dry glance. 'So am I getting coffee too?'

* * * * * * * * * * * *

Marisa was standing in the kitchen doorway, looking out across the stoep, with a blaze of flowers and paper in her arms. It was clear she imagined she was making an entrance.

'What do you think, everybody? Aren't they the most beautiful things in the world?'

Richard raised an eyebrow in André's direction, as if inviting him to share in his disdain. (André declined to side with him.)

'Don't you think Chris will love them? Hang on, I'll be back with you now, I want to come and arrange them out here.'

André put aside the newspaper, resigning himself to

the coming interlude of frivolousness.

When Marisa returned, she was carrying an assortment of vases on a tray. 'Practising for being a waitress again,' she joked. 'Traditional occupation of the budding actress.'

As she walked towards them, the hem of her skirt seemed to dance and flutter round her pale shins. It was an extraordinarily bright garment, André thought, noticing it for the first time; not sure whether to approve of it or not.

'May one enquire, Marisa, what this is all about?'

She was looking around for a place to work. 'We're celebrating, that's what.' She sounded as though she were determined to project an air of inspiration.

The sunlight singled out strands in her floating hair, honey-coloured and amber. As always, André found himself watching her.

'Can I use this?'

Without waiting for his answer, she took away his newspaper. Perching herself alongside the collection of pottery and glassware, she began to spread the pages out at her feet.

'Celebrating, Marisa?' Richard asked, with ominous carefulness.

She was busy now with the leafy bunches, pulling away the soggy wrappings, transferring the flowers to the dry newsprint at her feet.

'Oh,' she said with scorn: 'I kind of hoped you would say, "What is there to celebrate?"' She held up a spray of rather wilted looking flowers, admiring them before she put them down. 'That was going to be my cue.'

Calmly, Richard regarded her. 'That is more or less what I am asking you. It's a fair question, I think. Perhaps especially today.'

She was using the kitchen scissors to snip through the

string around the bundles, and the task seemed to take up her full attention for a moment.

Then she shook back her hair and smiled at them. 'Believe me,' she said. 'I haven't forgotten, I promise you.'

Her skin had a remarkable quality, André thought, perplexed. Almost as though there were light shining through it.

'It's Chris's last day. Remember? He's entering a whole new stage of his life, his whole career as a singer is about to take off. I just think we should be celebrating for his sake, to send him off properly, so he knows we're with him, all the way.'

She picked up another bunch and started snipping again. The twine seemed to be giving her trouble. She tugged, and drew away the wattle leaves that the flower-seller had used to protect the slender stems.

'God, do you know how lonely he's going to be? I wonder if you can even imagine it.'

She gave another little stab at the string, and the rest of the bright flowers came suddenly free, falling everywhere, over her lap, on to the ground. She gathered them together.

'I know you're thinking of the funeral. So am I.'

She leaned forward and fingered one of the flower-heads.

'I just believe that when someone dies, maybe there's more reason than ever – to celebrate. So we remember what it means to be alive. I think we forget, half the time. We forget we're creatures, living creatures, able to feel things, to touch, and see. Creatures that dream.'

She began to select flowers one by one, stripping each stem of the dark leaves at its base.

'Maybe it is difficult. Sometimes I think it's too difficult for words. But I believe in making an effort. And I do believe we should try to celebrate every moment we can – being alive, I mean. If we don't, I'm so scared everything is going to fall away, spill out of our hands – like that; before we even know it.'

There was a clumsy silence after she'd spoken. Even Richard seem hesitant to venture a reply.

Change the subject, André thought. 'Marisa,' he said. 'What do you call those?' He stretched out a hand towards a cluster of flowers with shadows at their centres.

'These?' she touched some of the petals. 'They're anemones.'

She managed to look at him, and he saw the light rushing gratefully back into her face. 'I love them, don't you? Look at these colours, the way they sing.'

The name reminded him of something. Eventually it came to him. 'What have they got to do with the wind?'

She was absorbed with her arrangement, reaching with her fingertips into its heart. Then she raised her face. 'The wind?'

'Well, an instrument that measures the wind – don't ask me what, its velocity, maybe – is called an anemometer. So 'anemos', or something like that, must mean 'the wind.''

A memory seemed to kindle up in Marisa, animating her. 'Oh, oh yes I do know that, my mother told me once. She saw them in Greece when they were there. I think it's because they grow in the wind. You find them all along the hills, under the pines. Or maybe it's cypresses, or cedars. Oh I don't know.'

She cupped one of them between her hands and held it close to her face. 'The colours are so clear, don't you think? Like children's paints.'

André had an impression that she was acting now. Feeling uneasy, he looked away.

Richard was sitting up. 'My dear,' he said, wrinkling his face as though the sunlight were blinding him: 'Where did you find those beads? At the bazaar?'

Blissfully careless, Marisa gave no answer, but murmured something to André instead, enquiringly.

Chris's recital? This afternoon. Oh hell, he had forgotten.

'You will go, won't you? Desi can't – you know she's back at that advice place from today. And I can't make it either, because of this funeral. We're all going to it.' Self-consciously she added: 'Our Area Committee, that is. I feel bad, letting Chris down, but I've made this other commitment. I really think it's important.'

Richard looked at her. There was something almost insulting about the candour of his amusement.

'Commitment, he said, making the word lilt. 'How fascinating to hear that word from you, Marisa.'

There was definitely something up between them, André thought. As far as this recital was concerned, well, hell, he would have liked to go. It was his last chance, probably, to let Chris know how much he did, deep down, appreciate his singing. The trouble was, Riaan was unlikely to get another pass for several months; and the whole point of seeing the kid was to spend time talking, catching up on things. When he rang the other night, asking if he could come over, there had been a hint of pleading in his voice – touching, and also faintly disturbing.

Something else occurred to him. Did Marisa really have to go to this funeral?

He interrupted Richard's droning sarcasm. 'You couldn't get out of it? All your other people will be there, won't they? They're not going to miss one person.'

She picked off a stray petal that had stuck itself to her hand. Her next words were almost inaudible. 'Actually I wish I didn't have to go.'

'Well don't then.' Richard spoke sharply. 'Don't go, and I for one will applaud you. It'll be the first authentic gesture you've made in your brief, ah, political career.'

Marisa began to dab at tiny drifting flowers, anxiously re-arranging them. The finished display, André surmised, was intended to seem artless.

'Look, don't get me wrong. I understand the arguments. You people think you're showing solidarity. But on another level – let's cut all this political bullshit – let's look at it on the human level. What right can you claim to belong in those processions? Those are not your dead; it's hypocrisy to claim real grief for those victims. How can you pretend to mourn people you never knew, who – let's be honest with ourselves now – who belong to a different community, who have experienced utterly different realities. If you ask me, it's an insult for you to claim that.'

Marisa stood up. She seemed to have recovered her poise. 'Okay,' she announced, 'I suppose I better go and get ready.' Without looking at Richard, she picked up her flower-bowls and disappeared into the house.

Richard watched her go. With a shrug, he turned to André and resumed what he'd been saying. 'It's like these people who pretend they really feel for "the masses" . . . the "toiling masses".' Raising his hands, he drew imaginary scare quotes in the air.

'All right,' André said quietly. 'All right, I'm going to answer that, heavy or not. I know it was chic a few decades ago to glamorise that sort of attitude. Call it moral torpor. I know people thought it was admirable, and honest, even if it was shocking. But I'm afraid I find it offensive – actually, yes, blasphemous – when crassness is elevated to some special philosophical category of bravery.'

In no rush, he shifted to a more comfortable position. 'Of course it's difficult. It would be shocking if it were easy to conceive of millions upon millions of people suffering. It takes a lot, one hell of a lot of mental effort to imagine it. But I believe we have a responsibility to try. At least we have the faculty, the potential. It's the other animals that don't.'

Richard waited a few seconds, as if to make sure that André was not merely considering his next sentence. When he spoke, he seemed hugely amused.

'I find it rather rich to hear you of all people going on so pompously about the power of the imagination. You wouldn't care – now that you're indulging in all this riotous free play – to invoke the human soul as well?'

André did not reply, still inwardly running over his own remarks. Could one really speak of an obligation to use one's faculties? Surely this only returned one to the swampy ground of moral necessity?

Richard persisted. 'How about a paradise? Angels? A god, even? Or would that be pushing it?'

Absorbed in self-interrogation, André only half heard the facetious gibes.

'Hey hey, joke, André. Oh boy. This is always the trouble with you poor Calvinists. No sense of humour.'

André tried to shake off the earnest mood he'd lapsed into.

Of course he was absurd. He didn't need Richard to tell him that. Vaguely, he constructed a grin. Yet his musings still had a momentum of their own.

It all begged another question: Why was it necessary to be fully human? Because reason, and rational behaviour, are kind of beautiful? Filled with obscure pleasure at that last notion, André snorted. Perhaps it was an aesthetic obligation, quite simply. No more than that.

Richard leaned back again. 'Seriously: how can you go

in for that kind of thing? I thought you . . . well, let me put it to you straight. You're a Marxist, right?'

This time André's mirth welled up and spilled over. Did Richard think it was that easy?

Richard stretched his arms above his head. Then, languidly, he stood up, and strolled over to the edge of the stoep, pretending to gaze bleakly over the yard.

When he turned round again, he had a smile on his face. 'Well, we've had some interesting discussions this morning. You know, André, there's no reason why we should disagree over everything. I mean, sometimes I'll even concede you have a point.'

Laughing, he held up his hands as if in surrender. 'I'll come quietly. Don't shoot.'

The man had great charm, it was undeniable.

'One last thing. Just before I go.'

There was that suave undertone to his voice again.

'I accept what you say – most of it. But I would like to ask you, just out of curiosity: what are you doing? You, personally. What role do you see yourself playing? Since you're so strong on moral responsibility.'

All the ready answers, long dried-out and harsh, shot up into André's throat, into that dry cavern of silence. Resolutely, though, he refused to utter them.

'Let's kill this subject,' he said.

'Oh come on. That's evading the question.'

André remained silent.

Richard, as if he knew he'd won the round, sauntered off into the house.

* * * * * * * * * * * *

The Union's reception room across the corridor was crowded with workers, sitting on chairs and benches. Cora was at the long trestle desk on her own. With a quick gleam of thanks she took her coffee from Desiree; and straight away gave her attention back to the man opposite her. (Hat on his knees, one hand resting on the knob of a stick.)

Desiree lingered, pretending to study the packed shelves along one of the walls. The Union was selling these booklets. Histories for workers: fifty cents each, available in English, Xhosa or Afrikaans. The 1922 strike of the white mine-workers. The strike of 1946. A history of the garment workers' struggle in the Transvaal. A history of the Industrial and Commercial Union.

A small office led off from this central room: just visible through the doorway, a pair of cotton curtains fluttered in the window, filtering the meagre light through a bright patchwork of checks. Maya had made them, put them up herself.

Cora was too busy even to glance her way.

Silently, Desiree made her way out again past the rows of waiting men. In the corridor, two women sat sharing a packet of hot chips with their children. She would have liked to wait a few moments longer before going back into that claustrophobic haze of smoke, and suffering.

Suddenly the smell of vinegar and hot grease provoked a lurch of queasiness. She forced herself to make an effort. Come on, who still needed coffee?

Vanessa held out a letter she'd just picked up from the pile of unsorted correspondence.

'Well, that's blown it.'

Her face had gone peculiarly pale. Bleached as a dead leaf, Desiree thought, feeling a tremor of obscure panic. Vanessa was looking at her, almost fiercely.

'I wish we'd gone through the correspondence at the beginning. I feel such a damn fool. I've just phoned this Mr McKenzie now, and he was incredibly rude. He said he'd already written to us, and that was his last word on the subject; and I went and got on my high horse and said we hadn't received anything – and that just put his back up more. Of course it was here all the time, sitting right on top.'

Vanessa took a small, grudging sip, and then put the mug down, as though the coffee were too hot.

'I don't know how I'm going to face Mr Langa.' Turning her back, she pretended suddenly to be looking for a file in the cabinet drawer.

'Thanks Desi,' Indran said, and whispered: 'Seems like an unfair dismissal here, and I still haven't got the hang of the new procedures. If you see old Kate, won't you ask her to drift in my direction.'

A small boy was standing next to his chair, staring up at him, with an air of obsession. Indran put his hand in the child's hair. 'Hey, Des, won't you ask him for me? What's his name?'

Crouching down, she tried to tease the tiny hand open.

''mTwan'am?'

Waveringly, the child stared at her.

'I think he's too little,' she said. 'He can't talk yet. *Ungubani igama lakho?'* The child tottered, and turned back to Indran, grabbing his trouser leg with both fists.

Kate came up and joined them, squeezing into the crowded space.

'Desi, could I ask you to see Mr Khetsekile? I'm sorry, but I want to work with Indran on this group case.'

Desiree took the file from her.

'Sisi?'

'I had a quick glance at it. It seems there's nothing to report yet. Just give him an update, I think, and tell him not to come in again till he gets a note from us. Okay? I think Liso is free to work with you, he was around here a second ago.'

'Sisi?' An elderly woman was trying to catch Desiree's attention.

Kate intervened. 'No, Mrs Siyaya, look, I'm afraid we've already explained to you, we've taken your case as far as we can. Really, I'm sorry, but there it is.'

She turned to Desiree, with a shake of the head. 'I've already spoken to her. She's trying to apply for more in death benefits and pension, but she has literally had every last cent she is entitled to claim.'

Pretending not to have heard Kate, the woman persisted with her appeal to Desiree. 'Now I am really struggling,' she said. 'I have got the two little ones still.' She held out a hand to indicate the heights of two toddlers. 'My brother's. And we are struggling for the rent, now for three months. So my trouble is bad.'

She reached out and touched a fold of Desiree's dress, softly stroking the blue print with its bleached parade of elephants. 'It is African. You are one of us,' she said admiringly.

* * * * * * * * * * *

After Richard's swagger off into the wings, André stayed outside on the stoep.

What was he doing? Not a bad question. You don't dismiss a reasonable challenge merely because you happen to dislike its provenance. Besides which, it was not as though he'd never asked himself the same thing.

The answer wasn't particularly hard to find, either. No great mystery about it: he was, in a word, thinking.

Put like that, it seemed risible. To be dithering with such earnestness, such bloody scrupulousness, over this ancient (no doubt eternally urgent) dilemma. Whether to act or not to act.

And if to act, then how? He turned his face upward to the sun, and stretched out his long arms, flexing them to ease out the small knots in the muscles.

In the lecture room after the past few months it had been hard to suppress the thought that his enthusiastic chalking up of problems was simply a way of diverting the students. Keeping their minds off more troubling concerns. He found himself constantly aware of his own voice as he ransacked his little repertoire of jokes. There was some technical term for it. For a soft, streaming hiss of steady noise. White noise? White sound? They used it sometimes to deaden pain.

But then perhaps it was not the teaching in itself that had this analgesic effect. Perhaps it was merely the fact of carrying on in the ordinary way, as though nothing were happening. Yet other people continued, after all, with their daily business. Baking bread, removing rubbish from the streets, seaming garments, selling flowers, printing newspapers, brewing beer, spinning yarn, canning fruit, making ice-cream, trawling for fish, delivering cabbages and pineapples to the markets, lugging in carcasses of slaughtered animals fresh from the abbatoir over the white tiles into the butcher's. Were those activities all merely variations on a theme – different forms, mutations of the same anaesthetic?

He'd taken to breaking off in the middle of his lectures with casual (stiffly casual) questions. Had anyone read the newspaper that morning? Had they heard? Merely (he would assure them afterwards) to illustrate *non sequitur*. And the third-years he might ask to quantify over 'Casspirs', or 'generals'; or he'd use the predication of Botha's existence to illustrate a point of notation.

At first the students said nothing; to him, at least. All the same, he guessed that his heavy efforts were angering them.

Eventually one or two found the courage to speak out. What did he expect them to do? They couldn't see the point in boycotting classes, it wouldn't help anything for them to sacrifice their own careers. They knew that the country was in turmoil. Maybe the emergency was necessary, because of that – all the unrest. Of course they were opposed to the government, they said, pointedly adding, with heavy emphasis on the pronoun, that *they* were not Afrikaners. *They* didn't believe in apartheid.

But that didn't mean they believed in violent revolution.

Glaring back at them, he'd toyed with an idea of lecturing them, there and then, on the breathtakingly fragile logic of belief. Fortunately he'd checked himself. They too were vulnerable.

Afterwards he reflected that he'd been guilty of bad practice, as a teacher. Behaving as though information (opinion, more accurately) forced on others would instantly, automatically constitute itself as 'knowledge' in their minds. (It was irrelevant, he had to remind himself, that the substance of it might be patently true.)

Who was he, in any case, to take on such a role? Some grand moral arbiter, the marshal of everyone else's conscience? André always pompous bloody Binneman.

He blinked. He was an angry bastard this morning, wasn't he? Uncomfortable at the thought, he got to his feet and wandered, restless, to the edge of the stoep.

Shake out of it, Binneman.

Where the vygies spilled down over the low wall, the brittle flowers shimmered with a glassy, festering mass of sunlight.

Out of the silence, Richard's question came back, voicing itself in his mind.

* * * * * * * * * * * *

Marisa carried the speaker out as far as the flex would allow her, and held it up in the doorway.

'André? I'm just organising lunch quickly. This is for the atmosphere. The mood music. I don't know about you, but I need something to cheer me up. Would you believe it's spring? No one would ever think we were young and rejoicing.'

André was standing up, staring morbidly out into the distance. Sometimes he looked like a complete nutter. With that broad, bulging forehead, the knobby wrists sticking out of his cuffs, the fair hair tangled and mussed; and his eyelashes constantly flickering, nervously. Loony. No, not a loon, a bat. 'The bat of erudition'. That was Desi's nick-name for him.

'Hey André,' she called again. 'Come on, come inside and give me a hand.' Under her breath she added, 'Batman'.

His eyebrows moved, and he frowned at her.

'Come,' she said, suddenly feeling an odd, apologetic tenderness towards him. She raised the speaker again, beckoning him to follow her inside.

André came indoors, still with that air of distraction. What was the matter with him, she thought, beginning to feel weary. Can't he talk? Can't he do something? Can't he help me?

Now he seemed to be fascinated by the lone speaker on the table.

'Don't you think,' she blurted out, 'don't you think it's like a giant nerve. Here, look, here's the head. A ganglion, isn't that what they call it? See, and the electrons come flowing along, until they leap across the synapse. We did it at school. Ssssnap BAM. Like that. Imagine, every time you think a thought. Oh well. I suppose that's how we know we exist. Crackle, ssssissle. *Cogito*. Bam bam. See? *Ergo:* I'm alive.'

To herself, she added, 'Yes I'm alive, André; what about you?'

Making herself be quiet, she started setting the table. (Secretly it appalled her to think of the brain as some fatty, close-packed lump inside the skull, with electrical pulses constantly shooting through it.) A longing rose in her, filling her lungs: to be at her parents' home again, in a quiet world, without this constant driving feeling that she was obliged to speak, perform, take a lead.

'Now where is Chris? He can't still be asleep. André, won't you go and call him; I'll just put some music on, and then we'll be ready.'

'Damn,' he said, with a sudden, awkward expression of guilt. 'Marisa I'm sorry, maybe I should have said before you went to all this trouble: Susan came to fetch him this morning. Ages ago. It must have been while you were out. I'm sorry, man. I thought you realised.'

The world took a slow tumble. Oddly, the light above the sugar bowl seemed to grow heavy, falling slowly over the grains, as though there were an infinitude of time for it to break over each glittering crystal. At the centre of the table, the anemones in their bowl looked almost ugly. Those sombre colours, like bruises, or shadows.

She shut her eyes fast. Come on. Say the right things.

'Oh well, we'll just have to have lunch on our own then. Heavens, André, it's all right. Or do you think you're not enough company? Idiot.'

She picked up a plate and passed it to him, with a piece of paper towelling for a serviette. 'Here, let me cut you some bread.'

For a moment she busied herself passing things to him.

'Some snoek will be delicious on that. Would you like to try it with some chutney?'

Finally she trusted herself to speak seriously again.

'Talk about non-communication. That's just typical of our house. Why is it we never manage to be together? I don't know. What do other people do? I'm not saying we have to have heavy conversations: you don't have to be talking all the time to communicate. But we really don't seem to know each other even. Everyone always seems to be on their way out somewhere. If you see what I mean. In transit. And I include myself, I know I'm as much to blame as anyone else. But what is the matter with us?'

André chewed steadily, nodding to show that he was listening.

'As for you. Call yourself a socialist – you're the most anti-social creature in this house.'

With a quiet groan he reached for the smoked fish. 'Ah, Marisa. Just because one is a socialist is not to say one has to be mindlessly gregarious.'

Despairing a little, Marisa took a bite of bread. The scent of the freesias was getting in the way, she thought. How could anyone taste food with so much sweetness drifting through the air. If only he wouldn't take things so literally. Couldn't he tell that she'd been teasing? Sending herself up.

'You still cling to this romantic idea that we ought to be living in some kind of hippy paradise – all communal bliss, all sweetness and harmony – understanding, light, love and lentil soup. That's the fantasy, isn't it? Deep down, you believe that if human beings would only sit down and talk to one another, all the planet's problems would be solved. You really believe it's that easy, don't you.'

'No, André, I wasn't actually . . . I didn't mean that at all.'

They'd had this discussion umpteen times in the past. Did he think she'd learnt nothing from him?

'I'm sorry,' she mumbled hurriedly. 'Forget it, I'm just

upset. I thought we'd have time together with Chris on his last day. That's all.'

'Well there's still the braai tonight. And in a way I think it's a good thing he's gone to the Fines. He seemed a bit jittery to me when I saw him this morning; and he's always said that Susan is the one person who knows how to handle him when he's feeling a bit on edge.'

Couldn't he stop talking?

'What's the matter, are you still mad with me because I'm not going to his recital? You know he'll be okay.'

It wasn't just simple stage-fright, she wanted to say. It was more than that. Here was Chris on the brink of a whole new life, his entire career was about to take off. Could André not imagine how terrified he must be?

He was busy removing transparent, needle-fine bones from another piece of the smoked fish.

And yes, she'd been two or three times to those afternoon concerts. Soirées, Susan called them, pulling a face at her own pretension.

It was true: for the performers, they weren't difficult occasions. Usually there were about fifty guests – mostly elderly people, with vestiges of some old, middle-European fineness about them. Murmuring to each other behind raised hands, they kept expressions of intelligent archness on their faces. They tended to offer applause frequently; light, brisk patterings of it.

As the afternoon wore on, the air would grow heavy, almost sultry with the sad, rich sweetness of the women's perfumes.

Afterwards, over the coffee, the chatter was dry, and generous – unstintingly generous towards the young pianist, or singer. Perhaps too generous.

'André can't you see? Those rich lady patrons of his are suffocating him. There he is labelled as the rising star, the young artist of brilliant promise. I mean, it just could kill him, being sent off like this, draped in other people's expectations. It's like some horrible burning robe they've wrapped around him.'

André was beginning to look uneasy. She had better calm down. 'Look I'm sorry. Maybe I'm going over the top.'

'Here,' he said clumsily. 'Easy. You want to try some of this snoek, come on, you've hardly eaten anything.'

'I'm sorry,' she repeated in a whisper. It's just that I'm so afraid for him.'

'Look, what about some music. Didn't you say you wanted something in the background? What shall we have? Come on, something that will cheer you up.'

'No.' She felt a fool. Suddenly the last thing she wanted was music. 'No – no no leave it.'

Quietly André handed her a piece of bread he'd buttered and spread with flakes of fish for her.

They sat in silence for a while. There was something touching about André's enjoyment of the food. Watching him, Marisa felt a warmth of gratification budding inside her.

'I suppose there's a part of me that's just jealous of Chris.' She would admit this to André. Let him see that there was this ugliness in herself. 'It's not nice, I know.'

Idly she tugged one of the flowers free from the bowl. She could imagine them growing high up on stony hills where the wind blew eternally, crisp with the spray of the sea in it, across wild herbs and wasps' nests.

'Why? Because he's getting out of this Godforsaken country?'

André's words were faintly shocking, she thought. 'No, no. That isn't what I . . . In any case, I don't believe he's abandoning us, the country. You'll see, he'll be back. Of course he will: that voice belongs to us; he can't just take it away, forever.'

André said nothing.

What I meant, she thought, what I meant was that I wish I was achieving the way Chris is; the way he is busy realising his gifts, that power in his throat. I wish I was on the stage again with a real role, and working, really working, driving myself, being pushed to the limits.

She felt restless.

'Here,' she said, offering André the petal she'd been spindling in her fingers. 'To nourish the rest of you.'

He gave her a sceptical look.

'Marisa. Tell me, why did you say, when we were outside, you don't really want to go to this funeral?'

He'd caught her by surprise.

'Oh,' she said, too quickly, too airily; and paused.

She looked at him. 'Because I'm scared, André. Plain chicken. What if something happens? I don't want to see people die. What if someone gets necklaced? The crowd can just turn on someone, anyone they think is a traitor, an informer, someone just has to point and say – that one; and they might kill him. It happens. It happened at that funeral Desi went to.'

'No. Come Marisa, you really are in a state. Besides, you know, that guy in Salt River wasn't necklaced. There haven't been any necklacings in the Western Cape.'

All the same, Marisa could see him wincing.

'This damned necklace. I do think the thing has been exaggerated. The media make out it's something planned by the Movement, that it's part of official strategy. Frankly I don't believe that.'

She longed to believe him. Stubbornly, though, she objected: 'André, it happens.'

'Yes yes I know it does, don't get me wrong, I'm not denying that. And of course it's horrible. What I'm saying is that the image of that violence is partly unreal. It's a spectre, something fantastical, projected by terrified imaginations. It's nothing new. You find it throughout history. The time of the Paris Commune, for example. You look at some of the right-wing cartoons of the time: it's the same thing. They made caricatures then of this monstrous female firebrand, *La Petroleuse*. In fact she was largely imaginary; an invention – unconscious, of course – of the frightened bourgeoisie.'

He seemed to misinterpret her quietness. Flushing, he reverted to apology. 'Oh dear. Am I being long-winded? Sorry. Maybe I'll just shut up for a bit.'

Marisa was still turning the strange name over in her mind. *La Petroleuse*. Part of her, she realised, yearned for a story.

'What was the Paris Commune?'

There was a quick gleam in his eyes. 'What is the Commune, that sphinx so tantalising to the bourgeois mind?'

Was he mocking her?

'Unquote,' he added.

He was getting boring again. 'Please,', she said. 'Please tell me about the mythical creature.'

He looked puzzled.

'The one you said. *La Petroleuse,*' she prompted.

Surprisingly, he seemed to soften. 'I can show you a picture,' he offered. 'There's a book somewhere in the living-room. Hang on, let me get it.'

While André rummaged next door, Marisa dabbed at a few fallen petals on the table: the colours of twilight, and blood dried on city pavements. Deliberately she placed one of the blueish scraps on her slice of bread, and took a bite.

The smell of the freesias was almost dizzying.

She did not want to see anyone die. Once, she nearly had. That time in Johannesburg, when she was living in that flat. The man had been their caretaker.

Perhaps they'd heard a commotion in the night? A scream? She could never remember. But in the morning they'd seen the stains in the stair-well: the dark brown smears where his hands must have trailed and battered against the walls as they carried him down, still bleeding from the stab wounds; all the way down from the workers' quarters on the roof of the building.

The murderers were his brothers, someone found out. Men who called themselves his brothers, because they'd all been members of the same singing group. The choir was famous in the district where they came from. They'd won competitions for years; national trophies, even. And then this brother, their star soloist, had deserted them, and come to Johannesburg to find work.

And so they killed him? For that?

Well, he had let them down, you see. Without him the choir couldn't exist any more. They must have felt he'd betrayed them.

Wiping her buttery fingers, Marisa took the book from André and began to page through it.

'Oh you'll see, the illustrations are all together in the middle.'

She found them: cartoons from the nineteenth century. As she studied them, she tried to shut out the sound of André's voice. One drawing showed a woman at a barricade, with a flag raised in one hand, and a smoking torch in the other. *'Types de la Commune.'* And here was *'une petroleuse'*, under the heading, *'Paris Sous La Commune'*. She'd expected a sketch of some demented hag: in fact, the satirist had drawn a creature with a round, almost pig-like head. She was clutching a fire-brand, and smiling. Smiling with a look of utter, serene stupidity.

Quickly Marisa turned the page and flipped through

the rest of the book. At the back there were maps. 'The Theatre of War, 1870-1871'.

Theatre, she thought. They do call it that, don't they.

'Marisa, you've got to listen to this. *"The Paris of M. Thiers was not the real Paris of the 'vile multitude', but a phantom Paris, the Paris of the francs-fileurs, the Paris of the boulevards, male and female – the rich, the capitalist, the gilded, the idle Paris, now thronging with its lackeys, its blacklegs, its literary boheme, and its cocottes at Versailles, St. Denis, Rueil and St. Germain; considering the civil war but an agreeable diversion, eyeing the battle going on through telescopes, counting the rounds of cannon, and swearing by their own honour and that of their prostitutes that the performance was far better got up than it used to be at the Porte St. Martin."*

'Are you listening? This is Marx on the Civil War in France. Great stuff.'

She stopped at another map, this one showing the city of Paris at the time. There. It even had the barricades marked in. Barricades. A civil war. And it was all true; it had really happened.

Somewhere out there in the world, Paris really existed. Her parents had even been there, several times. She had things they'd brought back for her. Silk scarves, and perfume.

It seemed fantastic. Barricades.

And last night there had been that man with his story about the long avenue of burning barricades stretching away into the twilight.

'*"The men who fell were really dead, the cries of the wounded were cries in good earnest, and, besides, the whole thing was so intensely historical."*'

'André stop it,' she said suddenly, astonished at her own sharpness. 'Please, please can't you ever be quiet.'

* * * * * * * * * * * *

There were flickers of dried-out white in Mr Khetsekile's close-cropped hair; and the broad bones of his face were prominent under the taut skin.

'Molo mNumzana.'

Politely indirect, his gaze swept her way for a few seconds. Long enough for her to make out the reddish sheen of permanent fever and weariness in his eyes.

Too late, Desiree remembered that Liso preferred them to address each worker as "*mSebenzi*". The usage had still not become second nature to her; and also, she thought, Mr Khetsekile, at his age, might even be offended.

While Liso asked after the old man's health, she skimmed through the documents in the file, trying to gather the elements of the case. There was a note from a doctor, scribbled on hospital stationery. 'Patient has tuberculosis. Recommend six months' treatment. Should stay off work.'

She was finding it hard to concentrate now. There seemed to be voices all around her.

Dave had filed carbon copies of all the letters he'd written to date.

'. . . on behalf of our client, Mr Alfred Mcebisi Khetsekile, I.D. No 742861, who was employed by you as a labourer from 1 March 1973 until 2 September 1984.'

At her back, Desiree could hear one of the workers from that group case. He was speaking in English.

'Of course, we understand the business is bad for the company at the moment. There is no work, in the building industry it is bad at the present time. So we do understand this. But now, in our contract, when we signed they told us we were supposed to be employ for a year. So when he wanted to fire us, this is now last Friday, we said no, we will not go.'

Shielding her eyes, Desiree bent closer over the file.

The old man had gone home to his family in the

Transkei, understanding the doctor's note to be permission, if not a command, for him to take leave. Once there, he'd found himself attending to all the long-neglected things. Christmas came, and the buses started bringing other men home; and since he was also due for the annual holiday, he stayed on. Then, throughout January, he continued to feel ill, weary and aching, persistently coughing. Yet it was becoming impossible to carry on without an income. He might be dying of TB, but his whole family would soon be dying of hunger. At the end of February, still feeling no better, he'd decided that he must go back to the city, no matter what the doctor said.

Back in Cape Town he'd reported for work at his old employer; hoping that no one would notice his cough and turn him away again.

But he'd been absent (the company noticed) for four months. He'd not even asked to take leave. What this meant, the company said, was that he had in effect dismissed himself.

Dave had been unable to fault the final pay-slip. The company had refunded their client's pension contributions for the past eleven years; and he'd been properly paid out for the three weeks of sick leave he was allowed by law to take each year.

Technically, the company had not behaved unreasonably. Not even in firing the man. Mr Khetsekile was no longer fit for work; and legally this was fair enough grounds for dismissal.

For a moment, Desiree's thoughts were invaded again by the clear voice of the young worker behind her.

'And then he says to us, he would let us to work to another company he also owns. But then, the money we were getting there would be less. So now we feel: if it was also his company, why should we all of a sudden be earning less money. So then. When we say to him that we will not take that other work, he is saying to us we are all fired. So now: we feel that this is breach of contract, because when we sign, it was to work for a year.'

Aware of her forehead tightening, she forced herself to focus on the file in her hands. Payments from Unemployment Insurance had come to an end. Meanwhile, at fifty-three, Mr Khetsekile was not yet eligible for a state pension.

Kate had suggested a couple of routes for Dave to try. One of his letters was an application to the Department of Manpower. Another was an appeal to the company. Under the circumstances, would they consider granting some form of ex-gratia pension, on compassionate grounds?

'Well, Desi?'

Liso had come to the end of a long conversation with the old man.

'He says, he is struggling badly. He says, he wants his job back.'

'Liso . . . no, look: this is what Dave has done so far. You can see he's written letters to all these places. But they only went off eight days ago. We haven't had any replies yet, it's too early.'

Liso took the file from her and showed the copies of the letters to Mr Khetsekile, translating them for him.

As the old man's gaze wandered from the papers to Liso, Desiree noticed again that hot glaze of exhaustion in his eyes.

'Yes.' Liso turned to her again. 'He says, it's okay, he is satisfied, he thinks the letters are good. But now, in the meantime, he has got no money. That is why he wants us to try and get his old job back.'

How could he possibly hope to work again? He'd been a labourer: one of those men who load heavy slabs of concrete onto trucks; who stand in human chains, catching and tossing along bricks. He could never do those things again. And there was no desk job, no soft job he could move on to now. The one gift, the only power he'd ever had was the youthful strength of his own body.

'So now, are you listening to the old man? He says he has got debts, he has got trouble with his rent where he stays in Crossroads. Also now his brother's child has got a baby that is sick at home, in Transkei. He must bring the child here to the hospital, the Red Cross. And he must still pay for funeral all the time.'

Liso leaned closer to Desiree, impatiently flicking his fingers at her. 'You know, that is the instalments. And he must still send money back to Transkei, for his family.'

Desiree felt scattered.

With a hint of coldness, Liso prompted her. 'Maybe we can phone them?'

'I'm sorry,' she said, nodding to Mr Khetsekile; getting to her feet. 'Liso, I'm sorry, I need to consult Kate, please just hang on.'

Kate was with Indran, still helping him with that group case. At first she paid no attention to Desiree hovering nearby. 'You see the trouble is, they're only entitled to a day's notice if they fall under the building industry. Although . . . hang on, hang on, if it's a paving company, it's possible they fall under cement products. As I remember you've got a notice period of a fortnight there. Mr Sentsili, the work you were doing, was it with bricks, or concrete slabs? Maybe slate? Does the company actually make anything, or did you just do paving?'

The tiny boy was still at Indran's side, clutching his thigh with one hand, swaying against him: clasping a paper bird, a folded paper toy. Where had he got that from?

'Hullo, yes Des, I'm sorry, did you want me?' While

Kate lit another cigarette, Desiree told her what the problem was.

Kate took one puff and put the cigarette aside. 'There isn't a hell of a lot we can do. Look, I'd refer him to the Black Sash. They don't give hand-outs either, but I think they do know channels, for cases where people are really destitute. They might be able to organise a food parcel or something, just to tide him over. Give him a covering letter, and just check that he knows where to find their office.'

It did not take long to write out the note.

When she'd finished, Liso seized the page from her. 'You can get him an envelope, they are over there,' he suggested; and turned to their client.

While the letter was being explained to him, Mr Khetsekile listened intently, peering at Liso's face as if he were afraid to miss any glint of information in the interpreter's eyes.

He nodded, and took the envelope. Yet there was something like disappointment in the way he stored it, so slowly, inside his worn jacket. Suddenly the film across his eyes seemed to take on a vivid shine. He turned his head away from them.

Alarmed, Liso questioned him again, reaching out with one hand.

It was a moment before Mr Khetsekile could speak. Then, when he did, Desiree saw the shock of compassion that flew across the interpreter's handsome face.

Turning at her, Liso began to blaze. 'The old man has been eating nothing, he says only bread, for five days now.'

He picked up an empty coffee mug and waved it angrily at Desiree. 'Can't you make some coffee for him even?'

* * * * * * * * * * * *

'So why are we still waiting, can't we get a move on?'

'Danny should be here soon, he went to collect the combi from campus. And Keir and Ryan have gone round to the Art Centre to pick up the tee-shirts: Pierre got a phone call from Rafiek about an hour ago to say please could we bring them through. Apparently Lucas was up the whole of last night screening them.'

Marisa recognised most of the faces, even if she could not put a name to each one. Someone waved to her. They were a friendly lot. Comrades, she thought, uncertainly. So far she was still unable to use that word without self-consciousness. It was useful, she could see. When there were people you hardly knew, and yet you shared a bond with them – you called them comrades. But the word still felt clumsy in her mouth, as though there were edges of its foreignness that remained.

'Are we just taking tee-shirts, then? Haven't we got any badges left, or stickers?'

'No. I'm afraid the media group's been a bit slack lately. I think it's because we haven't had a campaign on the go.'

'Never mind. We've got about five hundred copies of the last *Frontier* left over. The third one. We can't sell it, of course, now it's been banned. Journals Sub-Committee agreed we should just try to get them out to people as fast as possible. Give them away.'

A few more people joined them; some with packets of takeaway food in their hands.

'Still eating lunch?'

Rona was standing in a small circle nearby, listening to one of the students. He was telling them something about a lemon. Marisa moved closer.

The speaker lifted his scarf and covered his face with it, swathing the checkered black and white fabric around his forehead and nose.

'It's what you do, you see,' he said, muffled. 'And if you soak it first with some of the juice, it gives you extra protection.'

That must be why so many of them were wearing scarves. In case of tear-gas. Marisa felt a slight vibration of fear.

'But why lemon juice?'

'I don't know. Maybe because it's acidic. What the *mense* in the townships do, they also put Vaseline on their faces. You put it all around your eyes, and over your eyebrows.'

'Hmm, I reckon that's just to keep the sweat from getting in your eyes. But you've got to be careful; ey, Sally was just telling us: they keep changing the formula, and there's a new kind they've been using now, it seems to interact with the Vaseline, man. People are coming into the clinic with burns from it, these huge weals on their faces wherever they had the grease.'

'Here's Danny.'

A light blue combi had driven into the parking area.

'Viva Danny,' someone called out.

'Okay, we better work out a plan now, in case the *laaities* start stoning it.'

'Or what if they want to torch it?'

'No problem, we'll all just climb out and hand it over. Donation to the struggle.'

'Ja, I'm sure the comrades could find a good use for it. Maybe they could use it for an ambulance.'

'Well in that case we'd have to donate them Sally as well, so they've got a doctor to go with it.'

'Now comrades –!'

'Come on Sally, it would be your duty: we all have to make sacrifices in the struggle.'

'Okay, okay *mense*, look can we get going now.'

The speaker, tall and blonde, walked over to a

street-bin and tossed away the grease-stained paper that had wrapped his salomi. This was Pierre, Marisa remembered.

'Let's get a move on. Aviva? How many more cars do you think we need? The combi can't take more than twelve people.'

* * * * * * * * * * * *

Kate sat on one of the deserted benches, sorting through the stacked manilla folders. They'd closed the door at least an hour ago, yet the last clients had only just left.

'I do wish people would learn to take decent interviews,' she said, looking up from a page of scrawled notes. The hint of acidity in her voice was sharpened by tiredness. For a while, though, she said nothing more.

Then she made an obvious effort to lift herself. 'Right, let's get finished now. How's Mr Nkosi getting home? Vanessa, do you know?'

Vanessa had been busy sweeping the floor. Now, crouched down, she was using a torn-off flap of cardboard to collect up the heap of cigarette stubs, crumpled cartons, and fallen bits of food. She spoke without looking up. 'No no it's all fixed up, Solomon's taken him and Cora in the combi.'

'What about Liso, has he left already?'

'He's still around, downstairs. I think he's going back with Indran, I know he was looking for a lift to Observatory earlier.'

'Oh okay. Where is Indran, anyway?'

'He's just gone out for cigarettes.'

Watching Vanessa struggle with that improvised dust-pan, Desiree felt impelled to go to her help. What if her offer was refused, though? She had an uneasy feeling that Vanessa was angry with her about something.

(Inwardly, she could have shouted out in frustration at her own tongue-tied gaucheness.) Surely there was something she could do?

Kate glanced up again, still with a faint frown on her face.

'Des, I wonder, could you sort these into the groups?'

Handing over the files she'd already checked, she tilted her head to indicate another bench.

'Use that: you'll need space to make four piles.'

Finishing her task, Vanessa came over and joined them.

'Desi, by the way, I'm sorry if I snapped at you earlier. I don't know what got into me. Basically I haven't been a terribly nice person today.'

Satirically, Kate blinked at her. '"Nice"? What on earth is this sudden need to be "nice"? I ask you.'

Desiree felt her face growing hot. Filled with a surge of affection for Vanessa, she shook her head.

'No no it's fine. Everyone gets rattled in this place. It's one of the occupational hazards of the service, I know.'

'Well, anyway, I'm sorry. I'm afraid it really got to me, having that Mr MacKenzie shout at me over the phone. He's obscene. In fact, I don't think it would have made any difference if I'd seen his miserable letter first. He'd already made up his mind: that's just the way he is.'

Desiree shook her head again, lowering her eyes this time. She hadn't just imagined it, then: Vanessa had been angry with her. Her face was still flushed, she could feel.

'It's okay,' she murmured. 'Really, I didn't take it personally.'

Vanessa had gone quiet, as if she had more she was preparing to say.

'I'll tell you, though, it wasn't easy having to break it to Mr Langa.'

Waiting for her to continue, Desiree and Kate carried

on sorting the files.

'Well, maybe there's no harm if I do say this now. Might as well get everything off my chest. You know, I've been with the Bureau for three years now, and I'm beginning to think it's as much as I can take. I mean it. I've just about had it. All we ever do is we pick up the casualties. It changes nothing. After a while it all just begins to seem so damn . . . so damn futile.'

Indran returned, carrying a paper packet.

'I see you've cleared everything up already. Hey everybody, cheer up, what is all this? Who'd like something to drink? Kate, some orange juice?'

Vanessa managed a smile.

'I was just wailing a bit. If you want to know, I've had it up to here with the Bureau.'

'Ja. Ja I know.'

Indran stepped over and sat down next to Vanessa. Silently he offered her a cigarette from his pack.

'It gets to me too sometimes. Maybe there's a limit to how much suffering a person can sit and watch. I saw an old guy this morning, a petrol attendant. He'd been fired, but they wouldn't give him his notice pay, and there was some leave pay they also owed him. So in the end – because he was really desperate and they kept chasing him away at work – he went round to the manager's home one night to try and plead with him. And the manager actually took out a gun. Next thing he set his dogs on the poor guy. Can you believe it? I saw his leg where he was bitten, it's not even properly healed because he's scared now to go to the doctor.'

Indran seemed to be picturing it again in his mind.

'These petrol attendants have a rough deal, especially the guys on night shift. On one hand it's pretty boring, you just sit around all night long. But it's also damn dangerous, because they're sitting ducks for robbers. I had another client once who was mugged twice in one week. The robbers all carry guns; meanwhile these guys are lucky if they have sticks.'

Stretching out, he tapped cigarette ash into the bin Vanessa had filled with sweepings.

'Hey, where's that packet I brought? There's a chocolate milkshake, Des, won't you pass it to me?'

There was a rustle as Desiree handed over the packet.

Indran swallowed some of the milkshake, then held out the plastic bottle.

'Doesn't anybody else want some? Desi, come. Or have some of that orange juice. But anyway, to get back to this old man, the one who was bitten.

'He fought in the second world war, he was telling me: and he was saying how his life now is just the same, it's no different. He feels he is still like a soldier, fighting for other people, for things he doesn't understand. Everything seems to be out of his hands: he doesn't know from one day to the next what his future will be, if he will eat, when it will all end. He says it's like fighting a war again in peacetime. Only it hits him harder, because he's old now and the money gets less and less. Also, he says now it upsets him more than when he was young – that he can't see an end ahead.'

They were silent. When Kate finally spoke, it was to change the subject. 'Indran, I'm sorry, I meant to ask you, is Liso getting a lift with you?'

'Oh, no he's sorted out, don't worry. He was going to come with me, but then at the last moment he decided to go with Solomon and them.'

Desiree had not realised how thirsty she was. She swallowed another mouthful of the bright-coloured liquid before passing the bottle on.

'Orange nectar,' Vanessa said, reading the label. She had an air of mirth now. 'Why do they call it nectar, not juice? It makes me feel as though we're humming-birds, sipping this. Indran, for you?'

'No, no thanks, I'll stick to milkshake, that stuff's too acid for me. Stomach can't take it.'

'But you bought it.'

'For you guys.'

'Indran, you haven't got an ulcer?'

'No, but I worry a lot.'

'What, that you might get one?'

He joined in their laughter.

'All right,' Vanessa said, 'I'm feeling a bit more chirpy now. But I still meant what I said just now. I've been wanting to say it for quite a while. I really am planning to resign.'

'Ness? Are you sure you're not just over-stretched at the moment? Once your exams are over you'll feel better.'

Kate looked tired as well, Desiree thought. The blue of that dress emphasized her paleness.

'Today was a tough day, with only four of us. I've been meaning to suggest we should think about recruiting more volunteers. It would help to take off some of the strain. The other groups have all got at least six members; I think group D has eight people.'

Vanessa nodded. 'Mmmm.' (Her face showed doubt.) 'The trouble is, I don't know if it's even really the Advice Bureau that's getting me down. Maybe it's everything. The whole scene. This bloody country. You know, I always used to look down on people who left. I used to spout all the clichés about lack of commitment and so on. Kate, by the way, that's not meant to be a personal attack at all. I'm beginning to understand how you can reach a point where you wonder. You start to think, am I really helping to change anything? Here we are doing our feeble little bit. But it's a holding operation, isn't it? And maybe we're just prolonging the whole stupid agony.

Maybe it even helps the system – if we keep coming along to tidy up the mess it makes out of people's lives.'

She looked at them.

'I don't know. I'm sounding a bit bleak, I suppose. You know, for a while I thought it was getting better. I thought the government was serious about reform. Okay, probably you think I was naive. But I thought, give them a chance. Only now, there's no question, is there? I read somewhere some minister said they would fight to the last drop of blood to defend apartheid. I'm beginning to think they mean it. And meanwhile . . .'

Pausing, she tipped more of the fruit juice down her throat.

'I think my voice is going. It's all this talking. What I was saying: meanwhile, you just want to live a decent, ordinary life, like a decent, ordinary human being.'

'Vanessa, this isn't bleak, this is the death of the gods. Twilight in the desert.' Indran raised his hands, narrowed his eyes, conjuring up a desolate landscape. 'Scorching winds across the stony wastes. A sea of dunes. Imaginary horizons that shimmer and retreat, shimmer and burn in front of you.'

Reluctantly, Vanessa smiled.

'You know, I read you get these eland that live in the desert – in the Namib, up north. And they survive. They drink the dew.'

'Hey, you're making that up.'

'No, it's true, I promise you.'

Desiree wished for a moment that she was sitting at Indran's other side, leaning casually against his shoulder, the way Vanessa was.

'Wait, I've got something, I nearly forgot. Where's that packet again?'

He dipped his hand into the bag and came up with a handful of pale marshmallow shapes.

'Look, I got us sweets.'

'Fishes.'

Had he bought them on impulse, seeing them in a jar at the side of the till?

'There. Hnngh.' He bit off the lemon coloured tail. 'Well, it's somewhat leathery. But edible. Okay everybody, relax. I think we're going to survive.'

Vanessa lifted up a pinkish one and eyed it. 'Do you really expect me to bite its head off?'

'Yes go on, be brave.

Vanessa drew in a deep breath, then released it slowly. She was starting to look happier.

'Maybe it's nothing to do with this country, even. Maybe people are just basically bastards. Do you think that's possible?'

'Vanessa, eat that fish. Go on, rip its tail to shreds with your teeth. Act like a real bastard.'

'No no, I'm being serious. There's Mr Langa: he's never going to get his gold watch now. I know some people would say maybe it was an absurd thing to set his heart on. But it's what he wanted. He worked for those bastards for twenty-three years. So, okay: all he did was he swept their floors, scrubbed their loos. But that was his whole working life that he gave to them. And at the end of it, all he wanted . . .'

She blinked.

'I don't think it was even the watch itself. It was the recognition he really wanted. What's the phrase? "A token of the company's esteem". I know some people would say he's just one unfortunate individual. But he's a human being, isn't he? With just one life, like everyone else. Now it's almost over, and he must feel as if it's all been unreal. Worthless. And – I'm sorry, but if it makes me a bleeding-hearted liberal to care about the guy's feelings, then I don't mind; I'm happy to be one.'

Desiree felt the stillness inside herself deepening. Of all things to desire. When the hours of your existence have been measured out week after week after week in that small scribbled sum on an envelope – to ache for a gold-plated watch, with your name engraved in spidery italics on the back.

'Even if we had socialism tomorrow – which may God forbid.' Vanessa gave them a quick look of apology. 'I respect other people's ideas and theories and everything, but personally I'm all for free enterprise. What I'm saying is, supposing you changed the entire system, you would still have the Mr McKenzies. And what can you do? You can't pass laws that say people have to be kind. Decent. Human. And you can't force people to be generous. How much would that watch have cost?'

Desiree wondered again. What had Mr Langa really hoped? To capture somehow in a single bright, solid thing all the lost dignity of his life?

Vanessa answered her own question. 'Less than two hundred rand, I bet. Mr McKenzie's wife probably spends that on groceries in one week.'

'Hey talking of watches, someone – what's the time? I still want to get to that funeral this afternoon.'

'Heavens, Indran, haven't you had enough for one day?'

'Ja I am quite tired. Actually, I'm exhausted: I was up till three this morning.'

'Indran?'

'I was on a total high, man, I'm designing this computer I want to build. Anyway: I thought I might still take a quick drive out to Hanover Park and see what's happening there.'

'And Des? You're coming back with us? You said you wanted to go to your sister's place. We'll give you a lift to Salt River.'

4

'Me? Oh, I . . . I teach drama.' Marisa peered through the windscreen, frowning. 'It's surprising, this glare,' she said lightly. 'The sun doesn't look that bright.' Her grip on the steering wheel had tightened. Relax, she told herself.

What had made her give such a lame answer. She was an actress, damn it. Forget what Richard said. It was still her ambition, her dream to play a character with real life in her – complexity, substance. Yes. I want a role. (Where was all this aggression coming from, she wondered.)

Well, you had the chance, didn't you? In Johannesburg. You had the part. What was it? Cordelia. I still don't understand what possessed you to give it up like that. You were already in rehearsal.

No. He wouldn't understand, would he. It was useless trying to talk to Richard.

What possessed you?

She'd started trying to explain once. Telling him about her fright when she'd thought she was falling. And about the flat, with those mynah birds in the tree outside, and the caretaker who was murdered.

But he hadn't understood any of it.

Marisa, I simply cannot see how those things connect. You still haven't said why you walked out.

But that's not the point. They don't connect, maybe. It

doesn't mean they weren't all part of the reason.

It was true she'd had the chance. Why had she thrown it away? It wasn't that she hated living in Johannesburg. Many did, of course. Not her. She'd loved the flat she shared with two other actors in that unfashionable, outlying suburb along the stony contours of a ridge. She'd loved the early lightness of the mornings; she'd even loved the grimy miasma of exhaustion that filled the air by the end of the day. And she'd revelled in the summer storms, especially when they came bringing a crisp relief of hail. She still remembered the thick, sudden whiteness of the skidding stones as they pelted down, icy, into the grass and the earth.

'You'll have to direct me from here,' she warned the others.

'Easy, just follow that Casspir,' Mark joked from the back seat.

'You laugh?' Rebecca said, trying to make her voice sound theatrical with hintings of doom.

Rebecca was a teacher.

'And Mark?' Marisa tilted her head. 'What do you do?'

'Law. He's still studying, but this is his final year. He hopes.'

'And you, Lizelle?'

'Oh oh, this is Wetton Road coming up ahead. Can anyone see a roadblock, this is where they stopped us last time.'

'Jodie, genuine? When was that?'

'Watch out, *mense*, we're entering the war zone.'

'They were quite jacked up that time, stopping people. It was when they had that funeral in Crossroads, remember, about five weeks ago. Me and Gillian and Keir tried to get in, but there was no ways they were going to let us through. I will say: I felt sorry for those poor troopies. This one that came over and spoke to us, I reckon he couldn't have been more than eighteen – there was something in his eyes, you know – he looked confused, and you could see he felt bad having to play the heavy like that. He was blushing. And with his hair all short, he looked so vulnerable, you know.'

'But they are just kids,' Rebecca murmured.

'I feel sorry for those guys. You know how the army uses Buffels: usually you see them parked off at the side of the road, with the *ous* standing up in them, watching –'

'Yes, there's always one with binoculars.'

'But what I'm saying is, have you noticed how little space there is in those things. Okay, they're big, but the poor troopies are packed in there like sardines, man: and all they've got to protect them are those metal plates on the sides; they don't even come up to their waists. I scheme there isn't even room for them to duck, they're so squashed up. So you can imagine, these poor okes, ey, they get a stone coming at them –'

'Or a petrol bomb –'

'Or a bomb – there's not much they can do about it. It's no wonder they start shooting.'

'Talking of sardines,' Marisa said, 'how are you doing in the back?'

'No, no it's fine, Lizelle answered.' She was leaning back against Mark, allowing her hair to fan out across his thin sweaty chest.

Rebecca turned slightly. 'By the way, has anyone heard how Nathan is?'

'I went to see him yesterday,' Mark offered. 'He's going to be okay, he's a brave oke. The doctors still can't tell how many pellets he's got in there, they say there's still too much blood and everything. But they're optimistic, they reckon he probably won't lose the eye.'

Marisa felt an incipient stiffness of panic between her shoulder blades.

'What happened to him?' she asked.

Mark seemed willing to carry on talking. 'He was in Athlone, there was a lot of action going on out there and he went to take a look. You know Nathan.'

Rebecca made a tiny noise of exasperation.

'Apparently there were lank *boere* all over the place, but there wasn't much going on any more. Things were pretty tense in the morning – barricades going up, petrol, the works; but by the time Nathan pulls in, things had already quietened down: the *mense* were just standing around in the street. And then suddenly this one policeman turns round with his shotgun and opens up, straight into this group where Nathan was. He was already shooting as he turned, the pellets were just spraying – it was like he didn't care what he hit or who he hit.'

In the distance, way back across the flats, receding by the minute, Marisa caught a glimpse of blue-gums stretching away into the south. Somewhere out that way was an old cemetery, she remembered. And wasn't that the back of the Kenilworth racecourse. Perhaps there was horse-racing on at the moment. After all, it was an ordinary Saturday afternoon.

Another intersection was looming up. Marisa slowed down, trying to read the robots. As they drew up, she saw the jagged star of darkness in each glass disc.

'Check this,' Mark whispered, 'the lights are taken out.'

But why? It was deliberate? (She had better pay more attention to her driving, Marisa thought, aware of feeling increasingly confused. They were about to enter a built-up neighbourhood again.)

'Maybe it's to hold up the *boere*. Like they take down the streetsigns, or they paint out the numbers in the townships. Did you hear about that? You know how the streets in Guguletu have all these NY numbers, sometimes on the sides of the houses. The comrades have been going around painting them out.'

Marisa felt suffocated for an instant. Why was she the only one so ignorant? Many of the people in the Area Committee gave this daunting impression of being in touch; close to the heartbeat of the city.

'Look,' Rebecca said, lifting her hand to point out something on the roadside.

They all saw the neatly-piled cairns of stones and half-bricks.

'Now these Hanover Park *laaities* are really organised.'

Marisa continued to watch ahead, leaning close to the wheel; aware of children walking along the sandy verges.

High overhead, she caught a glimpse of something. Two kites were darting, careering and scything through the wind-scoured air. A paper shape with twin streaming tails, and something that sparkled black in the sunlight. They swooped and skimmed, and then went soaring up above the tenement blocks and the sand-blown stretches of emptiness.

'0 hel.'

Ahead of them, the combi was slowing down.

'What's the matter?'

'Keep going.'

'I've never seen so many Casspirs in my life.'

'Just keep going, Marisa. Follow Danny. He should be taking a left at this next intersection. After that it's not much further, you take the first right, and the church is two blocks down.'

'Check down this road. That's six, seven vans and four Casspirs just along there.'

'So what do you say, *mense*, I reckon this is what they call a show of force?'

* * * * * * * * * * * *

Under the rising wind the bougainvillaea was restless, struggling to separate shadows and shifting air from its own massy substance of sweet, dry, brilliant colour. Desiree clicked the low gate closed behind her. Out of habit she checked the post-box. The splintery wood was warm under her hand. But if there had been letters that morning, someone had already taken them inside.

Kate gave a farewell hoot from the street. 'Okay Desi, thanks again. So we'll see you at the meeting on Tuesday night, Vanessa's flat. We'll try to keep it short, I promise. Stay well then. Bye.'

'Bye, Desi, keep well.'

Ahead of her there was a flurry in the open front windows – and a dragging back again of sunlight and white net over the sills.

'Bye.'

Slowly, almost unwillingly, she walked up the narrow pathway. She could remember running, at the age of five or six, racing up to this front-door, after a morning spent in the city.

'See you.'

She paused, and leaned against one of the stoep pillars, remembering those Saturday outings to the Grand Parade.

Anthony used to stand next to their father, pretending to pore over the second-hand books just as he did. And Rosie would go off on her own, wandering up and down past the fabric stalls, running her small hand judiciously over an occasional bolt, as if to get the feel of the material. The trestles were too high for Desiree to see any of the wares, but she was content enough clinging to her father's trouser-leg. Sometimes there were books packed away in boxes underneath the stands.

They never came away without a present for their mother: a bunch of herbs, a packet of *botterpitjes*, a fluted, blue glass vase; and once a dozen roses, that their father chose with a strange, light-hearted reverence.

As they travelled home, by train, there would be the sharp, hot smell of steel flying in, until their father closed the window for them. Then, when they looked out, there was a sketchiness racing past of dry grass and the gold of vegetation; factory buildings, huge billboards – and in the background, always, the mountain.

Anthony and Rose felt the same dread, she knew, as they approached their station, where those fearsome smoke-blackened worksheds stood just across the tracks. Through the grimy windows they sometimes caught glimpses of fire.

While they were climbing out her father would hold her hand, though the other two laughed at her babyish anxiety. She dared not look down. And she used to try as well not to look up towards the top end of the platform, where the whites dismounted. They were dirty people, she knew; though she could not have said who had told her. Just as clearly, she knew how gravely her father would have looked at her if she'd ever put her guilty knowledge into words.

On the walk home from the station they would have to step over the ripe figs lying squashed on the pavements, oozing seed. Men stood behind huge pyramids of oranges, shouting. And ladies walked slowly past, with gold blossoms and medallions spattered on the hems of their floating saris. (Such grace, their father used to say, like Primaveras. And Primavera was the picture in the sitting-room.) Half-way up the street there was one shop she hated to pass, where the horrifying carcasses dangled in the window, with small nuggets of darkness crusted over the bleeding ribs.

Their front door would be standing open; because it's healthy, their mother said. We must let the south-easter through. (And it was true: somehow the wind seemed to scour the place clean, despite the grittiness at its edges, its hints of the sea and swerving, troubled birds.) In the room they shared, the two girls would find their bedspreads pulled straighter than they ever managed; while even, in the windows, the blowing lace was rustling with a crisper light. Their mother would have put the baby down on one of their beds: and Rose would pick him up, jigging him pertly till he blinked open his eyes and started dabbling at her face with his tiny hands.

She let herself into the house, calling out a tentative greeting.

In the sitting-room she paused, seized with a forlorn, cramping sense of longing, and loathing, for the familiar house. The carpet had been shabby for many years, worn away in patches, and stained by leaking rainwater. Yet as she looked at it now it seemed particularly threadbare. But then, hadn't it been once, in her child's imagination, a tapestry of birds and shimmering fantasies?

Her father's everlasting books took up one whole side of the room, creating a second wall with their paper masonry of dust and heaviness.

'It's me, is anyone home?'

* * * * * * * * * * * *

'No don't stop. Ignore them, Marisa. They're only trying to intimidate us.

At the corner a dozen policemen lined the street, watching the crowd and the cars go by. They held rifles loosely at their sides. Several police vans were parked along the verge, and near them a group of men in steel-blue caps stood conferring, one of them holding a walkie-talkie.

She drove very slowly now, bothered by the way the

residents paid no heed to the traffic. There were cars already parked all the way down the length of the street.

The combi's tail-lights had come on.

As Marisa drove up, she saw that tall, lean chap flagging her down. Ben, that was his name.

He leaned down to speak through her side-window. 'Marisa, is it? Could you do us a favour? We want to get the *Frontier*s out of the combi, just in case they search.'

He was blushing, she noticed.

'We were wondering if we could do a quick transfer and load them into your car. You're not as conspicuous.'

'Of course.'

Almost shyly he gave her directions. 'Okay, could you reverse a bit, just slightly, till you're parallel with the door of the combi. And then, if you could manage a spare rug or something, a jersey, to put over them.'

'Can we give a hand, Ben?' Mark was sitting forward, speaking over Marisa's shoulder while she changed gear.

'It's okay. Steve and Pierre are ready to sling them over. There are about ten packets. Can you just be ready to grab them?'

'This is the number that's banned? Why did we bring them, man?'

'Maybe it was dumb. I didn't think it was going to be this heavy.'

Gently she started to let the clutch out.

After she'd dropped the others at the church, she drove off to find parking; heading slowly, exploringly, down a side street. Perhaps there would be place under that tall blue-gum up ahead.

She travelled no faster than the pedestrians that milled around her, constantly invading the street; and now some children started to jog alongside the car – two small boys, and a little girl whose gold-brown plaits were weighted with tightly knotted ribbons. Daringly, one of the boys rested a hand on the side of the car for a moment.

'Nee,' she called out, alarmed. *'Nee, boetie, moenie.'* What if he fell?

The little girl's plaits swung to and fro across her shoulders as she ran on ahead.

Parking the car, Marisa started the walk back to the church.

In this part of the neighbourhood the flat-roofed brick houses gave way to row after parallel row of tenement blocks, each constructed to the identical plan: boxes, three storeys high, of unplastered brickwork; with a metal staircase jutting at each end, casting bars of rigid shadow. Groups of children stood on the iron landings, watching the crowd go past.

'Heeit, sister,' someone called out, waving.

'Troops out, yes.'

(She'd almost forgotten she was wearing the tee-shirt with that demand printed in giant letters across the chest.)

Cars cruised past, hooters braying, and their passengers leaned out, clutching on to roof racks to balance themselves.

'Viva UDF.'

'Viva.'

She was being jostled, but no one meant any harm by it, she knew. She ought to respond. She ought to raise a fist and shout back, Viva, Viva.

Suddenly, in the middle of the teeming road, she felt lost, seized with stirrings of dryness, doubt. What was she doing here in this alien suburb, amongst people she did not know. Maybe Richard was right. This was not her community. Perhaps it was true she was only here for the thrill, driven by some craving to experience moments of danger; to catch random, windswept glimpses of other people's poverty.

Or perhaps it was not true. Perhaps she set too much store by Richard's shallow cleverness. André thought so, didn't he?

Across the road, two Casspirs were parked along the sandy edge of an open field. God, those things were ugly. Like giant stinkbugs.

Ignore them.

For an instant she was lost in memories of the vines that grew over the pergola at home. There were always insects creeping in the wistaria, and the grape vine. Her father was proud of those grapes: small, glittering globes that burst in your mouth with a taste astonishingly smart and sweet at the same time.

She lifted her head; and the harsh sunlight made her eyes water for a second. High overhead, outrageously high, racing along an invisible vein of wind, was a scrap of scarlet, hurled so high, she imagined, by the brilliant, reeling strategies of a child.

People around her were pushing again. She hurried on, passing a yellow police van close enough to hear the crackle of voices coming from its radio.

* * * * * * * * * * * *

The two brothers stood facing each other across the doorstep.

'Well, Riaan.'

'Boet.'

André took in the slightly bulging forehead, the sea-coloured, restless eyes. It was disconcerting to be mirrored like this.

Reaching out, the boy offered him a quick, embarrassed handclasp. 'Hey, Boet, it's good to see you.'

André cuffed him lightly on the upper arm. 'Yes, well you too, Riaan. Come in, man.'

He turned to lead the way through.

'So how did you get here, the old man drop you off?'

'No, no I walked, I felt like some exercise.'

A quiet flicker of approval lit through André's thoughts. 'Well,' he said again, once they were in the kitchen. 'Some wine? I reckon you must be thirsty. It's only box wine, but it's drinkable.'

'No.'

(The refusal was meant to be obliging, André guessed.) 'Thanks, no, it's too early for a *dop*. Don't worry about me, Boet, unless you were thinking of making tea. If you've got rooibos? Otherwise it's fine, don't worry.'

Riaan stayed on his feet, leaning up against the fridge, watching amiably while André got on with the tea. Sizing him up, André supposed.

'So when did you get down? Hell, I don't even know where you've been stationed, Riaan. I'm sorry: you did drop me a line. I should have written ages ago.'

'Hey no, that's not a problem. I scheme you've been busy with all your lectures and everything. In any case, they would have censored out the names of the actual places.'

He did seem restless, André was thinking, noticing for the first time the slight tremor in Riaan's hands. High energy. 'Why don't you sit for a moment,' he suggested. 'We can go outside just now.'

'Nnnnn, 'ts okay. So who all stays here with you? This house seems amazingly spacious.'

André was distracted briefly by a small spill of the fine, rust-coloured tea. He used the edge of his hand to sweep it up while answering. 'Well, there are four of us altogether.'

'A quartet,' Riaan said, with an unexpected

impishness.

'Well yes. Of sorts.' (A quartet? André wondered about that.) 'Where was I? The people in the house. Okay, there's Chris. Chris Braaf. He's just finished his Masters at the College of Music. It's a performers's degree, in opera. He's a singer. But in fact today is his last day with us. He's got this bursary to go and study in New York. He flies out tomorrow.'

'New York,' Riaan said, exaggerating the tone of wonder.

'Yes. Exciting, hey? We feel kind of proud of him. Our housemate.' (Why did it embarrass him to admit that, he wondered.) 'I suppose we'd like to think some of the glory rubs off on to us. Reflected light, and all that. Of course he's thrilled about it. You can imagine: it's the chance of a lifetime.'

Riaan made a soft, sibilant sound of awe. 'He must be hell of a good?'

'Yes. He is. And there's Desiree. She's busy finishing a Masters by correspondence. Something to do with language, though I'm not quite sure what it all involves. She works part-time on campus, in the library; and she's been doing a bit of tutoring to keep herself going. Except the college where she taught has stopped classes because of the crisis. Here, do you take sugar?'

'Please. Three.'

'Digging your own grave, my boy.' André put in three teaspoons. 'And then there's Marisa. I'm not sure how you'd describe her. An actress. A bit flighty. She was giving drama classes until a few months ago, but that came to an end. She had a job as a waitress for a while, a few nights a week, but she didn't like it much. I think what she really wants is a career. She just can't seem to find her direction though. She's still looking. Actually, I would say that's her main occupation: searching.'

With some relief, André put the milk carton back into the fridge and dumped the used teaspoon in the sink. 'Okay, come on, you grab your mug, let's get out into the sun.'

* * * * * * * * * * * *

Inside the church the small porch was already packed with people.

A young marshal stood on a chair, reaching over heads to distribute leaflets. Taking one, Marisa pushed forward, struggling to get through into the main body of the church.

There, over there, in that side-pew. That row of heads looked familiar from behind.

One of the marshals noticed her trying to edge her way through the crush. Touching her arm, he raised his free hand and began to clear a path for her.

'Please, *mense, asseblief*, let the comrade through, man.'

His armband was made from crêpe paper: strips of yellow, green and black stitched together. It was a few seconds before that combination of colours took on a meaning. Startled, Marisa felt something rising, faintly effervescent inside her. She'd never dreamed a day would come when she would see the Congress colours worn openly like this.

'Hi,' Rona murmured.

'I suppose everyone's noticed the media around here,' Rebecca said cautiously.

'Ja, everything but UDF, isn't it.'

'You see the lectern?'

Draped over the rostrum was the same tricolour; sombre, except for the broad, singing streak of gold.

The first time, Marisa thought, slightly awed. This was the first time she'd ever seen the flag. The Movement had been banned the year she was born. (She'd not known of its existence even, until she was in her twenties.) Now, here, the symbols of the underground resistance were re-emerging into the light.

'Did anyone get an order of service?'

Marisa handed over the leaflet.

Behind the dais where the clergymen were taking their seats, the walls of the church receded and curved to form a quiet bay of emptiness. The apse, wasn't that the name for it? The term came back to Marisa from an almost forgotten course in art history. Through a rose of glass set high up there in the masonry, the sunlight streamed down; and below it, mounted against the wall, a wooden cross gleamed.

'Lot of people here.'

'How many do you reckon the church can hold?'

'I'd guess fifteen hundred, normally; but it'll probably be double that. They've opened the partition that goes through into the hall.'

In a way, the lack of adornment made this place more comforting, Marisa thought. She liked it that the glass in the high narrow windows was clear, letting in the ordinary light, unstained by mysteries or the gaudy drama of miracles.

'Comrade?'

Someone was speaking to her.

'Sister? Could you pass these along to the other comrades?'

She took the dozen stubby candles she was handed and, keeping one for herself, sent the others down the row.

There was a stir at the back of the church. Heads craned round; and people started getting to their feet. The bearers must be here. Somewhere a man began to sing.

'Senzenina?'

Briefly the voice threatened to crack; but then others joined in.

'Senzenina?'

'Senzenina?'

'Here's a light, Marisa.'

Pierre, who had already lit his candle, was reaching out, restlessly touching the small flame to everyone else's.

As the coffin was borne down the aisle, the voices of the congregation lifted.

'What have we done?'

'What have we done?'

Now everyone was standing, and trying to see, pressing shoulder to shoulder in the pews.

'What have we done?'

Moving from one to another, steadily increasing, the drops of quiet light lifted and dipped, joining and splitting.

'Mayibuye'

'Mayibuye iAfrika'

'iAfrika'

* * * * * * * * * * * *

Desiree found her sister in the kitchen, standing at the ironing board, with an open book propped up opposite her on top of the stove.

'Well, stranger.' Rose came over for a hug, using the flats of her hands to pat Desiree's back, placing a cheek close to hers. 'It's nice to see you, honey, come, why don't you sit down.'

Desiree felt her power of speech drying up again. Rose did not seem to notice.

'Why don't you put on the kettle? Or there's cold water

in the fridge if you prefer. You can even fetch yourself a lemon off the tree.'

Desiree felt a tiny stabbing of anger in her throat. Of course she was thirsty. And hungry. Trying to keep her face averted, she drew out one of the kitchen chairs. Then, kicking off her sandals, she stretched out her feet. At last she was able to manage a smile again.

She still did not trust herself to speak. Instead, she sat and watched her sister.

Rose had piled her hair on top of her head, probably for comfort, although the casual sweep of it had elegance. (Naturally.) To her shame, Desiree felt a trace of malice. Rose always looked so perfect. So effortlessly organised. Even in her jeans and that faded Indian top, she managed to appear neat and graceful.

'My word, I don't know when we last saw you. So what you've been up to? We heard that college has stopped classes.'

Desiree mumbled something. There were only five years between Rose and herself. A small gap, really; yet sometimes the distance seemed immense.

Everyone said: Rose had had to grow up before her time. When their mother died, two years after their father, Rose decided – on her own – that she would go out and work. (She'd done a year of typing at school already, and their mother had taught her the elements of book-keeping.) She was fifteen. What sacrifice, people said. When she'd been an A student all along, to give up her studies for her younger brothers' and sisters' sake. (Later, when Desiree and Anthony were old enough to help with the babies, she started going to night classes at the school up the road. In the end she managed to matriculate in the same year as Anthony; with distinctions, like him, in three of her subjects.)

And yet: knowing Rose's history did not make it any

easier to understand her now, from moment to moment.

'You've gone back to the Advice Bureau? Well, that's good news.'

Rose gave a slow, pleased nod. 'I was wondering what you would do.' She arched her back, and eased out her shoulders. Then she took another shirt from the pile and placed it over the board.

Silently Desiree shouted back. But I don't know if it's what I want. Please, Rosie. I haven't decided anything.

Almost as if she had heard her, Rose put down the iron. Going over to the fridge, she took out a Coke bottle filled with water, collected a glass and a packet of ginger biscuits, and quietly came over to put the things at Desiree's elbow.

'Come on now, it's not that bad.'

Returning to her work, she licked a finger and touched it lightly to the iron.

'There are disprins in the bathroom if you've got a headache. Do those people still smoke so much at that place?'

As she sipped the cool water, Desiree felt her spirits reviving. 'Yes,' she said. 'Non-stop.'

Rose carried on peacefully ironing. The silence was friendlier now. Desiree dabbled her toes on the cool linoleum. Could she take one of those biscuits? She was so hungry (not far, in fact, from faintness, and the sudden, humiliating rush of tears).

'Oh well,' Rose said tolerantly. 'If it's not smoking, it's always something else, isn't it. I suppose everyone has their own form of self-destructive behaviour. Who knows. Maybe it's even necessary.'

She held up another shirt, frowning at a mark on the pocket.

'Maybe if it was built into us to survive at all costs – each one of us, personally – perhaps we'd never get very far as a species. Maybe we'd never make sacrifices, or have children, or fight for things we believe in.'

She glanced at Desiree.

'Oh dear, you're looking awfully solemn. It was just a notion. Skip it. You really are tired, aren't you, honey. Please do me a favour and eat a couple of those things.'

This time Desiree obeyed, and as the spicy biscuit cracked between her teeth, she felt a child's satisfaction in the act of biting.

'So Rose, how are the studies going?'

Her sister pulled a face, careful to show that she was sending up her own despair. 'Better not ask. I'm hoping this evening I'll get a bit of peace and quiet.'

'And work, Rosie?'

While she listened, she allowed herself to relish the fragrant, subtle taste of ginger.

It turned out Rose had been in to the office that morning.

'But you don't work Saturdays?'

'No. But I'm trying to tie up a few loose ends. Barney and Ghaironisa have been fantastic to me, they've said I can take a week's leave before my exams, with full pay. But I want to make sure everything will go smoothly for them while I'm away.'

She turned to lift another shirt from the pile.

Now might be the moment, Desiree thought, to put her suggestion. Rose, she wanted to say. Rose, if I were to work full-time next year, I could leave my thesis for a while, it would mean –

Rose cocked her head. 'Wasn't that the front door?'

What would it mean?

Both of them heard the sound of people coming in; and then Shireen's voice was calling.

Rose would be able to stop working and get on full-time with her studies. It was time she had a chance.

'Rose? Rose, where are you?'

There was a soft thud, followed by a rebuke, and high laughter.

Shireen sang out again. 'Rosie? It's us, it's me and Begum. Where are you?'

Side by side, the two teenagers came racing into the kitchen, self-consciously doubling and reflecting each other's gestures. Between them they carried a bursting paperbag filled with fruit.

Shireen caught sight of Desiree. 'Oh. Hullo, how are you?'

Softly, Begum echoed the short greeting.

Shireen turned quickly. 'Look, Rosie, look what we got. Mr Ebrahim gave them to us. He said there was such a glut at the market today he's never going to sell them all and by Monday they'll be pap. He's given to everyone in the whole street. I think we should bake banana bread, don't you think that would be a sensible idea?'

For a moment Shireen had the tone of voice, even the considering expression, of a housewife.

'I know we've got a . . . there is a old recipe for it somewhere, isn't there?'

'*An* old recipe, Shireen. Why don't you look through those ones of Mommy's. You know where they are, on the top shelf.'

Desiree watched her sister clamber down with the old-fashioned tickler box. After fumbling for a moment, she drew out a card. It had a translucent blotch in one corner, Desiree noticed. Perhaps a butter stain, left there by someone's thumb.

Smartly, Shireen turned to Begum. 'You see I said, I knew it needed – it's not like you make ordinary bread, with yeast.'

Once, all those years ago, their mother must have picked that card up in the middle of her baking, to check something.

'Okay, cinnamon we've got, and nutmeg. Rosie, is there any baking powder?'

What was all this business about, with its elusive undertones of narcissism? Were they trying out motherly roles? Desiree doubted it. Perhaps they imagined themselves gracefully doing the rounds of the neighbourhood later, taking offerings of cake on Shireen's favourite, flower-bordered plate.

'Well all right, why don't you go down to Mr Davids on the corner? I know he keeps baking powder. And while you're there you can do me a favour and get us an *Argus*.'

Shireen offered them a delicate look of bliss and affection. (Knowing, no doubt, how her smile always came as a small, unexpected gift.)

'Take some money, you know where it is, sweetheart.'

Shireen took down the cracked jar. Suddenly, though, she turned.

'But Rosie when am I going to bring you the *Argus?* We're going to Begum's now. You know this stupid old oven doesn't heat evenly, you can't bake anything in it.'

Rose ignored the caprice of temper. 'There's no hurry for it. But Shireen: Uncle Theo did phone to say he's coming round later. About half-past four. You'll be back by then won't you?'

With a wave, Shireen turned and flounced away; unable to hide the delicate suffusion of delight in her face.

'I'm worried about that child,' Rose said, after the two girls had gone out.

Desiree looked at her sister.

'Don't be fooled by all that flitting and smiling. She cries at night. She thinks I can't hear.'

Desiree struggled to find her voice; but the questions came out small, and dry.

Rose closed her eyes for a moment. Then she shook her head.

'I think it's simply that she can't stand what is going on around her. You know she wants to leave school? She keeps saying it as though she's joking, but I think she really means it. I think she feels desperate. They haven't had proper classes for weeks now. The police are in the grounds every second day. Last week they came with their damn dogs and tear-gas again. And of course Mr Fortuin was detained three weeks ago. I think that was what really got to her. The vice-principal. He's also her class teacher. She worships him – well, they all do at the school, of course.'

* * * * * * * * * * * *

All the candles were burning now: a thousand petals against the muted light inside the church.

'Friends, comrades. Sometimes when outsiders come to our funerals, they are surprised. They see us singing and shouting, even dancing; and what often bewilders them, I think, is the joy, the very real joy that we express, even in the midst of weeping.

'Now you know, there is nothing disrespectful in this, or heartless. No: far from it. And that is what I would like to talk about today, comrades. I want to talk about the reasons why we celebrate, even as we mourn.

'Of course we are mourning. Our brother is dead. I do not hesitate to say that he was murdered, destroyed by the pointless, stupid actions of a bunch of uniformed, armed thugs. And let there be no mistake: this terrible death – like each and every violent death – this death fills us with a heavy sickness of outrage and grief. I mention this; even though it is something which hardly needs mentioning – should hardly have to be said.

'This man was not what we call an activist. He was an ordinary person. Not young. Not old. He was a nightwatchman: which is to say he worked long, cold hours – twelve-hour shifts – in return for a meagre wage. I just mention this, brothers and sisters.

'On Tuesday this week he came home at dawn as usual, and fell, in his exhausted state, straight into bed.

'Now I have to tell you that home for this man was a lean-to shack in one of our backyards, where he lived with his wife and their two small children. You see, in terms of the racists' laws, this man was supposed to belong to a category of people that could not live here in Hanover Park, even though his wife could. I mention this.

'Anyway, brothers and sisters. What happened on Tuesday this week? By the time the barricade was up at the end of his street, he was fast asleep. By the time the Casspirs started to arrive, a few hours later, nothing could wake him.

'Now apparently these thugs came with their shotguns and tear-gas; and when the kids scattered and started running, they went down the streets after them. It seems that a couple of these youngsters, looking for sanctuary, raced through the front door of the house, out across the yard, and then ran into the shack where this man lay sleeping. A policeman meanwhile cut across the yard to try and catch them. Now this man's wife was in the shack, busy cooking a meal for her husband. When she saw what was going on, she got the children to crawl out through the back where there was a zinc sheet missing, and just a bit of loose sacking.

'So the children got away. Meanwhile, perhaps because he felt sour, the policeman decided to throw tear-gas into the shack anyway. We don't know exactly what happened; but it seems the canister exploded, and the spirit stove then ignited. This poor woman managed to get her two babies out in time; but when she tried to go back for her husband, the flames were already too fierce.

'And, with all those police running amuck through our neighbourhood, there was not one who came forward and tried to help. I just mention that.'

The minister stopped and looked out across the congregation. The pause lasted a while. 'Brothers and sisters,' he said eventually, as though it had been a struggle to find his voice again. 'Let us pray in silence for a moment.'

Flushing slightly, Marisa kept her eyes open, her head unbowed. She was not 'religious' – whatever that meant; and though it made her feel awkward to stand there in rebellion, she could not bring herself to fake a thing like prayer.

A bead of hot wax spilled down, stinging her palm. She continued to stare straight ahead. At the edge of the dais, a row of schoolchildren stood on either side of the coffin. A guard of honour. Someone had placed a mass of pale flowers on the closed lid.

The minister moved closer to the microphone again.

'A moment ago I mentioned that our funerals are also occasions of rejoicing. Today is no exception.

'As we are assembled here, mourning the death of this one man, we do so together: people from all walks, people from all parts of the city, and even from the rural areas united in a single grief. And I believe that our coming together, this amazing capacity for unity today is a reason for rejoicing.

'Now, our young comrades have organised candles for all of us here today. I think those have been distributed. Does everybody have one?

'As we stand here, holding our lighted candles, let us think about the meaning of the light that we have taken, each one from the other. Of course, these are only small simple pieces of wax; and of course, in a few moments we will all snuff out the little bit of flame – like that. But let us remember that fire itself is something that inheres. It is not any of these individual pale flickers – even though it is in all of them. Fire itself is a process: it is not a thing. Above all, it is not something that you or I or any human being can "put out" or destroy. I'm sure I do not need to say that this is how we see the human spirit – the soul, if you like. And this is what I want to say, brothers and sisters. Yes, we are mourning a death. But in our mourning, what we are rediscovering is the great, the amazing truth: that life itself is indestructible. That is a reason for rejoicing.

'And I want to say furthermore, I believe the spirit of resistance is like that everlasting fire too. In the face of the utmost evil there is a human capacity to resist and to resist that is indestructible. And it is this capacity, this truly amazing power that you give witness to today, in coming here; and the sign of this power present here today is a reason to thank God and rejoice.

'Now, as you each look down at the small stick of wax in your hands, you may think its flame is feeble. To be honest, I think so too. Look at it. It gives out only a miserable little warmth, and the wobbling light of it hardly falls further than the cup of our hands. It is true that today we are mourning a single life; one small candle that has gone out. And you may think that our brother's death was a cruel waste. You may think it has shown us nothing but the bitter insignificance of individual existence. I for one will not pretend that I do not feel those things.

'But at the same time, brothers and sisters, think what a light has been cast by that death. And I mean a great illumination. This man, while he lived, was living in our midst, in our own neighbourhood. He lived here against the laws – their racist laws; lived amongst us in some kind of animal's *hok*, made from a few sheets of zinc and sacking. But it took his death to reveal this – to show us how he lived, reminding us of the simple, elemental reasons for our struggle.

'And another thing. This man was a watchman. A worker. In return for a pittance, he was on duty for twelve-hour stretches at night, six nights a week. That is, seventy-two hours a week. It is no wonder he was too exhausted to be roused by the screams that day. But it took his death to remind us that it is above all the workers who form the suffering heart of our suffering nation; and that until the last one of us is free, none of us will be free.

'If we can only keep alive the light of this knowledge, then our brother's life of suffering, and his death, will not have been in vain.'

Briefly, the minister stood silent. Then he looked out across the church.

'Brothers and sisters, there is one last thing I have to say. Take a look at the massed light around us. As each of us holds up our small flame, it seems to me that together we are creating an amazing candelabrum, a gigantic tree, thick with a fragile, blazing mass of blossom and leaves. Tell me, whose heart cannot find a reason to rejoice in this?'

He raised his hands. 'Let us pray together.'

* * * * * * * * * * * *

'Hey, this is grand out here.' Riaan stretched out his long lean legs and put his arms behind his head for a moment.

André took another covert look at the boy. His brother was leaner than he was, with a surprising hardness to the contours of his face. And the hair, bleached white by the sun, was cut close to the skull.

'So, well, Boet, to answer your question: I've been mostly based in Durban – or, not Durban itself, but just outside the city. That was quite *lekker*. In fact, grand. We were right on the beach, and most of the time we were doing nothing. I mean I did a bit of guard duty every third day, but I was out surfing, like, every single day: just check my hair – and it was even whiter, a few weeks ago. But anyway, they decided to close down that place. Which I can understand: I mean it was ridiculous, the money they were spending just to keep us there, it was something like a million rand a year.'

As he spoke, Riaan kept trying to catch André's gaze, as if he were searching for some answering lightness of attitude.

'Then, on the other hand, you think of all the money they wasted building the place. You should see this set-up. It's all the latest electronic equipment, nothing but the best. It must have cost a fortune.'

'I'm sure of it,' André murmured. (He was wondering what market the South African military had managed to buy such things on.)

Riaan gave him another uncertain look, and ducked his chin, almost bashfully. 'Ja well, so anyway, then you see we were all sent to different places, and I ended up going with a couple of other okes to South West. That's where I've been for the past three weeks.'

It was becoming easier to follow the erratic stabs and runs of Riaan's speech.

'It wasn't so bad, really. Okay, the situation itself is pretty horrible, I mean: it's a war. But still, at least I got a chance to see something of South West. That is an amazing country.'

André stirred, irritated by that use of the colonial name for Namibia.

'And the conditions weren't exactly uncomfortable. Okay it was hot, but from my point of view that was grand. And what we were doing in our section, we just used to lie around most of the day in the back of this open truck, you know, waiting. It was so hot we just used to wear shorts, nothing else. And these weird fruit things used to drop off the trees, they'd land in the back of the truck, and they make this loud, sharp sound, you think it's a stone coming at you.

He wriggled suddenly, reaching deep into a pocket to retrieve something. 'Here.' He held out an object. 'Here. We got into carving them, to kill the time.'

André palmed the small, hard globe, rediscovering an old pleasure in the leathery smoothness of the tough pericarp. Vegetable ivory, they called it. You worked it with your knife, peeling away parts of the dark outer skin to expose the pale, glistening core below it.

He nodded and returned it, not trusting himself to speak.

The emblem Riaan had gouged into it was the same one he and his mates used to carve, eleven years back: that circle crossed with the print of a dove's foot. Even then it had been slightly dated – a quaint relic from the peace marches of the previous decade, in America and Europe.

Riaan seemed hesitant to take it back. For a moment he kept his long fingers wrapped uncertainly around it. Then, abruptly, he reached over and placed it on the ground at André 's feet.

'So anyway, I was telling you. We weren't exactly suffering up there. Hey, we ate. You should have seen. Meat – every day. Fruit, fresh salads. You think, no man, you're supposed to be in the middle of a desert.' He widened his mouth into a mock gape.

For all his nervous mannerisms, Riaan was a bit of a

comic, it seemed.

'They were flying food in every day. Pineapple, even. I've never eaten so much pineapple in my life.'

He stretched contentedly, candid as a child about his happiness.

'For now I'm on leave. I got five days. Well actually I've got to hit the road again first thing tomorrow. Heading back to Durban. I'll be based there for a short while, until they post me somewhere else.'

He cocked his head. 'No, I scheme I'm a fortunate boy. I've had the best on all sides. Even in South West: okay, our camp was virtually on the border, but you never had a sense you were in danger. Of course the real action will only hot up in a few months' time when the rainy season starts. That's when the Swapos mainly move. Their tracks get covered up more quickly in the wet.'

In all this time it seemed the lore had hardly changed.

'Did you have any contacts?' André asked, curious.

* * * * * * * * * * * *

Victor walked into the kitchen.

'Oh hullo Desi. Hi Rosie.'

He pulled out one of the kitchen chairs and sat down.

'They haven't been round here again, have they? You hear they were at Mrs Peters again last night?'

Victor looked at his sisters.

'They were threatening to take away Nazeem if she doesn't tell them where Taliep is. Can you believe it? They wanted to hold his brother, like a hostage.'

There was something burning him up, Desiree thought.

'It's heavy for Taliep. You know his granny stays with them: now she's had another stroke because of all this. Taliep knows it isn't his fault, but of course he feels bad.

And it makes it worse because he can't be around to help his mom with her.'

Stretching across the table, he reached himself the packet of biscuits.

'So, Desi, how's it with you? I thought you would be at the funeral?'

Desiree felt a heat envelop her. 'No,' she said. 'I've been at the Advice Bureau all morning. But Marisa's going, from our house.'

'The Bureau. You're back with the Union again? That's good news.'

He went quiet again, as if he were still brooding on other things.

'I heard about Teach Zwakala. And that girl, also – Maya what's her name.'

'Greenbaum.'

'Yes. Are they still inside?'

Desiree nodded, and Rose looked up for a moment from folding shirts.

Something seemed to swell and rise inside Desiree. The thought crashed down, surging through her. If only Maya had been in the office. She always did their sorting during the week. She'd have gone through the correspondence. That stupid business with Mr McKenzie would never have happened.

'Well, how are things otherwise with the Union? How's the merger going? Are they going to be ready in time for the COSATU launch?'

A warmth of interest had come into Victor's voice now, Desiree thought. He was beginning to look less strained.

'I don't know, it seems to take so much consultation. It's not something you can hurry. Every step has to go through the factory committees; and there are a lot of factories involved, especially on the General Workers' side.'

Suddenly tired again, Desiree stopped. Victor knew all this. He was just looking for something to argue about.

'I'd give anything to be in Durban next month for the launch. I heard some people talking about the preparations. Just the interpreting alone is a massive thing to organise. You can imagine. They need to have everything in Xhosa, Zulu, Sotho, English and Afrikaans. They're hoping to have that system – what do you call it, when people have headphones, and you have –'

'Simultaneous translation?'

'Yes. That. But they don't know if it'll come off, because of the cost. You can imagine.'

'Mmmm.'

Rose broke in, changing the subject to the question of the boycott.

Victor's voice had deepened over the past few months, Desiree thought, as she listened to her brother answer their sister's questions.

There was something about a final decision that still had to be taken. But the signs were clear. A boycott was on the cards.

Then what about him? He wouldn't be writing his matric?

'That is what it would mean, Rose.'

Silence seemed to float across the warm kitchen, uniting rather than isolating them. Their father, each of them knew, would have been appalled.

Victor kept his eyelids lowered. 'Look. You know how I think. I don't forget I'm a September.'

When he looked up again, his eyes were clear.

'Desi, Rose. This is my own view. Please – don't go telling anyone else. But if you want to know: in principle, it seems to me that to wreck our own education is wrong. It flies in the face of reason. It destroys our very means of liberation. So it is deadly.

'But what I also want to say is, sometimes there can be a world of difference between the correctness of a principle – and the correctness of an action.

'And I know that's a hard thing to grasp. It took me a long time to see it. People want to tell you you're being contradictory. But I think that is a simplistic response.

'The reality is: this particular boycott is necessary. Rose, believe me, I'm sorry. But politically it is correct. There is no way, after everything that has happened this year – 1985 – that we in the Western Cape can go back to classes now, when meanwhile we've got the police still coming into the schools every week.

'And if you accept that, then you must accept that it would be a mockery of education to go and write exams now, when we are not prepared, and no self-respecting teacher is going to say that we are prepared.'

Rose eventually found a mild question to break the silence.

Victor seemed to relax again. 'Well,' he said, 'I suppose I'll just have to get a job. I was thinking of applying to the City Libraries; if you don't need a matric for that. Or maybe I could get a job as a clerk. I don't mind what, as long as it's with the municipality.'

He gave them a smile.

'Mainly because I'd like to get involved in the union. Once a trouble-maker . . . I suppose it runs in the family.'

Rose laughed too, 'There now.'

Over the years they had often, so often, lingered around this table, discussing the merits of different jobs. Library work was the answer (they'd decided) for anyone who planned to carry on studying part-time.

'There, you see. And you're so critical of Shireen when she talks about getting a job.'

'Oh Rosie.'

Victor only ever seemed to be in good spirits when he had an argument going.

'You know perfectly well Shireen just wants to earn a whole lot of money so she can buy herself fancy clothes and smart shoes. That's all she's interested in. In her case it's just naked bourgeois aspiration.'

'Now Vic.' Refusing to be drawn, Rose answered him mildly.

'Don't you think you're being a bit hard on her? She's only fifteen. Of course she wants nice things. It's not unnatural at that age.'

'At that age.' Impatiently, Victor reached into the packet for another biscuit. 'You weren't like that, Rose.'

He'd caught her off guard. Exposed, she stared back at him, her look of irony mixed with vulnerability.

Victor seemed to sense his advantage. 'Come on Rosie, you know it just perpetuates false consciousness – that sort of thing. People just want to look after themselves: they just want nice clothes, nice food, a fancy car, a TV and a hifi; and as long as they can get ahead, they don't care who else gets left behind in the ghetto. They can't see that if they worked to change things for everybody it would be better for them too in the long run. The idea of collective bargaining power – that means nothing to them. So they stay uninvolved.'

'Oh Vic.' Rose shrugged; but there was a soft expression in her eyes. 'Vic, I'm sure that is all true. But even so, I can't see the harm in Shireen's wanting. Look, I don't for one moment intend to let her leave school. That's a different issue again.

'But aren't there simple things that everyone is entitled to? Or else what is the struggle about, hmm? Isn't it to free humankind? I know: beautiful words, a beautiful dream. But I always thought it meant quite simple things. A world where there aren't millions with only rags to wear, and where a young girl won't have to feel guilty because she wants a pretty blouse. I'm not saying it must be costly.'

Desiree was gazing absently at the worn linoleum on the floor. There was that familiar place where the pattern merged into a dark fibrous mess, encrusted with sand and the grain of the underlying Victorian floorboards. Where the sunlight fell, it showed up a faint tracery of stylised leaves. For the second time that day, the quotation from Goethe came back to her. "The greyness of the dogma . . . "

'Is that really such a terrible thing? Or do you think if she can afford a nice pair of shoes one day, then the next day she won't want to walk anywhere, she's going to want a Mercedes Benz?'

'No man Rose, credit me with some intelligence.' Victor was trying to look pained; but could not help starting to smile.

Something light and glistening seemed to lift through Desiree's thoughts.

Victor stared at her. Then he was laughing too.

'Hey, Rose.' He stood up, still grinning, and went to the fridge. 'Can a person get something to eat around here?'

They heard the front door opening again.

'Hullo, it's me.'

There was something faintly disingenuous about the eagerness of Shireen's voice.

'Is Uncle Theo here yet?'

Discovering Victor there, Shireen adjusted her look to reflect a kind of proud indifference. Avoiding his eyes, she tossed down a newspaper, and – with a hint of self-conscious virtue – opened the fridge to store away the milk she'd brought.

Rose gave her a tiny nod. 'You got milk. That was

thoughtful of you, sweetheart; thank you. Are you going over to Begum's now?'

Vaguely, Shireen shook her head. She must have lost interest in her earlier project. Still refusing to acknowledge Victor's presence, she headed slowiy back towards the door, fingering her hair, as though something else pre-occupied her now.

Rose called after her. 'Shireen? If you're thinking of disappearing into the bathroom, please remember Vic might want a bath before he goes.'

Victor stood up and stretched his lean body. 'Okay.' (There was regret in his voice.) 'I actually can't stay much longer. If nobody minds, I think I will just take a quick bath.'

In the doorway, Shireen raised her eyes to meet his. Delicately, with exquisite grace, she offered him a smile, and left the room.

Rose glanced from Desiree to Victor. 'All right. Your clothes are ready for you, Vic. I've just finished ironing them. Why don't you change into one set now, and I'll put the other shirts and things into a plastic bag for you.'

'Thanks, Rosie.' Blinking quickly, he shook his head. 'Thanks,' he muttered again.

* * * * * * * * * * * *

'No. No, I didn't have any contacts. Which I must say I'm glad about. We did have one incident at the camp; but I slept right through it: you must know how I can sleep, hey.'

Riaan blushed slightly, though whether out of embarrassment or pride, André could not decide.

'The Swapos came right into the camp. Apparently they got off fifteen shots, but only eight of them actually hit the camp. Nobody was hurt or anything.'

Cautiously Riaan added, 'I reckon those Swapo guys aren't too well organised or something.'

'And then? What happened?'

'The police went after them. The Koevoet guys. That's what usually happens. But they didn't get anything that time. They said the Swapos got away in a bakkie.'

With a careful lightness, he added: 'Which was quite unusual. Most of the time they get those guys. It's almost always just a few of them, and the transport they've got is primitive, man.'

He peered at André, as if once again searching for clues.

'In a way, it's kind of painful.'

Certainly, there was something endearing about the boy's transparency.

'You know what they mostly use for transport?' He offered André a look of conspiracy.

'Of course I shouldn't be telling you this. It's all highly classified information. 'He shrugged. 'But there was this one guy I met, he was in EW, that's electronic warfare. He was telling me, his job was to pick up all the communications, stuff from the Soviets – especially off the coast, although ninety-nine per cent of the time he reckons it's just fishing boats, you know they're talking about some shoal they've spotted. But up there on the border, he was getting stuff from the Swapos. And these messages, this is unreal: he says it's mostly requests to send two bicycles ahead to some place. Or to send donkeys. This is how they operate. And he's just picking it up all the time, they know exactly when those okes are going to come in, how many of them, where they plan to move on afterwards. You'd think, surely they would use code. Or they do, according to this guy, but it's like some elementary code that you work out in two seconds, and you're laughing.'

Riaan shook his head. 'I don't know.' A private thought seemed to have quietened him. 'No, I don't know. It's frustrating, that's all. I mean, wouldn't it be quite easy to get better codes? You could use a computer, or something?'

André remained silent. He was remembering those stifling attacks he'd used to get in the army: a sensation of being gripped by anger, loathing, homesickness, and boredom.

The idiom of the camp was disgusting to him, composed (as he saw it) of violent curses and belches, with bigotry or sexual dread at the heart of every utterance. He'd tried hanging around with a few English-speaking guys, thinking he would have more in common with them; but after a few weeks he'd tired of having to clench his jaw each time they referred to him – because of his name - as a tame *takhaar*, or rock-spider.

When his first leave came up at last and he was able to go home for a few days, it had not put an end (as he'd hoped) to the throat-drying attacks.

Riaan was about seven at the time. (André could remember him scampering around in a bathing costume, so awed at first by the return of his big brother that he could hardly speak.) Looking over the child's head, he'd stared at their mother. And Pa? Swiftly he made a grab for Riaan, pretending to wrestle with him. *Mother? Has Pa gone off again?* The small arms could hardly reach André's waist, and Riaan had to resort to butting him in the belly. (You forget how small little kids are at that age.) Suddenly Riaan was shouting imperiously to their mother to bring him his towel. Nothing would deter him, either. How long had his father been away for this time, André was wondering, savagely, as he hoisted his little brother up on to his shoulders.

Their mother went to make coffee; and André carried

Riaan outside to the swimming pool, where Riaan wanted to show off his butterfly stroke.

Watch this, Boet. The skinny shoulders pumped up and down, creating spectacular wings of beaded, thrashing water. *Now watch me, Boet. Watch me this time, I'm going to do another length.*

Roaring, André shouted encouragement, shading his eyes against the metal-bright sharpness of the light on the water.

Did you see me that time? Wait, wait, I'm going to do backstroke now.

André cheered him on, enjoying his little brother's rich, honest boastfulness. Then, all at once, the sickening bitterness swarmed in his mouth again. To his dismay, and for perhaps only the third or fourth time in his life, he'd found himself appallingly close to tears.

Riaan was looking at him, sideways.

'Anyway. I've been talking about myself all this time.

What about you, Boet? You still busy with your thesis? Oh, hey, the old man reckons he saw your picture in the paper. Was it you? He says there was some protest march at UCT, and he swears that was you in the front row. Is it true?'

What was the boy really asking, André wondered slowly.

Riaan laughed. 'The old man reckons you're a Commie. You know that? He didn't want me to come and see you. In fact, I must tell you, he was hell of a mad with me, because I told him straight I was going to make my own decision. I said to him: you're my brother. I need to get to know you.' There was a trace of seriousness in the boy's eyes.

'It's crazy. I mean, here we come from the same family, but we hardly know each other. I often think that. I've never really sat down with you and had a long talk. It kind of worries me sometimes.'

The words touched André, more than he cared to show.

Riaan went on. 'In the army too, these guys believe anyone from varsity is a Commie. A *Kommunis*. And you know what they call UCT? Moscow-on-the-Hill.'

'Well.' André relaxed, letting his shoulders heave as he laughed with Riaan. 'Well, things haven't changed much then. The old man used to threaten me that if I joined Nusas he would throw me out of the house and never speak to me again.'

Riaan offered him a sombre look, uncertain, perhaps, how much sympathy he should register. 'So then didn't you join?'

André was amused. 'Oh no of course I did. After a challenge like that, wouldn't you? Or rather, no, let's be accurate here. I tried to.'

Now, of course, he could see how gauche he must have seemed; perhaps downright strange, with his lumbering, pathetically over-eager presence. Always hanging around the student offices, trying to find a way in to that crowd. Occasionally they would give him a small task, setting him to collate pages, or to letter a caption that someone needed in a hurry. In fact, they always seemed to be working at speed. That was half the trouble. They were quick and light; they knew so much. And it was made worse by the presence of the girls. Some of them frightened him with their sophistication. Others, he used to think softly, seemed like wild creatures who might be frightened of him. Fragile gypsies, with tiny metal stars tinkling in their hair, dressed in filmy tops that gave hints of small, naked breasts. He never could bring himself to speak to them. Indeed, he'd found it difficult to start a conversation with any of those Lefties (as he took to calling them privately, in his frustration). It was no wonder, perhaps, that they had made few overtures to him.

Riaan was waiting patiently for him to continue.

'Perhaps they were afraid I was a spy.' He let his smile expand, and sniffed lightly, to show his good humour. 'There I was with my clumsy questions, and an Afrikaans name . . .'

'But you did leave home, André. I remember when you went away. So didn't the old man throw you out then?'

Their father had persisted with his suspicions, convinced that André was defying him.

The times when he bothered to come home for supper, he would take his seat and stare heavily across the table at André. Then, as soon as his food was in front of him, he would begin the interrogation, always benign to start with. Smoothly the questions would flow. (Oh yes, their father had had a real love affair with words. And with himself. The old ham saw himself as the stern patriarch: god-like to his family.) Then he would begin to rant, working himself up until he drew some response; and that would be the cue for him to throw back his chair at last and come round the table, demanding that André repeat what he had just said.

It was remarkable how much force his father had been able to cram behind the knuckles of that broad, freckled fist.

Then one morning while he was sitting in a lecture, André flipped over the page of his note-pad – and his hand had reached through a shaft of sunlight, finding no resistance. In that same instant, he'd recognised something. Whatever childish regard he had ever felt for his father had finally withered away. The fact, like the fact of a death, was terrifying in its simplicity. For a moment he'd thought another of the old attacks was on its way. Instead, he was overwhelmed by a sense of immense calm as he regarded the implications. To have lost, irredeemably, every vestige of respect for another human being: this was what had happened. Morally, it seemed to him untenable. It tore away a part of his own humanity.

A week later, without saying anything to his parents, he'd left home and moved into digs; taking everything that he cared to keep from his boyhood packed into a rucksack, a togbag, and two suitcases.

André shifted. 'How is the old man?' he tried, cautiously.

A doubtful look came into Riaan's face.

'He's terribly overweight. I can't understand him, really. He knows his heart is going to give in, he knows he should eat less, but he just carries on stuffing himself. And drinking. He has to have two whiskies at lunch-time, and then it's another couple before supper, then he has more, and after that it doesn't seem to stop, he goes on all evening. He didn't always drink like that, did he?'

André felt tired. He had not wanted to hear this.

'He's killing himself, if you ask me.'

'Listen. Riaan. Sorry, I'm changing the subject, but I've had an idea. I must confess I'm starting to wilt slightly. I was up early. But why don't you stick around till supper? We're having a braai here this evening, for Chris. It's nothing formal – just our house. Then we could carry on talking.'

Riaan hesitated.

'Hey, Boet, I'd like that. But I don't know, the old man might not like it. I told you, he wasn't pleased – at all – about me coming here.'

'Come on, you're your own man, aren't you? What right has he got to interfere? If you like, you can phone him.'

'You know, I'd quite like to play around with your computer for a bit. I mean, if you want to take a rest for a while, or something. Would that be okay with you?'

* * * * * * * * * * * *

'Viva UDF!'

'Viva!'

'Viva ANC!'

'Viva!'

It seemed that this round of calls and responses was going to go on for a long time. While the congregation chanted, there was a wisp of conversation around Marisa.

'Who is it? It can't be an Exec person, they're all in hiding.'

'No, looks like we're having someone from the youth.'

The interpreter pulled the microphone towards himself again. 'Is the comrade from CAYCO here? Can we have the UDF speaker to come forward, please?'

A young man sprang up on to the dais and went to join the interpreter. The two spoke briefly to one another, and then the speaker stepped forward, raising one fist to punch into the air.

'Amandla!'

The shout was a massive thing, metallic, echoing with confidence; and the response came rolling back as if some earth-encrusted boulder had been dislodged: *'Ngawethu!'*

The cries and answers went on and on in the standard patterns.

'Inkululeko!'

'Ngoku!'

'Ngoku!'

'Inkululeko!'

Around Marisa, everyone from the Area was joining

in, raising and dropping their fists in rhythm. Yet she could not bring herself to shout along with them. She knew the words: she'd heard many of these chants before. Often, in any case, you could guess the responses. (There must be a name for it – for the structure of these cries.) Well then, why didn't she join in? The faces of her comrades shone as they shouted back one hoarse chant after another.

Trying to block out the din of the crowd, she let her thoughts drift. (No: it was the pettiness of her own words she was struggling not to hear. There was a tastelessness about this mass behaviour, all this jubilant automatism: wasn't that what she really thought? She was a prig then. Too proud of her privateness and her own ideas.) At last she managed to distract herself, remembering terms she'd learnt once. Strophe and antistrophe. Lines out of old Greek dramas; ancient verse. Imagine, she thought: reciting in the open air, in stone theatres open to the drifting light and the shadows of clouds.

'Mayibuye!'

'iAfrika!'

'iAfrika!'

'Mayibuye!'

The speaker was signalling that he wanted to begin.

'Comrades . . .'

Keeping an eye on him, the interpreter repeated the greeting in Xhosa, also holding a hand high: *'Maqabane . . .'*

'Roar, young lion', a single voice sang out; and other voices, laughing, followed it up: 'Roar!'

'Yes', someone shouted; and there were whistles of agreement. 'Roar!'

'Comrades. The government is trying to divide us.'

The phrase had a trace of a lilt at the end. Taking it as his cue, the interpreter quickly took the microphone.

Then, as the last syllables of the Xhosa faded, the young speaker came back in, in English.

'The government comes into our townships.'

Catching fragments of the translation, Marisa heard the interpreter choose a different word for 'government' this time. *AmaBhulu*. Literally it meant *'boere'*, she knew. And that meant the Afrikaners, really; or the police. (Although someone had told her that the word was used more and more these days to mean, simply, 'whites'.)

'They try to tell us that the people who say the troops must get out of the townships – that those people are our enemies.

'But we know who our enemies are. The enemies are the people who are shouting at our children, the ones who come with guns, in the Casspirs.'

'Phantsi Botha!' someone shouted.

'Phantsi!'

'Down, down!'

The speaker nodded. 'Today we are meeting because these enemies of the people have killed one of our brothers.

'But we say: it does not matter how many of us they kill. Despite their deaths, in spite of these deaths, the people – we who are the people – are united.

'And nothing can destroy our unity. Their bullets will not destroy our unity, their tear-gas will not destroy our unity. Not even when they come with their Casspirs. This is what the UDF has to say today: that the government will never destroy the unity of the people.'

The speaker paused until the translator had finished. Then he gave a sudden shout. 'Longlive UDF!'

'Longlive!' the cheer came back.

Inspired, a group of teenagers at the front started a new round of calls.

'Inkululeko!'

That word for 'freedom' again. And the response meant 'now'.

'Ngoku!'

She still could not join in. Trying to keep a smile on her face, she stood there, rocked by the movements of the people around her.

'Aluta!'

'Continua!'

'Forward to socialism!'

'Forward!'

'Forward to freedom!'

'Forward!'

'Victoria!'

'E certa!'

'Freedom is certain, victory or death!'

'Freedom is certain, victory or death!'

It was several moments before the speaker could get himself heard again.

'Today, comrades, we are burying one of our people. But there are also two other comrades we have said farewell to this week.'

He paused for the interpreter.

'One is a comrade, an old comrade, who died this week, overseas in Havana. That's the capital city of Cuba – another country, across the sea.' With a sweep of one arm, he indicated how remote that other country was.

Across the aisle, an old man breathed out with audible regret.

'Now the name of this comrade'

'Igama lakhe'

'was Alex la Guma.'

'bengu Alex la Guma.'

'Now, most of us have never even heard this comrade's name: that's because the government of this country has kept us from knowing about him, and from reading his books.

'But he was one of this country's greatest writers. Now what the government did to him – they put him under house arrest.'

Someone gave a whistle of dismay.

'So then in the end he had to leave this country, to take up the struggle . . .'

As he waited for the Xhosa phrase to die away, the speaker pointed to some imaginary region, using the curve of his whole arm.

'. . . from outside.'

The gesture made it plain that 'outside' was somewhere almost fantastically far away, hidden beyond the bulge of the planet's vast, curving surface.

'And when this comrade died, he was the representative for the ANC, he stood for the ANC in Cuba.'

'*Viva* the African National Congress!'

'*Viva!*'

'So today, as we are mourning the death of our other comrade, we are also mourning the death of Alex la Guma.

'But this is the message we have today from the UDF: One day, when we have a people's government, and the people decide what we will teach, and what we will read, and what we will study – then we will read the books of this comrade, Alex la Guma; and his name will not die.'

Fists shot up, and the pent-up shouts were released, ringing through the stony spaces of the church. '*Viva Alex la Guma! Viva!*'

Marisa shivered. The building was cold after all, despite the long, amber shafts of light streaming down.

'*Longlive La Guma!*'

'*Longlive!*'

The Muslim priest had come back from his consultation with the group of marshals. Now he was standing near the lectern, lightly fingering his beard with one hand. Marisa saw him trying to take a secret look at his watch. Maybe he would hurry things up? There were still hymns to sing, according to the order of service. (Although no one would have any voice left if the shouting carried on much longer.)

'Longlive!'

'Longlive!'

The moulana had managed to catch the speaker's attention, and the two men leaned close to hear one another's words.

'Something's up.'

Marisa felt the shimmering lightness of fear race through her again. If everyone would be quiet, they could get this ceremony over with, and leave. She looked down at the stub of candle she'd placed on the ledge in front of her. Where the wax had spilled, it had left greyish blotches.

Eventually the young man took the microphone again.

'Now, there's another comrade we are thinking about today. He died this week, in Pretoria, where he was put to death by the regime: our comrade Benjamin Moloise.'

The audience grew silent again.

'We all know his name I think. We know why the racist regime hanged him: for his part in the people's struggle to end oppression.

'But he was very strong before he died. And he left a message for us, comrades. He wrote a poem, that is – some words, a message. Now in this poem he said he was proud to be what he was. He said he was not afraid. He was proud to give his life; his one life.'

People sat in stillness. Many kept their heads bowed, though others stared forward with the blinded, momentarily rigid expressions of grief.

One of the Christian ministers came over to the

microphone now, with the moulana. As if to steady them all, he raised the open palm of one hand.

'Brothers and sisters. Some of you may have been wondering about the occasional noises coming from behind that door. Now, I have to tell you that the church is surrounded. There is a large police presence out there; but at the moment they are just standing around. They have given us five minutes to conclude our service; and then, I am afraid, we have to leave the premises.'

Marisa felt her body tighten. Along with the people next to her, she sat forward, listening intently.

'Now there is no need to panic.'

Briefly he turned his head away from the microphone, as he consulted the small group that had gathered near him. A scouring electronic sound chased after his words.

'Before we go out, we will ask someone from the youth to lead us in the singing of the national anthem. After that, we will please allow the bearers to leave first with the coffin. Then, as we follow them, we will depart calmly, in an orderly fashion. There is no reason for any panic.

'All right. Can we ask the marshals to start taking up their positions, please?

A young woman dressed in khaki detached herself from the group and went to stand at the edge of the platform. Pinnned to her black beret, a tiny, tricoloured dab of paper formed a badge.

'Brothers and sisters, please: let us show these people outside that we are people of dignity. Let us show the world that, if there is any violence here today, that violence does not come from us. Let us show them that it is not us who are the barbarians. Please. Let us remember that we are here today in peace. '

* * * * * * * * * * * *

Desiree contemplated the long rows of the bookshelves. Somewhere in all her father's writings there must be a paragraph that crystallised his beliefs.

The papers were all kept together on the bottom shelf: newsletters, minutes, journals and pamphlets – some tied into bundles, others left loose in precarious stacks. The family album lay here too, bound in dark leather, corded, and tasselled. Desiree crouched down; and as she threw out a hand to balance herself, her fingertips brushed across a shining, sapphire-coloured bird in the carpet. She could smell the acrid reek of old ink, and a stifling dustiness. Dreaming, she looked up.

The sunlight was skittering over the silk threads and tiny mirrors in the cloth over the bed in the corner. It suited her to have this room, Rose claimed. Never mind if it was a bit of a thoroughfare: at least it gave her the afternoon light and warmth. (While Victor and Shireen were still babies, it had been easy enough to put their cots in their mother's room, or in with the two older girls. But the two teenagers each needed privacy now; and really it was better if Anthony slept in the front room, since he had to come and go at all hours, working at the hospital.)

She reached for a set of roneoed foolscap pages.

Her mother would have typed the stencils for these. She was always typing for organisations, or doing their books.

She had gone to find her one night, wanting to take Shireen to her. (The baby had woken up, racked with tiny, shuddering sobs.) With her little sister wrapped in a blanket, sagging down against her own childish hip, she'd wandered down to the back room. Their mother was there. She was always there, working late at night.

But the typewriter keys did not stop clattering.

Mommy, please I'm here. Shireen's crying again.

She'd been thinking only, indignantly, of the clumsy

bundle she wanted to be rid of. Then she saw her mother's face: with the skin glistening; and that mouth stretched open. Blindly she carried on typing, keeping up a mechanical din; and meanwhile there was a low, grotesque sound coming out of her mouth.

Instantly, Desiree was suffocated with shame. She knew this was something she should not be witnessing. It was unspeakable.

Unseen, she'd managed to back out of the doorway, with her burden drooping in her arms. Taking the baby to bed with her, she'd lain there smoothing the small head of sticky hair. *There Baba. Mommy's going to come now. There, it's all right.*

A spasm of cramp pain was shooting through her calf. Quickly Desiree stood up to flex the foot. The old accusation was stirring in her mind, hardly even forming itself into words. It was my fault. I should have said something. Spoken to Rose. I should have told someone.

What does it mean, if you know that someone is suffering, and you say nothing, and then they die?

Picking up the album, she went over to sit down on the divan.

That was her mother at eighteen. Younger than me now, Desiree thought, making her thoughts centre on the photograph. The light gleamed on one temple; and on either side of the high forehead the hair fanned out in a glistening cloud of tiny, drifting curls. So like her own. People often said it. Rose took after their father – a September, no mistaking; and Shireen was the pretty one; but she, Desiree, was the image of their mother.

There were other brownish photographs lying loose between the stiff pages. (The glue of the old silvery mounting corners had dried out years ago.) Desiree picked one up and turned it over. On the back, the inscription gave it a date. 1956. The picture was a group shot, taken at a conference. Her mother stood there shyly, embarrassed, it seemed, by the plate of food in her hand; while in the background near her a tall slender man was partially obscured by shadows.

Desiree remembered. When she and Rose were children they had demanded over and over to be told the story of that courtship.

Did he really call you Miss Heldsinger?

Oh no, Mommy.

It was part of the game that they should fall into a giggling, scandalised fever of mirth each time they heard this; while their mother was never allowed to revise her telling.

Well in those days people had respect, you know.

And you called Daddy Mr September.

Their father had been much older than her: a teacher at one of the leading schools in Cape Town, he'd been in the profession for ten years already by the time they met.

And at the dance that evening – they had a social do, to end off the conference – I couldn't believe it when your father came up to me. This tall, elegant man . . . and so kind; I couldn't think why he should ask me.

This was always their father's cue to look up from his book and murmur soberly, *I believe it had something to do with the polka dot ribbon, my dear.*

Their mother would pretend not to hear, though she had to fight to keep a certain light from filling her eyes as she continued the story the girls knew by heart.

He was such a gentleman. After we danced he fetched me my supper, and then he stayed at my side, asking me what I thought of the speeches and the discussions and everything. You can imagine how shy I felt afterwards when the others told me I'd been talking to Martin September – the *Martin*

September, from Trafalgar High. And he was asking me for my opinions. Of course I'd heard about him. He was always writing articles and pamphlets, and his name used to come up quite often in the minutes I was typing for the Teacher's League. Meanwhile I didn't realise it was him; and he just stood there. He was really listening to me, he even forgot to finish eating the chicken on his plate.

Hmmm, their father would interrupt comfortably at this point. *Was it really chicken? Funny how I don't remember that at all. Smitten, I must have been. Completely smitten.*

The pages felt clammy under her fingers. Fighting, Desiree tried to focus again on the spilling photographs. She ought to stick these loose ones down. They would get lost some day.

Always remember: the finest aspects of a human being never can die. Her father had said that once. *The qualities that make us human are precisely those qualities that are immortal. Think of the things that lift us above the beasts: and aren't they precisely those things transcending the immediate, the individual? They are the things that bind us; the things that only exist where we hold them in common. Language, now. And think how language in turn depends on – or maybe it creates – the gifts of memory and imagination. Empathy. Speculation. Logical construction. Of course, for each of us, so long as we are alive – awake to the times, living through our days – there will always be urgent, immediate, possibly even ephemeral questions. But what humankind possesses, everlastingly, is a sense of its own history, and its dreams of a different history.*

* * * * * * * * * * * *

Outside, the sky was overcast with cloud, and the vestiges that remained of the sunlight were raking the pitted sand with cold, metallic streaks, picking out clumps of weeds and rims of discarded bottle tops.

Caught up in the middle of the fast-moving throng, elbowed and pushed, Marisa had already lost sight of the people she knew. The coffin up ahead was obscured. Around her she sensed the springing tautness of people's bodies as they strode. She skipped quickly forward, afraid of being knocked over. The head of the column must be out on the street now.

She glanced sideways at the woman she'd come up alongside. She held a scarf over her mouth and nose and walked fast, keeping her head down. Marisa longed to catch the woman's arm, to meet her eyes; but she was pushed aside by a younger comrade.

Suddenly there was a loud thudding noise. And again.

The screams were swarming in the air, clouded and blazing; and people were turning, racing back.

The short, cracking sounds went on. Something came flying down, hard at her feet. There was a pale filament rising.

Her eyes were swimming with the fire. Blinded by the acrid smoke, she reached out her hands. Run, for God's sake. The corrosion was scouring through her nostrils, her throat, seeping down into her chest.

All around, bodies were hurtling. There were more shots. Someone's hard shoulder sent her flying. She was on her knees; the knuckles of both hands were kneading the sand. Get back on your feet. The smell of the dry, powdery earth was choking her. Get up. She could see nothing, yet she knew there were people still running, pounding past her. She was winded, all the breath burnt out of her by the harsh spume. *Hou aan*. Behind the church was a small stoep, sheltered from the wind by the shapes of the buildings. Through scalded eyes, she could make out people, comrades gathering on the raised terrace. *Hou aan*. Keep going.

'Here sister, okay, it's all right.'

Someone was helping her, reaching down to lift her up the steps. Strong arms.

'It's okay now, take it easy, it goes away.'

She was sinking. She leaned against his chest, clasping his arms. His body was warm. Someone else's arm came around her; but she did not lift her face from the young comrade's shoulder. The woman huddled next to her was trembling. *'Fok hulle,'* she cursed. *'Fok hulle.'*

'You'll be okay, just rest there, lean on me.'

Where had everybody else got to? she wondered. What was happening out there in the streets?

The smarting fire in her eyes began to die down. (She had not believed it would pass.) Now there were only stinging traces left on her face, in the drying smears of mucus above her lip. Humiliated, she felt through her pockets for a tissue; but she found nothing, apart from the car keys.

For another moment she let herself lean against the comrade's khaki-shirted chest. People were still coming up on to the stoep, but they were no longer running.

'Sister, you okay now?'

He was trying to disengage himself. Marisa sensed him looking over her head.

'Thank you.' She drew away, taking a deep breath; and nodded. 'What has happened to everybody else, do you know?'

A helicopter was flying over the church grounds, dipping down almost to the rooftops and then lifting sharply up again, bucking and veering.

'No,' he answered her. 'Maybe they're going to tell us now.'

'Okay, comrades.'

Two marshals had been conferring with a group of

people at the end of the stoep.

'Comrades, can we have your attention. Just so you know what is going on: the coffin has been taken by car to the cemetery, and most of the clergy are on their way there. Apparently they got through the gates just before the tear-gas started.

'Okay, firstly, if there is anyone in need of medical attention, we have a first aid post set up; and if you will report to Nabil here, he will see to it that you are taken across.'

The helicopter's juddering noise made it difficult to catch some of the words.

'Now, secondly, I think most of you know that it was our intention to march to the cemetery. However, comrades, we wish to stress that it is too dangerous now. We are asking everybody please to go home quietly instead. Our marshals will escort people back to the transport, for those of you who came on the buses.'

People began to move away, heading for a sagging fence that picked out a boundary between the grounds of the church and the open field next to it.

'Ja, please, everybody, can we move along. We'll go around the back way, we can get over the fence.'

The gathering clouds had deepened, and now there was a faint light in them. Or was it smoke hanging in the air like that? In the distance, a second helicopter seemed to be circling the area.

Marisa, walking on the edge of a group, turned briefly aside and lifted a corner of her tee-shirt to try and clean away the stains on her face. Now she noticed her hands too. They were scratched and filthy, covered in earth and a thin, drying wash of purplish brown.

And her necklace was gone. The clasp must have flown apart. She had not even felt it slipping. It must be lying in the yard, trampled into the sand.

Two young women were helping people across the fence, holding down the wire strands. As she sprang down, Marisa saw the bush growing there, with its limp, multicoloured flowers crushed against the fence post. She knew its name – 'yesterday today and tomorrow'. All at once, the rust along the wires had a smell of rain, or blood.

As they moved across the vacant land, people joined together in casual clusters. Others fell behind; and the thin column lengthened. One of the helicopters flew up and down, keeping patrol above them; casting flickers of teetering, blade-thin shadow.

Underfoot, the fine grey sand kept yielding and spilling back. The grass that grew here was scrawny: the real vegetation seemed to be the weeds, Marisa thought. Weeds that would be prickling with hard dry thorns in a few months. And the daisies were out all over the place, thick on the ground, right here in the track. Bending quickly, she tugged and broke off a few of the bright *gousblomme*. Then she ran forward a few steps, to catch up with the group ahead.

One of the women had taken off her shoes and was carrying them. Looking down, sideways, Marisa saw that her pale stockings were shredded and laddered into cobwebs. Her shins were crusted with blood and grey earth.

The air had turned cool.

Marisa played with the light flowers in her hand. The stems were firm, robust things. They made her think of a game from her childhood. Using her fingernails, she pierced a small slit in one of them. The rank juice seeped out. She took a second daisy, and pulled its stem through the incision she'd made.

Her hands were trembling, though, from exhaustion. In any case, the activity bored her after a moment or two.

She raised her head. In the distance were two yellow Casspirs, drawn up on to the verge of the field; but the people in front were walking on past them.

There. Wasn't that Pierre, down there at the end of the street. She caught sight of other familiar figures, Steve, Rebecca, standing in a group. God. Thank you. They were all safe. She started to run, breaking free from the column. If she'd had the breath she would have shouted. (The childish soaring of her heart disturbed her. She ought to be feeling awed, or frightened. After all, there was smoke still hanging above the streets, making gigantic canopies of shadow and burnt, sombre light. Yet she was longing to sing.) *Liewe Here, dankie*. Stricken, she carried on running, holding down the keys in her pocket with one hand.

'Marisa. You found us. That's great, that's everybody then.'

'Ey, man, what happened to you? Your eyes look terrible.' Mark seemed to wince as he looked at her face.

Casually, Steve put an arm around her shoulders; and for an instant she was flooded with a profound feeling of love for him.

'Marisa, hi.' Rona had come across. 'Listen, you came in your own car, didn't you? Are you okay to drive back on your own, or would you prefer to have somebody with you?'

She had begun to shiver. Longing for warmth, she moved in closer to Steve.

'We decided it's best if we all leave together, so everybody's going to squeeze into the combi. Danny should be here in a moment. Sally's still busy giving first-aid, so Aviva's going to stick around until they've finished; and Pierre and Simon will probably stay as well, just in case.' Marisa tried to listen; but her chest was beginning to ache from the jarring, unstoppable tremors.

'Is that okay with you? How are you feeling?'

Rona, please, she wanted to say; but she couldn't get the words out.

'Are you all right? Do you want someone to go and fetch your car for you? Where are you parked?'

This time she managed to speak.

'No, I'm fine.'

As she shook her head, she felt the tightness of the tendons in her neck.

'I'm okay. Really. I can manage on my own.'

The gears felt stiff. As she battled to find reverse, Marisa was angered to find herself on the brink of tears. Breathe. Just breathe slowly. Drop your shoulders. (Her collar bones had risen up into hard ridges.) She'd been avoiding the little mirror against the windscreen, but now she caught a glimpse of her face.

The burning eyes were not her own.

Where the whites should have been, there were two bright ovals of blood red. The irises, by contrast, were a harsh, almost mineral green.

The eyes stared back at her; stark with recognition.

Shaking, she reached for the gear shift again. Get out of this place. She had to get moving, or she would find herself stuck here, trapped in the car with those hideous eyes watching her.

* * * * * * * * * * * *

There was a loud, long battering at the front door.

It must be Uncle Theo, hoping the elaborate syncopation would announce him as a friend. Desiree stood with a bundle of dusty papers in her hands. There was still time to disappear into one of the bedrooms. But Rose had taught them too well. *You be polite to Uncle Theo, he has been very good to us.* All right, all right, she would answer. (No one else seemed about to go and let him in.)

He stood there wiping his boots on the doormat, looking at her. There was a faint tang of brine about him.

'Desiree. What a nice surprise, I didn't expect to see you.'

He could not hug her right now: his hands were full, clutching a long, bulky object wrapped in sheets of newspaper. She caught a glimpse of a fish-tail.

'Come inside, come in, come in.'

Uncle Theo never arrived empty-handed, she was thinking. And the gifts, though they were for the family, were always formally presented to Rose – as though he still sensed a need, after all these years, to placate her.

His talk seemed to fill up the small hallway.

'Well, Desi, I see your arms are full too. What is it? Books again. Don't you ever stop studying?'

She nodded, trying not to seem rude. Loudly she called out, 'Uncle Theo's here, everybody.'

'I've brought the family something for supper,' he announced as they entered the kitchen.

Rose was getting slowly to her feet.

Bravely their uncle traversed the narrow, crowded space to reach the sink. Then, laying down the fish, he turned.

'It's a nice firm one, Rosie: came in this morning off the boat. They say the snoek are running like crazy.'

Rose was already switching the kettle on. 'Sit, sit. Please Uncle Theo, take a seat.' She had never quite unstiffened towards him, ever since the time he'd offered to take Shireen into his own home.

Desiree remembered Rose's despair. *He wants to destroy our family,* she'd shouted, in front of them all.

No. No Rosie, please, all I meant . . . I only wanted to do what was best. Grieving, Uncle Theo had struggled in his lumbering way to embrace her. He'd only wanted to lighten their burden, to help them.

Now, while he made himself comfortable, he could not stop himself from glancing around, as if he were longing to see the rest of the family.

In the silence, Desiree found herself staring at the gift he'd brought. The newspaper wrapping had come away, and she could see the fragile, sheeny web of the fish's skin.

A drawn look had come into Rose's face. Desiree felt a prickle of guilt: she wasn't helping her sister. 'Rosie,' she said quickly. 'Please, just tell me what needs to be . . . I'll do it.'

'Would you, honey, please.

Gratefully, Rose yielded and slid herself on to a chair again.

'Well, so how are you? And Auntie Vivienne?' With one slender hand pushing against the side of her face, she gave her attention to Uncle Theo.

He seemed to be ageing at an accelerating pace. There were deep wrinkles around his eyes. He'd been ten years older than their mother. He must be nearing sixty, then.

'Are the kids around, by the way? How's my sweetheart?'

As if on cue, Shireen appeared.

All surprise and radiance, she darted across the kitchen, singing out Uncle Theo's name. His face softened, instantly warming; and he put his huge arms around her.

When he released her, she came skimming over to the dresser.

'Oh Desi let me do that.'

With a tiny, pinched look of disdain she took the plate of biscuits out of Desiree's hand and opened a drawer to fetch out the paper doilies.

Something about her appearance was different. Maybe it was the ribbon in her hair. And she'd put on her pearls. (Uncle Theo had given her that little string for her fifteenth birthday.)

As she arranged the biscuits she kept glancing up, offering flashes of her dark, shining eyes.

'Oh I nearly forgot, your Auntie Vivienne sent a present for you, Shireen. It's a skirt. My hands are too dirty now. But it's on the backseat of the car, in the packet. She wants to know if you can use it. She bought it ages ago – in a fit of optimism, she says – but she knows she'll never get into it now.'

He winked at Rose. 'Once you've had a couple of kids, you know.'

Shireen's face shimmered with delight as she went to collect the car-keys from him, and left the room.

The tea was ready. Desiree brought the things over to the table, while Rose moved aside a few parcels.

Uncle Theo looked at the plastic bag containing Victor's neatly folded change of clothing.

'Is Vic on the hop?' he asked. 'I know he's on that SRC at school. I suppose he's one of the ones behind this stupid boycott.'

For the first time, his good-naturedness was strained.

'He's on the run, isn't he? I know the police are going around picking these kids up.'

Both sisters remained silent, not denying his charge.

'I'm sorry, Rosie, but you know my views.'

'Yes,' she said, 'Uncle Theo, we do. But I'm afraid it is Victor's life; and he makes his own decisions.'

'Rose. I want you to know, that boy can come and work for me any time he wants to. I mean it. Any time. He just has to come and ask. He's got a fine brain and he's damn well wasting it. If you ask me, it's a sin to throw away gifts like his.'

Uncle Theo took a sip of his tea, obviously making himself keep a look of gentleness on his face.

'Aaaa Rosie,' he said. (He never could hide it when he felt bewildered, or hurt.) 'I know. I understand you have your pride. You never would come and work for me. I offered, but you refused. Stubborn, like your mother. But even she wasn't too proud to come and do my books for me. She wasn't a September. Although your father managed to change her, in the end. He made her like the rest of you.'

Desiree knew what her uncle thought: their father had failed to provide for them.

He, Uncle Theo, had worked his own way up in the world, without begging from anyone: making sacrifices, he'd waited to marry till he was past thirty.

I didn't go to university, I never belonged to any glorified debating society. What was that grand club of theirs, their New Era Fellowship. At that age I didn't have time to go round criticising everything and everybody. So-and-so is a quisling; somebody else is a collaborationist. And we must boycott this; and you don't co-operate with that lot, because they're part of the system. And those ones have joined forces with the "Herrenvolk". And this was wrong – and this and this. Oh my word. On and on. Everything was always so damned negative.

He was not one to knock others, just because their talents were of a different kind from his own. But sometimes, you know, it wasn't easy to see who *was* acceptable to those people – outside of their own little coterie.

Look, I grant you they were eloquent types, well I suppose, after all they were teachers, intellectuals. I don't mean to run them down, really, I'm grateful there are people like that to educate my kids.

And as for your father now. I don't think it's right to speak badly of the dead. I think he was a genuine man: all his life he believed in what he was doing. Yes. I will say he was sincere. And they say he was a very fine teacher too, they say that. They should never have banned him from his work.

But he had no right to drag your mother into his politics. She was a child, just a girl when he met her. If he had stayed a single man, all his self-sacrifice would have been fine. But he chose to have a family, he should have had more responsibility.

You know, your mother was always so busy looking after others, giving, giving – that she ended up unable to look after herself. And then she couldn't look after Shireen either in the end, she couldn't even feed the little thing. She must have been in such pain all that time, and she wouldn't tell anyone, in case they took her away from you children and put her in hospital.

(I should have told someone. If only I'd told Rose what I saw. They might have saved her.)

And for what? In the end, what was it all for?

Victor appeared in the doorway, freshly bathed and shaved, dressed in a tracksuit. Seeing their uncle, he went over to greet him, stooping slightly as he held out his hand.

Uncle Theo seemed to consider saying something, but then merely nodded. Victor must have sensed the stiffness. Shrugging, he went to Rose and put an arm around her neck for a moment, giving her a quick smile.

'I'll be around.'

He took the bundle she held out to him and slipped it into his canvas rucksack, turning away to re-buckle it. Then he gave her another hug.

Pausing a last time in the doorway, he called back to his sisters, dead-pan: 'I see Shireen got a new skirt. You better watch her. Day after tomorrow she'll be angling for a Merc.'

Then he was gone.

It was getting late, Desiree thought. All afternoon she'd failed to find the right moment for her offer; and now Uncle Theo was in the way. Rose, she wanted to say: give up your job for a year and go to university. Of course she would get a scholarship; and the family would manage. She, Desiree, could get a full-time post – the library had already offered her one.

She could guess how Rose would respond, of course. (Desiree had better finish that Masters, or else. How dare she even think of giving up her studies?) In a way, it was a pity they'd had that conversation earlier with Victor. All those convictions would still be in the forefront of Rose's mind.

At the edge of the sink the newspaper steadily soaked up a watery pink stain from Uncle Theo's fish. Some of the words stood out on the newsprint, while others seemed to be turning transparent under the slow disturbing seepage.

Surely she should still ask; even though she knew Rose would turn her down. Or would that make the question false – less than sincere? Wasn't some part of her secretly depending on Rose to say no?

Desiree stood up.

'Excuse me,' she said. 'Please won't you excuse me, Rosie. Uncle Theo. If you don't mind, I want to carry on looking through those papers. I was trying to find something for Chris.'

'That's all right, honey. By the way, Anthony and Soraya said they might drop round. I'm sure Soraya would give you a lift home later, if you want one.'

'Well,' Uncle Theo turned to her, with a slight clumsiness. He was still hurt. 'You know, I could take you, Desi.'

'No. Thank you, it's kind of you, Uncle Theo, but I'd

like to walk, it's only a few blocks. I need some fresh air.'

* * * * * * * * * * * *

André poured himself a glass of wine and went to drink it outside on the stoep.

It was still light, but the earlier lustre had faded from the sky. Now a mist was beginning to invade the suburb, pale as smoke, but moving fast.

Chris had seemed in a bit of a mood when he came in just now. Tired out, probably. Suffocated by all those gushing ladies. That was Marisa's theory, wasn't it? Oh well. One thing: at least he'd carried that box of records off to his room with him. For a moment, as the two of them stood facing, he'd been on the point of saying something about the gun. But then he'd thought better of it. Chris really hadn't looked too good right then. Anyway, he was leaving: it wasn't as though the problem was going to be around much longer.

André swallowed some more of the wine. It must be getting late. He'd slept for a couple of hours at least, needing it. He hoped Riaan hadn't minded entertaining himself.

So where was everybody else? Chris had asked where Desiree was. Come to think of it, he'd sounded upset, almost, that she wasn't back yet.

And Marisa? Nothing could have happened at that funeral, surely? All those stricken, trembling poses of fearfulness this morning had simply been fabrications of hers, dreamed up to add some glamour to her little role. She'd never been in any real danger.

In the meantime he could get the coals underway. As long as it didn't rain, they could probably still have the braaivleis out here.

He did not move immediately. Some notion had been

groping through the mass of ungathered sounds and images in his mind as he fell asleep. There was a mistake he'd been making all along in his thinking. A serious one.

Riaan emerged suddenly from the outbuilding and stood in the doorway, silhouetted by the light behind him. Seeing André, he called out something, and came quickly over the grass.

'Hey Boet, I got it to work. It's giving me random numbers.'

He looked happy, André thought, watching his brother bound up the steps.

'Twin columns,' he boasted. 'I reckon you could use them for a code, don't you think? But now the only thing I can't seem to figure out is, how do I get it to print a copy, I mean onto paper?'

'Okay.' André nodded. 'I know – that manual isn't the clearest guide in the world. I'll help you now. But won't you go and give the old man a ring first? Go on, the phone is in the sitting-room.'

Riaan frowned. With a shrug of reluctance he started backing off towards the door. 'Suppose I better.'

André went back to chasing his own elusive argument. When it first came to him it had seemed as plain as tapwater.

It had to do with reification. All along, this was the mistake he'd been making. It was fine and well to talk about the 'power of speech'. But such concepts – gifts, faculties, powers – were mere abstractions; generalisations dreamed up by observers. If they existed anywhere, it could only be in the minds of their inventors.

It was an elementary mistake. But he'd made it all right; never questioning – simply assuming that the 'gift of language' could be treated as a thing; as if it were somehow packaged up in the human beast along with the heart and kidneys.

Bitter with himself and weary, André felt on the verge of sagging again. If he'd wanted to theorise so grandly about the nature of 'humanness', it might have helped if he'd started by studying what was actually there. How did people behave, in reality? What was all that making of sounds and gesturing about?

And where was his noble argument now against taking up arms?

* * * * * * * * * * * *

Down that way, to her left, was the church, its walls already in shadow. There was a Casspir pulled up outside it. So what, though. They were everywhere. Perhaps if she went back in that direction she'd find a way out onto the main road.

As she approached the building, she slowed down. That was Aviva standing there in the dusk: dark red hair, candy-striped dress. She was watching something behind the Casspir.

Travelling still more slowly, Marisa managed to get a look too. They had someone. Tall, fair-haired. It looked as if they were searching him. Three or four policemen. They'd got him standing up against the side of the Casspir, with his hands reaching up to touch the metal. He had his face turned slightly to one side: Pierre.

The road was almost empty. Stopping immediately, Marisa abandoned the car and ran over.

'What's happening?'

Aviva turned. 'I thought you'd gone already.'

'I couldn't find the way. What are they doing with him?'

'They're talking about detaining him. Simon's gone to try and find Omar, in case we need a lawyer. But I think they'll let him go. They're just being heavy.'

'Why?'

Aviva was looking away again, keeping an eye on the policemen.

'Why would they want to detain him?'

'Oh you know. Pierre's always out in the townships. He's a known activist. He's been inside twice already. Last time they beat him up quite badly. That bastard Major Buitendag has got a personal vendetta against him. He told Pierre once he had a bullet he was saving for him with his name – Pierre's name – engraved on it.'

Something was happening. The small group had broken away from the Casspir and Pierre was walking out into the middle of the street. Marisa thought she saw him give a small grin in their direction.

'I'm going to go over and ask one of the *boere* what they think they're doing.'

Aviva walked up to a policeman.

Pierre was still surrounded. Watching him, Marisa noticed that the skin along his pale, muscular arms had tightened, raising the blonde hairs. All he had on was a pair of khaki trousers, and a thin tee-shirt that had come untucked, exposing his lean belly. She herself was shivering again. He must be freezing. Then she remembered: there was someone's anorak lying in the back of her car, draped over those parcels.

Running back to the car, she hauled out the heavily padded, khaki-coloured jacket. Inspired slightly by Aviva, she walked straight up to Pierre with it, ignoring the two young policemen at his side.

'Pierre, here, you'll need this.'

Quickly he heaved it on. Then he puffed out his cheeks and nodded. 'Feels a lot better. Thanks. Jesus, I was cold. But you don't have to worry, I think they're going to let me go. Here comes Buitendag now.'

A policeman was approaching them. He seemed older

than the others, and the slow confidence of his walk suggested that he was senior in rank as well. 'Is that your car over there?' He was speaking to her. Patiently he repeated himself in Afrikaans.

'Yes,' she said, alarmed to find she was frightened. 'That is my car; and I prefer to speak English.'

'All right.' He gave a shrug. 'Follow me, please.' She had to walk back to the car with him. Three policemen were already there, unloading the brown-paper parcels and stacking them on to the roof.

'Will you open the boot, please.'

She closed her eyes for a second. Let them look, there was nothing in it.

'You can open it yourself. Here.'

Trying for an air of pained fastidiousness, she tipped the keys into his palm.

He handed them over to one of his men.

'What is your name, please?'

Behind him she could see a policeman paging through one of the *Frontiers*.

'Marisa, just relax.' Aviva had come up, fast. She was standing close behind her. 'Remember, all you are legally obliged to tell these people is your name and address.'

The man looked at Aviva. Under the peak of his cap his eyes were narrowed and flickering; as if he were amused.

Marisa gave him her name.

'Siervogel. *'n Goeie Afrikaanse naam.*' He nodded, almost approvingly. 'But you prefer to speak English. I see.'

She wasn't going to rise to his bait.

'Well now, Miss Siervogel. Perhaps you can tell me about these magazines that were found in your car. This *Frontier*. It's a UDF publication I see.'

He smiled at her as he spoke. 'I take it it's banned, of

course.'

His eyes – humorous, clever – had a restless, blue-grey light in them.

'Yes, *Frontier* is a UDF journal. It says so quite clearly on the cover.'

(Aviva, thank God, was doing the talking.)

'As I'm sure you know, the United Democratic Front is not a banned organisation. It is perfectly legal; and as you might therefore expect, its publications are also perfectly legal. '

He looked Aviva over, almost amiably. Still holding his ground, he began flipping through one of the magazines, pausing every now and then to stare at a page, exaggerating the look of contempt on his face.

'Are you quite sure?' he asked, sceptically.

'You may not like its contents, but that's hardly the issue. I can assure you, *Frontier* is not banned.'

Leaving them, the major went over to speak to the young policemen who'd been searching the car. It was obvious they'd found nothing else.

Marisa turned slightly towards Aviva; afraid to say anything. (The truth seemed to be hanging between them, suspended in a fragile balance with silence.)

'It looks like they're going to let Pierre go,' Aviva said quietly.

She is a comrade, Marisa was thinking. A real comrade. The word no longer seemed so strange.

'Hang on, here's Simon.'

Across the wastes of cold-shadowed sand, people had begun to turn on lights in the tenement flats, creating pale squares of yellow in the solid blocks of darkness.

Pierre and Simon both came towards them out of the deepening twilight.

'So, what's up? What's with them searching that car?'

'They're bothered by the *Frontiers*. '

'Oh shit. And I couldn't get Omar. Apparently he went with the clergy to the cemetery, in case they had any problems there. So what do we do now?'

'I've told them the journal is legal.' Pierre gave Aviva a cautious glance.

(It wasn't a lie, Marisa thought. Strictly speaking, only one number was banned.)

'Simon, shut up.'

'Oh. Well. But I've also just been speaking to Sally. She says the medics are going to be busy for some time. So far they've had nothing serious, they're mostly dealing with cuts, sore eyes. They had to treat one old woman for an asthma attack. But they might still get people coming in later with more serious injuries. Ey. They're just getting reports now the *boere* have been using shot – you know, pellets; but sometimes people are afraid to come out for help while the Casspirs are still around.

'So, anyway: she says we mustn't wait for her. She's prepared to stay overnight, or else Sedick will give her a lift back later, when he gets a chance. Personally, I reckon we should get the hell out of here. What's the story with the *Frontier*s now? Why don't we just tell them they can have them? Let them confiscate them and we'll take a receipt.'

'Ja.' Pierre nodded. He seemed faintly confused; perhaps from exhaustion.

Major Buitendag was coming back.

'All right. You people are free to go.'

His face made it clear that he had no liking for them; and little trust in them either.

'Don't let me see any of you in this area within the next twenty-four hours. You know, you people cause us a lot of problems, running around in your UDF tee-shirts. Unnecessary trouble.'

Aviva stirred. 'I beg your pardon,' she said. 'But if

anyone has been causing any trouble around here it's – '

Touching her arm, Pierre tried to silence her.

'No, I want to ask this man. Who's been the cause of the problems today? Who's been throwing the tear-gas? Who's been swaggering around the streets with guns, terrorising people?'

'Come, Aviva, you're not going to win this one.'

'Answer me.'

The major let his eyelids droop, as if he were bored.

'Lady, please. I've been very patient with you. But just don't make me lose my temper now. Take my advice and get out of here.'

Turning his back on them, he walked off.

On the freeway, Marisa glanced sideways, trying to see beyond the reflected light on the inside of the glass and the darkness outside.

Across the fields, between the low houses and flats, she caught a glimpse of fire: a rack of amber shimmering up into the darkness. A street barricade.

Then the barricades would be going up all over Cape Town tonight. People who lived on the slopes of the mountain would come out onto their patios, to watch the rags of fire spreading across the city's grace of a million lights, necklaces of light as white as moths.

Suddenly she noticed the three figures racing over the wide stretch of vacant land, coming towards the road. A streetlight flooded them briefly in a blaze of shadows, and she saw them more clearly. They were young – no more than teenagers.

Arching his chest, one of them slowly drew back an arm. Time seemed to grow heavy in that moment, tumbling slowly over and over. Imagining she heard the stones hailing down, Marisa accelerated. The figure froze as she flashed past: a dancer, or an actor – caught in the spasm of light from a stroboscope.

When she looked back in the mirror, she thought she saw an object flying through the night; slowly, as though it were a dream, or the blurred edge of a memory.

Keeping her eyes on the mirror, she saw something else. In the distance, a solitary Casspir was coming up behind her on the freeway. The three figures were already running along the verge to meet it; each with an arm pulled back, and a fist about to rise, filled with stones.

5

Up ahead was the familiar landmark of the jacaranda tree, the tips of its branches faintly brushed with traces of white and lilac light. Nearly home, Desiree thought.

There was a slight, welcome chill in the air. (More often there was a listlessness about the neighbourhood in the evenings: grease-stains in the narrow, pitted roads, a tired reek of steel and dust.) The small gardens had begun to burst with spring growth: where the bulbs had come up too early, there were long, torn leaves lying flattened and tangled by the rains – with sprays of buds lifting from beneath them, nonetheless.

In the dusk, the white-washed walls down the street had a mild, almost elusive gleam. Perhaps it was the tranquillity of those surfaces that provoked the local graffiti-writers to cover them with scrawls.

Where is the border now, Boetie? On top of the low wall, above the writing, someone had left out a colony of tiny succulents, planted in a rusted hub-cab.

So what?

Most of the messages were political; but a few seemed to be merely the pert, inscrutable comments of teenagers.

No time for words.

What did that mean. Or this one, painted in a neatly cursive script, like the magnified writing of a child: *I have a headache.*

Who had a headache, she wondered. The high wall, perhaps, with its sulky fringe of jasmine creeper. The graffiti artist? Or perhaps the whole series of exclamations was addressed to that writer – bookish, and austere – who lived in the road. It was possible: some of the other messages seemed to have personal targets. Once she'd seen *Be Bop Speed Cop!* sprayed up in cheeky, racing letters opposite the house where a motorbike leaned heavily in the driveway.

She reached up to touch the pale, sweet-scented mass of flowers. What was it again. There was something Chris had been telling her about jasmine. *It was the thing my mother felt most bitter about. That the whites had to take that away from her. I don't know. I know my Dad said she only dreamt that jasmine. But for her it was real.*

Of course there were other things. She blamed the whites for the wind too. Out there, you know, where we had to move to, you can never get away from it. It gets into everything. And the dust comes with it; hot, and dry: it stifles you. She used to say: the whites – they wanted Claremont, so they came with their Group, to murder us all. They pushed us out into Lotus River, Hanover Park, Belhar. Into the sand, where the wind is, and you can't grow anything. Not like we used to.

It was the jasmine that really hurt her. Losing that.

Desiree walked on, still thinking of that white cascade of imagined, fragile, scented light.

The end of the world is naai.

Nigh. A clever pun, she thought quickly, embarrassed that she knew the coarser sense of the last word.

Ahead of her, a cat came running out from an alleyway full of weeds.

* * * * * * * * * * * *

'André?'

Riaan had come back. André noticed the awkward,

bashful look on his face again. God, had he also been that young once?

'The old man sounds really mad. He wanted to know what you've been telling me.'

André looked steadily back at him.

'I think maybe I better not stay too late,' Riaan went on, almost apprehensively.

'Okay look, don't worry. I can take you, if you don't mind travelling on the back of the bike. I've got a spare helmet. You just say when you'd like to go. Or do you want to leave straight away? That's fine with me.'

Uncertainly, Riaan shook his head.

André found himself wondering whether the kid was frightened of him now. Maybe he believes I'm a Communist. Swallowing another mouthful of wine, he tried to persuade himself that the idea was amusing. He was starting to run out of ideas.

'Do you want to get back to the computer, then?'

'No. Ja. No, just now. Boet, I still want to talk, you know.'

'Well how about making yourself more comfortable then. Pull up a brick. Chris will probably come out and join us in a moment; and the other two should be home quite soon. Maybe Chris will even let us play his demo tape. Then you'd get a chance to hear his voice.'

'A demo tape? You mean, like a band makes when they want to get into recording?'

Riaan was looking half impressed, half doubtful.

'No. That's a joke. It was a cassette he made for his audition.'

The wind was tousling the leaves of the honeysuckle over the old outdoor shower. Or what was it, jasmine?

'Look, I think I'm going to get this fire started in the meantime. If you want to give me a hand you could start crumpling up those old papers in that box.'

André picked up one of the wired bundles of rooikrans and ran his hand over the fibrous wood. Bit sappy. Maybe this was the time to use that branch that had come down from the tree in front. He began to drag more wood out from under the canvas sheet.

At first the small flames shot up erratically, sending out smuts and flying ash.

'Hey, Boet, what is this? It looks like old biology notes.'

Crouching beside the fire, André wiped his face with his hand. 'Those notes? It's old stuff of Chris's.'

'But are you sure it's okay to just burn it? Look at this.'

André glanced at the small, sketchy diagram of the respiratory organs. Scribbles in pencil labelled the various sections. *Trachea. Larynx. Pharynx.* The rest of the page was taken up with a scrawl of incoherent notes. (Lecture notes, André guessed.) *The vocal cords are tiny, just over 1 cm (about half an inch) in a man, shorter in a woman. In order to produce the sound, you need a strong chest and diaphragm that will supply a a strong column of steady air. This stream is then modulated so that the resultant sound is at a pitch predetermined in the mind (very NB). The sound produced is actually quite small, depends upon resonating cavities for its amplification and timbre. These cavities are the throat, back of the mouth, nose, back of nose, the forehead, and the upper chest. (NB, be able to give diagram.)*

He was beginning to share Riaan's misgivings about burning this. But Chris had been adamant, insisting it was all wastepaper. André crumpled the sheet up again.

'No, I suppose it's okay. He was pretty definite about being finished with this.'

Really, I'm never going to need any of it again. I want to get rid of it; I actually need to chuck everything out. It's symbolic, and all that: clearing away the dead growth, preparing to start a new life. That sort of idea.

'Boet, you think it'll rain?'

'It might drizzle a bit. Won't you have a drink now? It's getting on for sundown. Come on, let me get you something.'

'No, no Boet, I'm fine, stay there. You need any more of this paper? You know, you forget what the Cape rain is like.'

André nodded again. 'Keep sending. Ja, it is good, hey. Clean. When you get that smell of the wet earth, it's as if you feel yourself breathing properly for the first time.'

For a while they both worked in silence.

'Boet?'

The hesitancy in Riaan's voice each time he spoke was beginning to move André, for no earthly reason. He hunched his bulky shoulders, resolving to be more gentle with his brother.

'Ja?' he said, with a nod that he hoped was peaceable.

Riaan was peering at him again. 'Boet, do you think the ANC will ever win?'

André waited, not sure where this question was coming from.

'I mean, do you believe the good guys always win in the end? Because, you know, I'm starting to have my doubts. Sometimes I lie awake and these thoughts get into my head; and they kind of sit there, trapped in my skull, like . . . like these giant birds.'

There was a shaken look in the boy's face.

'Maybe you'll think I'm being pessimistic. But I can see this government getting to the point where they'll use nukes. I mean, what's to stop them? I don't think they care. I'm talking about the military now. Even if it means they go up with it too, they couldn't care. I'm working with these guys every day. I see them. I listen to what they say. I tell you, they're insane, Boet.'

What could he say, André thought.

'I just don't know anymore. I mean: don't get me wrong, it's not a problem for me to fight. I believe in defence and all that. Only, I suppose I'm on the wrong side.

'I don't know. Sometimes I even think: it's all so mad and sick anyway, maybe it would be for the best if they do just blow everything up. Let the whole place go to hell. Then at least something clean could come out of it afterwards, out of the ashes. Like those flowers, what do you call them? They only come up after there's been a veld fire; and they're the colour of fire.'

'Fire lilies?'

'Fire lilies, yes.'

André had no heart to offer pedantic corrections. He should be pointing out the depth of difference between the seasonality of vegetation, and the rough, singular course of human history. Part of his mind was even framing the questions. Think, Riaan. Why is it that the substance of hope is so often nothing but a symbolism – images, spuriously invoked images of cyclicity, and rebirth? Why do you think hope always has to be manufactured, whipped up?

Oh Christ, he thought suddenly. He was sick to death of himself.

'Ey, Riaan – cheer up. Come on. Here. Here's a riddle for you. What's a featherless biped?'

Riaan's eyes lightened, and suddenly he had the look of a small boy laughing. 'A biped? A biped's a human, isn't it?'

'A human being, yes.'

'But why the 'featherless'?'

'Well, think.'

'Oh I get it, because birds are also bipeds. Technically.'

The notion seemed to tickle Riaan. Then his eyes glinted with a look of query. 'Hey, but what about the apes then? They're also bipeds, and they haven't got feathers.'

'True. It was only a try at a definition. Actually, it's ancient. It doesn't really work, does it.'

André heaved himself to his feet. 'Okay then, let's go and get that machine to print for you.'

* * * * * * * * * * * *

Marisa heard the tape playing as she let herself in. It was Chris singing, she knew immediately: that soaring of amber sound, the subtle, ethereal sculpture of his phrases.

The sound seemed to wash over her, stunning her with its weight. She leaned for a moment in the doorway, feeling strange: transparent, almost, as though she were made of glass. In her mouth there was still the taste of tear-gas, she discovered; a taste like the acrid smell of an ant swarm.

Hurrying on to her room, she was glad to close the door on the sound of Chris's voice.

On the floor next to the bed, a few sprays of honeysuckle lay already withered and creased. At the sight, she felt a wave of distress (exaggerated, she knew; yet unstoppable). She would have to get a grip on herself. (As she thought it, a part of her was wounded by her own hardness.) Rest for a moment.

She sat down on the edge of the bed, wondering what to do next. Her knees were hurting stiffly, stinging. Carefully she lifted the crimson birds of her skirt to examine them. Nothing. It was nothing – only grazes. A few shreds of dead-white skin, and blood that had long since dried.

Afraid that the trembling might begin again, she lay back, lifting her feet on to the bed. Once again she tasted the tear-gas. It was in her lungs, her throat, her nostrils, her mouth. Her entire body was permeated with the reek of dying fire.

Remember that time when we went walking on the mountain in the twilight. Past the stone pines, with their warm, dusty bark, and the squirrel-chewed husks of cones fallen at their roots. And there was that fragrance from the dry bushes; and a smell of foam and salt, we thought, rising up from the darkening ocean below us. And Braam, you said: *fireflies, look*. They were, too: flitting and dipping there in the darkness between the trees, pulsing with a living chemistry of light.

She would have to get up soon. Overhead, the bleached ribs of the candelabra lily were turning slowly, casting their spokes of criss-cross shadow on to the wall.

She needed a jersey. Suddenly, pushing herself, she stood up and went over to the chest-of-drawers.

Once there, she paused though, wondering again what her next move should be. She looked down at the childish jewellery box on top of the chest. The toy ballerina reached out with her stiff little arms. Unable to resist the mute plea, Marisa wound her up.

Accompanied by a slow, precise tinkling, the miniature dancer began to revolve. Somewhere underneath the lid there must be a hidden cylinder, turning so that its small sprigs would catch against the tines of a metal comb.

Calmed, Marisa went back to her search. Then, as she was turning over the clothes in the bottom drawer, a few glistening threads caught her eye. Chris's scarf. His present.

She hauled it out, cursing herself. She'd nearly forgotten. It still needed to be wrapped, as well, and there was no paper – unless Desi or André had some.

There was something ringing: not this music – something else, in the background. The phone. No, well she wasn't going to answer. It might be Richard. She would rather pretend she wasn't here. She had nothing to say to him now.

The music box was beginning to give its last slow twinges of sound.

* * * * * * * * * * * *

With a towel wrapped around herself and a noisy hairdryer in one hand, Desiree sat on the chair at her desk, running her fingers through her wet hair to expose it to the draught of heat.

The brief shower had revived her. Earlier she'd not been sure she was in the mood for a celebration, however small. But her headache had gone, and her shoulders were beginning to unclench themselves. She was glad, she thought, letting the warm air play over the back of her neck. André had given her a message when she came in. Apparently Chris had been asking for her. *Something's eating him, Desi. I don't know what it is, but he seemed upset when I told him you weren't back yet. He just went straight to his room.*

She switched off the dryer for a moment, distracted by its high-pitched sheen of noise. Perhaps she should go and find him now. *I got the feeling he wanted to talk. Only he wouldn't to me, of course. I know he's closer to you.'*

Someone had put on Chris's audition tape. She sat for another moment, stilled, listening to the rising voice as it streamed through the air: liquid gold, but with an added texture, the faintest shadow of wind-swept, dry grass.

The last of the tightness in her neck disappeared.

* * * * * * * * * * * *

The blaring noise seemed to be coming from the street outside. Someone was leaning on a hooter. Students, perhaps, or apprentices – on their way to the pub on the main road.

But the sound wasn't moving away. Across the semi-darkness, André looked at Riaan. In the light of the falling, quietened flames, his brother's face was an assemblage of glistening planes and shadows.

André found himself on his feet. He knew what this was. He started running, pounding through the kitchen and living-room, down the passage to the front door. A car had driven into the yard. For a moment he was blinded by its headlights. Then he could see the shape of a man getting out. The hulking figure was unmistakeable.

Okay, Pa, André thought. Okay.

'Waar's my seun? I've come to fetch my son. *Jou blerry Kommunis, where's Riaan?'*

So the old man had come to save Riaan from André's diabolical influence. He had already staggered over close enough for André to smell the blast of blue heat on his breath.

'Go and tell Riaan he is coming with me now.'

André kept one arm braced across the doorway. His father's face was looming out of the darkness, with a drunken, ironic expression of politeness. (He still affected sideburns; still let his hair grow over his collar, even though it was greying now and thin.)

Glancing back, André thought he saw someone standing just inside Chris's room. Where were the others, he wondered.

'Listen, Pa, if you are looking for Riaan, he's . . . .

Marisa must have come into the room behind him.

'André what is going on, who is this man, is it the police?'

André wished she would go back inside. Suddenly his father burst past him and rushed into the centre of the living-room.

'Who is this, who does he think he is? This is our house.'

The man stood there, panting and aggrieved.

'I've come to collect my son. You bastard, I know he's here.'

'André, what's happening?'

Desiree had come into the room now too. André saw her hesitate at the sight of his father.

'Jou fokken Kommunis, what have you been telling that boy. Just go and fetch him. Now.'

Like spiders, the words fell into the room. There was a bleak incomprehension in Desiree's face. She's frightened, André thought. In a few strides he crossed over to her side.

'Jy, jou donder. Leave your fucking Coloured girl alone and get my son here.'

As the insults scurried over them, André felt something clawing into his very being. His hands were terribly hot as he faced his father. 'Now you have gone too far. I must ask you to get out of this house.'

The man tried to lunge at him, but staggered off balance. André took his chance to grab one of the thick wrists, and then wrenched him up by the back of his jacket.

'Riaan, come and help me,' he shouted, staggering with their father past the furniture.

'You bastard, you fucking bladdie bastard.'

Feeling his father threatening to twist round, André tightened his lock around the broad neck. For an instant he thought he heard his brother in the background. He could see nothing, though. (And on second thoughts, let Riaan keep out of this.) This game was nearly over, he didn't need help now. There was a crashing sound, and he seemed to hear screaming. But they were moving now. Oh Christ, what was this all about. Struggling to keep a grip on the hulking, fleshy shoulders, André dragged his father across the yard. He would force the man into his car and tell him to drive off.

He pulled open the car door. Finding a massive strength in himself, he lifted his father off the ground and hurled him down into the driver's seat.

For a few seconds the old man sat there, stunned, staring up. It seemed to André that there was terror in the man's enormous, glistening face.

'Pa, I'm warning you. Get out of here.'

'You bastard,' his father whispered, while his fingers struggled with the bunch of keys. 'You bastard.'

He looked up at André again, with eyes that were beginning to water. Suddenly, as if he were panicking, he stopped trying to start the car and wound the side window up, fast, leaning away from André until he was protected by the sheet of glass.

Get out of here, André mouthed at him. He noticed his father fighting to press down the lock on the door. Why was he having such trouble?

Finally he drove off, accelerating too fast across the gravel in the yard, then slewing to one side before he turned out and went lurching off into the road.

André took a few steps, surprised to find his face and shoulders whipped by the drooping branches of the pepper tree. The stillness had come too quickly. After listening for another moment, André walked to the gateway.

The car had stopped a few hundred metres down in the middle of the street. He could just make out the shape of the driver's head. It seemed to be at a strange angle. He took a few more steps down the road, staring. Then he broke into a run.

Getting up close, he peered through the window of the locked door. Inside, his father was leaning over, groping at the air with his hands. As he looked up at André, his lips moved. Was he merely gasping, or trying to say something. The pale eyes were watering again.

Baffled, André leaned down.

Now he could see that the man had his right hand clamped over the upper part of his left arm, as though he were trying to raise it. For some reason it was taking a huge amount of effort: sweat was beading, trickling down the puce-coloured face.

Watching that effort, André had the notion that his father was trying to show him something – a catch he had just made with his bare, triumphant hands. Yet the massive, flailing creature kept slipping out of his grasp, falling back below the surface.

He must do something to help him. André looked around. The quickest would be to smash the window in.

He found a broken brick in the gutter and grabbed it. Moving around to the far side, he poised himself to bring the stone crashing down against the window. Quickly he looked at his father again. The old man was staring up at him, in agony, with bright water streaming down his face.

Oh God, he thinks I'm going to kill him.

Wait. He shook his head, then bent close again, trying to signal reassurance. He would have to go and phone for help.

'Nee, Pa, wag net, orraait?' He would be back. Cupping his hands to his mouth, he shouted, close up against the class. 'Pa, I'll be back now, okay. Just hang on, Pa. Please.'

He gave the side of the car a quick slap of encouragement, and as he turned to race back, he raised his fist, and nodded, smiling.

'Please, just hang on, Pa.'

Desiree had her arms around Marisa's shoulders, but the screaming seemed to carry on spiralling through the house, independently of either of them.

Riaan stood in the background, shifting helplessly.

'Quick, please out of the way, I've got to use the phone, we need help fast. I think the old man's having a heart attack.'

'André, please, you try to calm her. She found him: she was the one who went in there. I'm going to phone my brother.'

'What?'

'Boet . . . '

He grabbed Marisa, seething with impatience. 'What's the matter?' The words were thick in his mouth.

She was still screaming, drawing in small, hard nuggets of breath, and releasing them in terrifying, painful wires of sound.

'Stop that, Marisa. Stop it.'

She was quicker than he was and managed to stab her fingers at his mouth and nose, forcing him back for a second. He pushed away her hand, deliberately rough.

'I never knew he had a gun, he . . . ' Her voice continued to rise. André could feel the vibrations right through her taut body as the sobbing broke, hard and brittle in her upper chest.

In the background, he heard Desiree's voice.

'Rose, it's Desi, please is Anthony there? Please tell him to come. It's Chris, there's been an accident. Please he's got to come quickly.'

'Boet, what must I do?'

Marisa was rocking against him, still trying to speak, a thin reed trembling with hysteria. Her face had a sickly sheen to it, and her tight, fast breathing had become even shallower.

'André, we didn't . . . we didn't . . .'

He tried smoothing her hair.

Suddenly the tears were springing from her eyes.

'We forgot his scarf, André. We didn't even give him his present. And now . . . and now . . . '

'Boet, please.'

Now Desi was asking him something.

'You said you wanted to use the phone. Didn't you say?'

No. Why? Who would he want to call? He reached out to put his free arm around Desiree's shoulders, drawing her into a huddle with Marisa and himself. It shocked him to feel the smallness of her bones. She was light as a bird, as paper.

'You said something about the old man . . . needing help.'

In the background, Riaan kept calling him, going on like a bloody stuck record.

'Boet, what are we supposed to do now?'

